Pomegranate Dreams
& Other Stories

Happy Reading.

May Lakshmi

Dec - 31, 2002

INDIALOG PUBLICATIONS PVT. LTD.

Praise For Vijay Lakshmi

Pomegranate Dreams is a story of remarkable poise and balance. By turns hilarious and wistful, darkened by necessary touches of loss, it is told by a zesty if disaffected teen girl Juhi whose family has lately come to live in Philadelphia.... The stories included in this collection with the novella are bittersweet explorations of Indian women's experiences that are rich with the themes of cultural displacement; marriage; compelling illicit love; and above all, with identity. They are both painful as well as lyrical. Lakshmi is an economical, incisive story-teller. This entire volume is a pleasure to welcome.

    – Richard Wertime, author, *Citadel on the Mountain*

Whether she is writing about a Hindu girl's nostalgia for Christmas, a mother's first attempt to put aside her sari for a western dress, or an encounter between heartsick immigrants on a commuter train, Vijay Lakshmi writes with sorrow, humor, and tenderness about what people lose when they come to America. In these remarkable stories, marriages falter, children grow up, and loved ones die, but what lasts is the power of our dreams.

    – Simone Zelitch, author, *Louisa*

She explores the isolation of immigration.

    – Erin Kennedy, *The Philadelphia Inquirer*

Working and reworking immigrants' experiences, Lakshmi creates characters whose isolation we understand because we are all partners in living ... their insecurity and their alienation are a part of the human condition.

    – Anne D. Ulrich in *Writers of the Indian Diaspora*

Pomegranate Dreams

& Other Stories

Vijay Lakshmi

First published 2002 by Indialog Publications Pvt. Ltd.
© 2002

Indialog Publications Pvt. Ltd.
O-12/A, Lajpat Nagar-II
New Delhi-110024
Tel: 29816778

ISBN 81-87981-25-9

INDIALOG PUBLICATIONS PVT. LTD.

Published in India by Indialog Publications Pvt. Ltd.,
June 2002.

Indialog Publications Pvt. Ltd.
O - 22, Lajpat Nagar II
New Delhi - 110024
Tel.: 91-11-6839936/6320504
Fax: 91-11-6935221
Internet Addresses: http://www.indialogpublications.com
                    http://www.onepageclassic.com

Cover Painting adapted from "Pomegranate Tree" by
Seeroon Yeretzian

Printed at Chaman Offset Printers, Darya Ganj, New Delhi

ISBN 81-87981-25-3

For my mother Subhadra Devi,
the source of my stories, and
for her grandchildren, Prabodh and Nidhi

Acknowledgements

To my husband, Pradyumna Chauhan, for his faith, his love, his companionship, his mentoring, his incisive reading and exacting criticism of my work, I owe the fruition of my dreams.

To Paule Marshall, for her thoughtful guidance,

To Richard Wertime, for initiating me into the art of fiction writing and for his continued interest in my work,

To friend and fellow writer, Simone Zelitch, for her astute comments,

To Michel Fabre, for introducing me to *The Paris Transcontinental* and Claire Larriere, who gave me my first break,

To Dorothea Fischer-Hornung, for her friendship and for the gift of magical moments for readings,

To Song Wen Wei and Ping Hou for translating my stories into Chinese,

To Seeroon Yeretzian of Roslyn Art Gallery, for permission to adapt her design "Pomegranate Tree" for the cover page,

To friends and colleagues: Elaine Atkins, Paul Bolledu, Pat Delrio, Grace Flisser, Emilie Harting, Camen Flys Junquera, Alecia McKenzie, Katie Mckay, Tom Ott, Amritjit Singh, Carol Stein, Don Weinberg, Narcisa Williams and Ronald Williams, for their encouragement and constructive criticism,

To Shantanu Lal, for searching the "Pomegranate Tree," and his suggestions for the cover design,

To my uncommon readers: Nidhi, Punita, Laurie, Rekha, Manisha, Raghavendra, Suneet, and Prabodh,

And to Chandana Dutta, Editor-in-chief, Indialog, for her meticulous attention to detail and her patience,

I am immensely grateful.

CONTENTS

POMEGRANATE

It is a cluster of deep red or pink juicy berries tightly packed inside a thick hard shell. When the fruit is ripe, the shell splits open or "laughs."

Pomegranate is called *punica granatum* in Latin because of its grain-like seeds; *pome granade* in French; *anar* in Hindi; and *dadima* in Sanskrit. Pliny called it *malum punicum*, the Apple of Carthage.

Considered to be a symbol of fertility, prosperity, and abundance, the pomegranate figures in many cultures. The motif can be found in temple carvings of India and the Moorish palaces of the Alhambra in Spain.

Parsis use its twigs to make their sacred broom. They shower its seeds over a child's head – during the Sacred Thread ceremony – to ward off evil. The juice is used to sanctify the dying.

To the Armenians, a pomegranate represents the "essence of life." During the Matriarchal Period, it was considered to be the symbol of womanhood, "the sure parent."

It is said that the Prophet Mohammed asked his followers to eat pomegranates to cleanse their spirit of envy.

A saying in Sanskrit – *dadima mani dansh* – equates performing a hard task to "biting into the pomegranate."

"The pomegranate represents a hero's journey of life, death and rebirth, whether it is Persephone's journey from the underworld, or Jesus' Passion and Resurrection, or our own. This small globe carries the power to transform and renew our souls. The seeds of change lie beneath its blood red surface. We need only look within to find all the strength and life we need."

– Kathryn Hadley

POMEGRANATE DREAMS

I thought we had arrived at the edge of
the world, the bounds of beyond. One
step more, and we would plunge into
empty space. Except for a small clearing
where my father had parked the car, and
except for a huge brown rock with tufts
of grass hanging from the crevices, we were surrounded on
all sides by nothing but a mass of towering trees that blocked
the sky and cast moss shadows on the ground. I still remember
the splintered sky above our heads, the dandelions at our feet.
And I can still remember the taste of fear in my mouth as I
imagined reptiles, dinosaurs, and winged beasts lurking in the
undergrowth.

Suddenly, a bird flapped its wings and let out a long shrill
cry. Soon the woods began to echo with a cacophony of bird
calls that rose above the tree tops and reached the sky. The
green curtain around us shivered as if alive, then lapsed again

into emerald silences. I clutched my mother's hand and wished we were back in the safety of the city with its tall concrete buildings, its neon lights, its humming traffic, its jostling humanity.

Then I heard Papa clear his throat. "This is how the land must have looked to the Pilgrim Fathers when they landed here centuries ago," he said in a hushed voice, as if afraid of disturbing the silence. "So pristine and so wild. Remember the stories of the men who tamed the wild Frontier?" he asked me and Bansi.

We nodded. Our education in American history had begun months before we boarded the plane in New Delhi. "You must know about the country you are going to live in," Papa had said. I sucked in my breath, hoping he wouldn't start on his history lessons now. Mercifully, he was too engrossed with his Pilgrim Fathers to do so.

My mother, obviously moved by the surroundings, breathed in. "Never saw so many trees in my life. They're so beautiful!"

"Awesome!" Bansi said.

I remained wordless.

I don't know how long we stood there before Papa came out of his reverie and said, "Okay, let's get moving."

We got into the car. Papa spread out a road map against the steering wheel, and traced the thread of a route with his finger. "Let's see. This is Brink Road and this park is where we are. Here." He circled a tiny green area that looked like a butterfly's wing. "Actually we're quite close to the house."

I peeped over his shoulder. The distance between where we were on the map and where we were going wasn't more than one tenth of an inch.

"So we're not lost!" I sighed.

"Who said we were lost?" Papa said, folding the map and reversing the car. "I wanted you to see the America that is more than steel structures."

The green mass receded and, with it, my fear ebbed too. We got back to the road we had left. The wilderness was behind us, the city ahead. My mind was already racing to the house which none of us, not even my mother, had seen. An American home, Papa had assured us after signing a year's lease last week, was an American home. Three bedrooms, two bathrooms, a kitchen, a living and a dining room, central heating, running cold and hot water. "What else can one want?" he had asked.

Yes, what else could one want? "Nothing," we had agreed.

I spent the whole week dreaming of a house with roomy rooms and leafy trees and grass like crushed green ice. Big, beautiful, and spanking new, it replicated the ones that had leaped out from the pages of glossy magazines.

"We turn somewhere here." Papa's voice was a ripple in distant waters.

"Yes," I heard Ma say. She had been reading the directions. "We turn left on Lincoln Avenue."

"There! Next to the mailbox." My brother squealed. "That's Lincoln Avenue."

I pressed my face against the rolled-up car window and laughed. The sky was ocean-blue, the trees copper-green, and the sunshine liquid-glass.

Papa turned into a windswept street lined with giant trees whose thick branches formed a canopy over our heads. We drove through a tunnel of filtered green light. The mansions that stood farther away from the street, ducked behind the trees, as we swept ahead. I waited for Papa to slow down, to turn into a driveway, to claim one for us. After what felt like ages, he finally slowed down.

"Make a right on Brink Road," Ma said, folding the map and putting it away in the glove compartment.

I held my breath and counted.

One. Two. Three.

We turned.

I blinked at the rows of identical houses that stretched out like multiple reflections caught in a twofold mirror. Papa drove around the block. I stared at stunted front lawns with some clusters of black-eyed susans nodding in the wind, midget backyards cramped with picnic tables, inflatable pools, and tiny patches of tomatoes and cucumbers along link-chain fences.

"7957-55-953-" Bansi was half hanging out of the car window like a schoolboy, his thick unruly hair ruffled by the wind, back counting the house numbers. I wished he would shut up and act like a grownup. He was nineteen and in college. "Seven-Nine-Four-One! Here it is," he shouted in triumph, as if he had discovered a lost continent.

Papa pulled up along the curbside in front of a twin house. "Here we are," he said. "This is the house!"

"This?"

I stared at the house with a tamarind-green front door and windows.

"This."

"But Papa we —"

I might as well have protested to the winds. Seatbelts snapped, doors slammed, everyone got out of the car except me. I couldn't. I took off my glasses, which had suddenly misted up. I was still rubbing them clean when my brother poked his head through the car window and asked. "Now what's holding you back?"

I squinted at him. "This can't be our house! This small shabby and —"

"You didn't expect a chateau, did you?"

"What's a chateau?" I asked.

"It's — never mind," he said.

"I hate this house."

Bansi gave me a long look. I knew a lecture was in the offing. He looked so much like Papa when he was serious.

Even his voice sounded like Papa's when he started telling me what to expect from America. "Mansions don't come with the Green Card. You have to work hard, and once you have saved money, you can buy as large a house as you want to. I see nothing wrong with this place. It's better than Patel's Motel." He paused. His eyes glinted. "May be you prefer Patel's Motel. It's big, right?"

I felt the blood rush to my head. Bansi knew how I had detested being cooped up in the two rooms in Patel's Motel which is where we had been living for a month, ever since we had landed in this country. Mr. Patel was a nice man. He had made special concessions for us. His wife, a short plump woman who wore her thinning hair rolled into a tight bun had placed a hotplate in our room for Ma to cook a quick meal. That, however, hadn't made the rooms less cramped, nor taken away the smell of spices hovering in the air. It was embarrassing to see people stop and sniff the air when they walked by.

Bansi must have noticed some pain in my face, for he smiled. "Come on, Grumps," he said a trifle kindly. "Let's go inside."

Reluctantly, I slid out of the car and followed him into the house.

My mother was standing in the kitchen, examining the ugliest wallpaper I had ever seen. A design of bright-red raspberries and strawberries nestling in tiny baskets of green leaves spattered across it. I was sure my mother was going to walk out of the kitchen in disgust, any moment now. She didn't. On the contrary, she smiled and said, "It's cute! Don't you think so? Very unusual. A nice change from flat paints or paisley designs."

I backed out of the kitchen without a word and climbed the stairs. Bansi was standing in one of the box-sized rooms, measuring the floor with his eyes. "What do you say?" he asked, as soon as he saw me. "The sunlight from the window falls straight here and if I put my desk –"

Without waiting for him to finish his sentence, I spun around and ran down. If a modest house on a nondescript street was all that Ma, and Papa, and Bansi had wanted, then we might as well have stayed in India or gone to live in the Gandhi Ashram to spin cotton and drink goat milk. Why did we have to leave our house with big windows that opened onto a garden teeming with the fragrance of *champa, mogra*, mango and lemon blossom? Why did Papa have to show us pictures of grand houses with gleaming windows and green lawns when this tiny house was all he could manage?

"This isn't an American house!" I blubbered, when my parents stepped into the small backyard made smaller by the fat roots of a lone cherry tree that had usurped all the space. "We can't live here."

No one paid me any attention. Ma and Papa had walked over to a pink man in orange shorts who was waving at us from the other side of the fence. Bansi was contemplating a squirrel trapezing across an electric cable. I stood glaring at the grass at my feet till I heard Papa calling me.

"Did you hear what Mr. Mikulsky said?" he asked me as I approached him and the pink man.

I shook my head.

"I was telling your dad about the school bus." The pink man spoke with an accent. "Is a pity it doesn't enter our street."

Papa frowned. "I should have thought of that!"

My spirits soared like a balloon that had slipped out of a child's hand and was sailing away into the blue skies. Maybe I was going to like the pink man, after all.

The illusion didn't last too long, for he was quick to assure Papa. "No! No! No! The bus stop is just two blocks down the street. On Lincoln Avenue – that big street with big houses. You can walk. Isn't that far, really."

Papa's eyes cleared. "Surely you can walk two blocks," he

said to me. "We used to walk miles to get to our school when we were your age."

"Two blocks!" the pink man sniffed. "Is nothing for a young girl like you."

I knew then that I was going to hate him for the rest of my life.

The globules of sunlight trembled as I stomped back to the cherry tree. The cascading branches shrank as I tore off a handful of leaves and threw them on the grass for the wind to lift and scatter. Swallowing the tears that were threatening to spill out, I swore. When I grow up, I told myself, I would never live in a twin house with a tiny backyard and a tamarind-green front door. Never would I live on a street called Brink Road. And never with a pink man in orange shorts for a neighbor. My house, I resolved, would rival the grandest mansions I had seen in the movies. My garden would resemble the Brindavan Gardens in Mysore where Bollywood shot its song sequences. Flowers, musical fountains, lights, and all. I would also have a heart-shaped swimming pool, a snaking driveway, a backyard filled with apple trees, and a deck jutting out into the woods. I swore I would have it all, one day.

One day? The wind laughed in my face. But what till then?

Till then? The question drummed in my ears like hailstones on a tin roof.

Yes, what till then?

Till then, I tossed my answer back to the winds, I will live with my dreams locked inside me like kernels compressed inside a pomegranate. Like pearls in oyster shells. I will wait for my dreams to ripen, to swell, and to burst out of their casing, gleaming like rubies, glowing like pearls.

My pomegranate dreams!

The cherry tree nodded. The wind chuckled. It's going to be a long time, they whispered.

I can wait, I said.

We moved into the house on Brink Road, the following

weekend. My prayers, offered in earnest to gods and goddesses, went unanswered. Not a single miracle happened to make Papa change his mind. The motel account was cleared, the suitcases packed, and we were ready to roll, as Bansi put it. Papa had decided to make four trips to transport us and our baggage in the used Honda Civic he had bought. Sitting in the motel lobby, near our piled-up suitcases, I felt like a lone traveler on a railway platform, waiting for the train to arrive. America was a lonesome place, indeed, so unlike my home country where we would have been surrounded with friends, relatives, and servants on such an occasion. Someone would have brought a truck. My grandmother's astrologer would have determined the auspicious time to enter the house, which he would have sanctified by sprinkling sacred water and rice in all corners. An aunt would have carried an earthenware pot filled with water and placed it in the house on the eve of our moving in. Later, amidst much laughter and ceaseless chatter, everyone would have sat down to a feast of *halwa* and *puri*.

I was sitting in the motel lobby, feeling homesick, when I saw a pickup truck drive in. Grandpa and Grandma Miller had come all the way from Lancaster to help us move. I still remember the silver-haired man with laughing blue eyes and wisps of silver hair neatly combed away from a shining forehead. Dressed in his Sunday best – a white shirt, navy-blue suit, and a red tie – he looked ready to play the organ in his church as he always did on Sundays. Instead, he was ready to load our suitcases into the truck. And I still remember his rosy-cheeked, stocky wife, a grown-up Cabbage-Patch doll, who wouldn't stop talking from the moment she got off the pickup truck to the moment she climbed back into it in the evening to return to Lancaster.

Mr. and Mrs. Miller had been my father's hosts when he had first come to America as a Fulbright scholar. Papa said they had represented for him an America he had only read and dreamed about. He never tired of talking about their generosity, their trust, and the love with which they had taken him into their home and hearts. Mr. Miller had driven some three hundred miles in a blowing snow storm to pick up Papa from JFK International Airport. And not knowing what would appeal to an Indian's taste buds, Mrs. Miller had cooked him a feast. Mashed potatoes, sweet corn, beef roast, spicy chicken, steamed cauliflower, boiled spinach, glazed carrot, and much more. It always tickled us when Papa narrated how, tired from his long flight from New Delhi, and relieved at finding such kind souls as his hosts, he had fallen asleep over a bowl of sweet corn. Grandpa Miller always teased him about that meal. Since Papa addressed them as Mom and Pop, they became Grandpa and Grandma Miller to me and my brother Bansi.

Grandma Miller lost no time in taking charge of the kitchen as soon we entered the house on Brink Road. She had brought some pots and pans, dishes, bedsheets, a big basket of fruit and vegetables, and a table with four chairs as housewarming gifts.

"You can start unpacking," she told my mother. "I'll have supper ready by the time you're done."

And she did.

By the time we had emptied our suitcases and hung our clothes in the closets, supper was ready. Grandma Miller had spread a red checkered tablecloth on the table and dished out Papa's favorite sweet corn, vegetables, meat loaf, and iced tea which she made from homegrown mint leaves. "Eat. You need to eat more," she said, passing around thick slices of warm bread. We ate.

And then she brought in her apple pie, which was to become the mother of all my pies. The aroma of cooking apples, sugar, and cinnamon and the taste of a warm flaky crust dissolving in the mouth still hauls me back to the day I first tasted Grandma Miller's apple pie.

After the Millers left that evening, we rolled out our beds

on the floor, and got ready to sleep our first night in our first American home. The good food and the pleasant visit by the Millers had left us fulfilled even though we had no regular beds and the windows were without curtains. It was a relief to be away from the motel, from the sound of doors banging, from voices murmuring in the hallway, from the noise of someone taking a shower in the middle of the night, or some insomniac watching TV at full volume in the room next door. Wrapped in a light blanket and watching the play of the street light on the ceiling, I dozed off. Sometime, in the middle of the night, I woke up to see a full moon smiling through the window. I slipped back into deep slumber. In my dreams I was lying curled up beside Dadi, my grandmother, who had started sleeping on the floor after my grandfather died. I inhaled the fragrance of sandalwood and butter that always clung to her. She was singing her favorite hymn to Rama. I was back in Jaipur, my hometown in India, and yet the house was the one we had moved into on Brink Road, in America where the rooms had grown bigger, the ceilings had risen higher, and the windows had grown taller. In the backyard, pomegranates were laughing on the spindly branches and apples were beaming in the thick leaves. Two landscapes and two houses – one familiar, and the other unknown – had fused into one. Like the mendicants in my grandmother's stories, I seemed to have overcome the barriers of time and space. I was in two places at the same time, straddling two worlds. I didn't know then that it was just the beginning of the kaleidoscopic formations and re-formations that my mind was always going to be subjected to.

When I woke up next morning, it took me some time to come to terms with the small, bare, unfamiliar room I had slept in. A babble of voices outside the window reminded me that this wasn't my home in India. I rubbed the dreams from my eyes. Somewhere, a lawnmower coughed. A car growled, a door slammed, and someone shouted. I scrambled to the window. Mr. Mikulsky, the pink man, was tinkering with his lawnmower while his wife, a ruddy woman with thinning hair and a swollen right arm, was hanging laundry on the clothesline. There were no pomegranates laughing nor apples beaming in the backyard; only the old cherry with its knotty trunk stood nodding in the morning sunlight. The rooms had shrunk back into boxes and the windows into small squares. Like all dreams, last night's dream had become just another memory.

The plain dull house on a plain dull street with a plain dull name soured my days. Distance endeared even more the home we had left behind in Jaipur. It may not have been centrally heated or cooled, but it was five times the size of the twin house on Brink Road. When it rained, we could play hide-and-seek with our friends and cousins inside the house without disturbing the grownups, who sat in cane chairs on the veranda, watching the monsoon clouds break.

Here, the paper-thin walls absorbed no sound. If Bansi so much as turned in his bed upstairs, we heard him. If Papa coughed, we knew. We could even hear the water running in Mrs. Mikulsky's kitchen and Mr. Mikulsky's Polish songs, which he liked to play on his cassette player at night. In the beginning, the slightest sound of the floor boards creaking or a door opening would scare me to death. I always thought that someone, a thief or a robber, was sneaking upstairs, while it was really Mr. Mikulsky or his wife climbing the stairs on the other side of the common wall. Ours was no American house, no matter what Papa or Bansi said. The real American houses were the ones on Lincoln Avenue, the street where my school bus stopped. Lincoln Avenue was no ordinary street. It was a dark river winding its way through ancient trees, behind which sat grand houses looking so dignified, so aloof, and so self-sufficient. They mesmerized me. They filled me with such longing that sometimes I felt my chest would burst.

I didn't mind the rain or the sun when I found myself on Lincoln Avenue. The massive sycamores threw sun-dappled shadows at my feet when I stepped off the bus in the afternoon. I would walk home with golden discs of sunshine dancing at my feet. A whiff of fresh-baked cookies often wafted through the light-footed afternoons. I would sniff the air and look at the shining windows of the mansions. I rarely saw anyone except the men who raked leaves and mowed the lawns, or the dogs that came out to mark their domain along tree trunks or a lamppost. The inhabitants remained distant like the rich in India who used to glide past us in sleek, imported cars with the smoke-glass windows rolled up. The only faces visible had been those of the chauffeurs in livery or the ayahs accompanying the children to school. The rich must be the same everywhere, I thought. Aloof and invisible. All that they did was talk on the phone, or drive around in cars with tinted glasses, or sit behind lace-curtained windows and drink tea poured from a silver tea-service by a maid wearing a frilled white apron.

There was a huge red brick house along the avenue with arched windows and doorways that had everything I yearned for in a house – a porch, a driveway, and a vast lawn. I would often see a girl on the lawn, throwing a ball for her poodle to fetch. She was my mirror image: dark-haired, brown-skinned, my age, and perhaps Indian. When I passed her house, my feet dragged, as if my shoes had filled up with sand. I would hide behind a sycamore and watch her chatting and laughing with a couple of white American kids, or hurling a stick across the lawn for the dog to fetch. The sight was enough to set my heart knocking wildly against my chest, as if a woodpecker trapped inside were trying to get out.

This girl had everything I longed for. I wished we could be friends. I wished I could see the inside of her house, smell the flowers, touch the exotic shrubs. I would stand with my heart throbbing, my eyes unblinking. And yet, had the girl looked at me, I would have walked away.

Slowly. Casually. Carelessly.

I would have walked away from her house with its arched windows and away from her lawn lined with neat rows of flowerbeds. I would have walked away from her friends and her dog. I would have walked away, pretending indifference to everything she had and I didn't.

The image of the girl and her dog would cling to my mind long after I had left the scene. It would linger there like the fragrance of flowers pressed between the pages of a book. Like the whiff of mothballs in the folds of old clothes stowed away in a trunk. Like the specks of a dream that never faded.

Whenever I came home with silken cobwebs trembling in my eyes, everyone knew I had seen the girl with her dog. Ma would open the fridge and stare into it as if she were seeing fruit trees growing inside. Bansi would remember some task he had to finish and disappear into his room. I sulked into the glass of milk Ma placed in front of me.

"Drink it! You must be hungry," she would say, holding a cookie jar in front of me. I would down the milk in a gulp, grab a cookie, and slink off to my room without a word.

One day, however, as I was about to leave the room, Papa stopped me. "You want to make friends with that girl, don't you?"

He pushed aside the papers he was always reading and grading, even when he was drinking his tea, or talking over the telephone, or watching the evening news. Sometimes, when he was not preparing for those extra courses he taught, Papa would sit late into the night pounding at the typewriter, working on a book. I had secretly centered all my dreams on that book. I was certain it was going to be a bestseller. The moment it was published, the treasure chests that lay buried under deep seas would float up to the surface. We'd be rich and we'd live in a house on Lincoln Avenue.

Papa repeated his question, tapping the table with his pencil. "You want to be friends with that girl, don't you?"

"Yes, Papa."

"Then why don't you talk to her?"

"How? How can I do that?"

"Very simple!" He leaned back into the chair. "Just say 'Hello!' Introduce yourself. And there you are. You're friends. We never had any problem making friends when we were your age." Papa made everything sound so simple.

"It's not that easy," I mumbled. "You don't understand."

He squinted at me. "What's so complex about it? She's your age. She's Indian," he said. "Like us."

"Like us?" I sprang up, as if I had touched a live wire. My back arched. "How can they be like us? Nobody's like us. They're – we're –" I fumbled for words.

Papa waited for me to finish the sentence.

"Yes?"

I took a deep breath. "She can't be like us, Papa. We don't live in a big house with beautiful trees. We don't have big new cars. We don't even have a dog. We're nobody. We –"

"Now wait! Wait!"

Before I could complete my list of deprivations, Bansi vaulted in. He always did that, especially if he heard me complaining about what others had and we didn't. He took advantage of being older and in college, but most of all, of being Papa's ambassador. He was cast in Papa's image.

"Don't be ridiculous, Miss Greedy!" He said, looking down at me from his superior height. Bansi was shooting up like a bamboo tree. He was all arms and legs and a big head, too. "What do you mean by a big house and two cars, ha? Everyone in America has a house and two cars. Don't we?"

Papa returned to his papers, leaving the field to Bansi – his Knight in Armor.

"Papa's car is ancient. And yours? You call that junky-jet a car?"

"It runs, doesn't it? Doesn't it take me wherever I want to go? Didn't all the girls look at me when I picked you up that day?" he asked. "The paint may be chipped and it may have a few dents here and there, so what?"

"So what? Is that all you can say for that scrap?"

He laughed. "It doesn't have to be a limousine, does it?"

I gave up.

I couldn't argue with Bansi, who believed he had resolved all doubts and who thought he possessed everything in the world though he didn't even have a pair of Nike sneakers to his name. Nor a Calvin Klein winter jacket. Not even a CD player. He didn't mind working late in the evening and on weekends while others his age were partying. He didn't have a girlfriend. "So what?" He would shrug when I teased him. "I'm happy. I have better things to do than to sit around holding a girl's hand."

Perhaps he was right. College and part-time work in a computer store didn't leave him any time for anything. The only thing for which he could squeeze out some time were his ships. Assembling and collecting miniature boats was Bansi's passion. He had a number of tug boats, sail boats, barges, liners, steamers and battleships lined up on a shelf in his room. I would watch his hands move with the precision of a watchmaker, a jeweler, an artist when he glued tiny masts, sails, rudders, decks, port windows to a vessel. And when it was completed, he would hold it in the hollow of his hand and look at it with eyes flashing like beacons.

He was content living simply and frugally, satisfied with the minimum, like Papa and his idol, Gandhi. I considered him strange. Wacky. My mother, though, doted on him. She called him her *sadhu*, her monk, her ascetic who demanded nothing, who desired nothing. He was like Baba, the mendicant, who used to come to our house in Jaipur for alms, an ascetic who had renounced the world. He never talked to anyone. No one knew who he was, where he came from, and where he went. We wouldn't see him for months. Then suddenly, one day, he would be standing on the front veranda steps, waiting for my grandmother to bring him whatever she could hurriedly pile up on a tray. Baba wore nothing but a loincloth on his ash-smeared body. Hardly a beggar, he asked for nothing. And he never stood still. Papa said he was one of those mendicants who had taken a vow to keep moving, who never sat down. Motion, he said, was one way of disciplining the mind and body. To stop was to cease. It wasn't for nothing that Papa had chosen to be a professor of philosophy.

In any event, Baba would keep treading the flagstones, as if he were warming up, or marking time to march off. Chanting some strange mantra, beating rhythm with a pair of iron tongs in his hand, he kept his bloodshot eyes fixed upon a point in the ceiling. Hidden behind a door, we would peep at him. Bansi was certain that tiny finches nestled in his tangled and matted hair. With mounting excitement, we would wait for the birds to pop out, chirping and fluttering their tiny wings. They never did.

From the tray piled high with fruit and nuts that my Dadi offered to him, Baba would pick out a banana, or a mango, or a handful of peanuts. Never more. Then he would walk away. Grandmother would beam with joy, for he had accepted a morsel from her home. She would clasp her hands and bow her head to his receding back.

And if my grandmother were late in turning up with the tray, Baba would leave. Without a word. Without a backward glance. Nothing could make him come back for his meager meal. Not his hunger. Not my grandmother's pleas. She would be miserable for days, because a monk had gone away hungry from her door. Not even a stray dog or a cat or a cow went away hungry from her house. How could a monk go away empty-handed? A monk, who had overcome hunger and desire. Who had renounced the world.

Bansi was like Baba. He had overcome desire. He needed no props to be happy. I did. Bansi could be happy not wishing for anything. Not wanting. Not having. But I couldn't. I wanted the whole universe. The sun. The moon. The stars. The wind. The earth. The sky. The rainbow with a pot of gold at the end of it. I wanted to clasp them all in my hands. Isn't that why we had come to America, anyway? I asked myself. Isn't that what everyone came to America for? Rushing in from all the quarters of the world. In boats. In planes. On foot, across the borders. From Africa. From China. From Cuba. From Haiti. From Mexico. From Russia. Ukraine. Yugoslavia. From all points of the compass. We wanted it all.

And if we couldn't have it all, then what was the point in our dreaming America? Wishing America? Craving America? Coming to America?

The first thing that Papa had done, as soon as he returned from his year-long stay in America, was to spread out a world map on the table and point out to us the huge land mass sprawling between the Atlantic and the Pacific oceans. "That's where we're all going," he had said, laying his finger on America. We had hung on every word of his as he spun stories about the beauty of the land, its abundance, its opportunities, its prosperity, and its people, especially about a Mr. and Mrs. Miller who had been his host family. Kind, honest, hardworking people, Papa had said. They were a beautiful people who represented the true spirit of a beautiful country. Visions of a distant land with a good people in it began to sprout in our minds. It was the land where pumpkins turned into crystal carriages and mice into white horses and cinder maids into princesses.

So powerful was its lure that, dreaming of America, we dreamed of nothing else.

Wanting America, we wanted nothing else.

·"Now to America!" Papa had said, one day, our visas fluttering in his hands like the sails of a ship ready to cross the bar. And we started packing our suitcases. Squealing with delight, at first. Then, squirming with woe, as Papa reduced to a small pile our rising mound of toys, clothes, books, and the childhood treasures that stood for souvenirs. We had to pack our lives into the two suitcases each one was allowed to carry into the new land. Bansi didn't mind leaving everything behind. In fact, he took off with three pairs of pants and the model ship that our grandfather had given him upon his tenth birthday. "New country. New life. New Dream." That was his motto.

But I was furious. Leave everything behind? Never.

Going to America couldn't mean dismantling our past and abandoning it like a charred building. The pile of things I couldn't carry with us grew bigger. If I had a genie at my command, I thought, I would transport everything of ours to America in the blink of an eye.

Papa looked at my pile and growled, "No. This is all trash now."

"It's not," I cried, clinging to my treasures.

Papa didn't recant. I wouldn't surrender.

Finally, my grandmother pulled out her trunk and deposited in it all my treasures – my dolls, their tiny china tea service, their bed, table and chairs, my glass beads, crayons, clay animals with chipped noses and bobbed tails, and reams of drawings I had done. "I'll send them by surface mail," she said. They were still there, in the trunk, under her bed when I visited her some years later.

When we set out for America, we left behind so much. Not just my dolls, my glass beads, my plastic jewelry, and the clay menagerie I had collected over the years. Not just Bansi's cricket set, his old Superman and Phantom comic books, and the radio he had assembled for his science class. Not just my mother's brocade and silk saris, her heavy gold jewelry, which she said she would have no use for in America. Not just the *koel* singing in the mango trees and the peacock dancing on the roof. Not just the friends and cousins we had grown up with. Not just the festivals which popped up every other day and provided us with an excuse to take off from school.

We left behind much more.

We left behind our grandmother with whom I had lived all the years of my life. Despite our pleas and despite her love for us she wouldn't accompany us. She couldn't leave her land behind. She couldn't leave the house with absurdly large rooms filled with wind and the echoes of the fifty-seven years she had spent there. She wanted to die among the familiar.

We left behind the stone house that was cooled in summer by the wind heavy with mango blossom, and warmed in winter by the sun.

We left behind our garden where *champa, chameli*, marigold and bougainvillea jostled to out-bloom each other; the pomegranate trees with slender spiny branches, from which parrots swung, prying the fruit open with their sharp beaks; the *jamun* and guava trees that yielded so much fruit that even the street urchins would stop to climb over the compound wall to steal some.

We left behind the monkeys that leapt from one branch to another, shaking the fruit down so that it lay staining the flagstones purple.

And we left behind something else, too, a sense of belonging, which seemed to have slipped off like a bundle from the top of a bus climbing a mountain road.

I couldn't believe that we had exchanged that bounty for a tiny house with a grizzly cherry tree whose gnarled roots were splayed like fear unleashed in the dark.

Bansi thought I suffered from inflated nostalgia. "What do you have to cry about, Miss Grouchy?" He chided me. "We have everything. Look at people like Chacha who have nothing. He's the one who's truly gotten a raw deal." Chacha was our uncle, my father's cousin.

My brother had this habit of pointing out to the deprived and the disadvantaged, but never to the ones who were privileged and better off than us. "It's Priya who should be complaining," he said. "Not you."

Priya was Chacha's daughter. Our cousin. Our sister. My friend. Priya was sixteen, but she acted as if she were thirty-six. Her enormous brown eyes, set in a thin face, framed by a mop of dark curls, hardly ever blinked as she looked at you. Her smile never faded. Priya never complained, never sulked. She laughed at everything. Neither her mother's mood shifts nor her father's stern look muffled her tinkling laughter. None of us could have believed that such sweetness would be sullied, one day.

Chacha lived in a small apartment on a scrawny street block weighed down with rusted, dented, battered, abandoned cars. Virtually all of the houses were mere shells now – dark and crumbling. Boarded. Wild grass and dandelions had pushed their way through the cracks in the steps and the crevices in the walls. They were houses without a soul, already food for the worms.

The first time we went to visit Chacha, Papa swore afterward, that he would never drive to that place again. As the street narrowed, as a car or a bus in front of us lurched to a sudden halt, and as those behind us honked or cursed or shook their fists, Papa's face grew red, then purple.

"What a place to live in! This is atrocious. Monstrous. Appalling –" His adjectives grew more complex. His voice more gruff.

Papa didn't lose his cool easily, but that day, as he drove through the maze, his temper shot up like mercury in the Indian summer heat. "What a place to live in!" he snorted. He never took his eyes off the road. Never stopped grumbling. Never stopped barking instructions at me.

"Don't open the window."

"Lock the door."

"Don't stare, Juhi."

I could hardly keep my eyes off the plastic bottles and empty cans rolling near the curb. Scraps of paper fluttered in the breeze. Garbage spilled out of lidless containers and the houses stared at us mutely as we looked for Chacha's brown stone building.

Finally, I asked him. "Is this America, Papa?"

He stepped on the brakes. He frowned at me in the rear-view mirror.

"What do you –" he began, but before he could complete his sentence, Bansi shouted. "There's Chacha!"

We stopped in front of a huge brown building. It had a brown roof, brown doors, and brown windows. Chacha was standing on the steps, flailing his arms like a windmill.

"Any problem finding this place?" he asked pleasantly as we got out of the car.

"Not much," Ma said.

Papa glared at her.

"Good!" Chacha said. "Getting here can be a little complicated at times."

"A little?" Papa choked, mopping his forehead with the flat of his palm. "I think driving across the country would be easier."

Chacha ignored the sarcasm. "Come! Come! Shobha and Priya are waiting for you and tea is ready," he said, leading the way.

Chacha reminded me of a big brown dormouse as he walked in short steps beside my tall, broad-shouldered, gray-haired Papa. Chacha's skin, his eyes, his clothes, even his shoes were brown. It was as if he had become a part of the building itself.

The elevator was stuck on some floor, so we took the stairs. By the time we got to his apartment on the fourth floor, we were all out of breath. Priya and her mother were waiting for us at the door. Shobha Chachi was a small pallid woman with a pinched mouth, and eyes that reminded one of moonless skies. She looked at us as if we were complete strangers before saying, in a listless voice, "Come in."

The two-bedroom apartment was small and stuffy. It was a drab place except for the hand-embroidered peacocks, roses and pansies that leaped at us from the cushions and tablecloths. My mother picked up a cushion and said, "This is exquisite!"

Shobha Chachi's eyes flashed as if a shooting star had sailed across dark skies. Then midnight closed in. She said in a flat voice, "What good is it? No one sees or admires my work here."

The air conditioner was pumping in stale air. Chacha turned on a table fan, saying, "It's a bit warm today."

His wife twisted around and pointed to the windows. "When you don't open the windows, it has to be warm, no? Where's fresh air?"

"If you open the windows you'll have uninvited visitors climbing in," Chacha explained. "You know how it is here.

Besides, with the air conditioner on, how can you open the windows?"

"The air conditioner doesn't always work." Shobha Chachi let out a big sigh. "I feel choked."

Chacha stood there cracking his fingers, looking around like a trapped animal searching for an escape. He shifted his weight from one foot to another. There was an odd silence in the room. None of us knew what to say. Then Priya came to our rescue. She turned to me and asked, "Do you want to see the building?"

"Good idea!" Chacha sounded relieved. "Go! Go! Show them around. It used to be a very fine hotel." He must have found it disconcerting to have all of us standing there like actors who had forgotten their cues.

Priya led us through the hallways, giving a commentary like a tourist guide. "It was a magnificent building, once. A grand hotel, really. Full of beautiful people."

Bansi and I tried to ignore the tilting hallway floor, the hair-thin cracks in the walls, the worn-out carpet.

Priya, oblivious of everything except what only she could see, continued. "You should see the dining hall – of course it's cluttered with junk now. Old furniture stocked there, you know. But once its walls were hung with gilt-framed mirrors and there were huge chandeliers –"

"How can you be so sure?" Bansi asked.

"There's one still in there. I saw it. It's pure crystal – like the one in the Gwalior Palace of India." Her eyes were shining like twin moons.

"But what about the beautiful people?" Bansi asked. He wasn't impressed.

"What happened to them?" I wanted to know.

"You know, people grow old. They die. They go away. So much happens in life. You're still too young to understand all that," she said sizing me up. "And guess what!"

"What?"

"One of them still lives here."

"Who?"

"One of the beautiful people. She's lovely, like -- like a movie star."

"She can't be lovely if she's old. And she has to be very old," Bansi objected.

Priya wasn't put out in the least. She pushed a loose strand of hair behind her ear and stood her ground. "What do you know? You haven't seen her. She's really stunning!"

"Can't be," Bansi shook his head. "She has to be a wizened old woman. A hag."

"A ghost!" I breathed. "Maybe she's a ghost!"

"That' right!" Priya's face lit up. "A ghost! Diamonds in her golden hair and diamonds in her ears –" Priya's imagination was going at full throttle. "I have seen her floating down the grand staircase –"

Bansi frowned. "You're making it all up."

"I'm not."

Priya swore that she had seen the woman with a sad oval face and corn-flower-blue eyes, wearing diamonds. She was always dressed in white.

"If you hear someone playing a piano in the middle of the night, you know it's the lady in white," Priya whispered.

"Nonsense!" Bansi said, but I felt a delicious shiver run down my spine.

What a ghost! Beautiful! Wearing diamonds! Playing the piano! I envied Priya her almost-sanitized ghost.

The one that I had heard about, but never seen, was a scary one. It was said to live on the tamarind tree at the back of our house in Jaipur. No one had seen its face. We had been warned to stay away from the tree because the ghost was supposed to change into a handsome young man at night and lure young girls away. My grandmother said that girls who fell under its spell lost their mind. It had happened to our gardener's daughter. The moment she walked under the tamarind tree at dusk, the ghost had grabbed her. Someone had really seen the girl locked in the embrace of a white form. So the exorcist had been called, and for two days the man had mumbled strange chants and poured water over this girl and whipped her to free her of the ghost. Had Papa not intervened, the girl might have been skinned alive. In any case, she lost her mind after that. She cried and laughed and talked to herself. I still remember a girl with a thin pale face, sitting under a tree and looking at us with soulless eyes. Within a couple of months, she was hastily married off to a man three times her age. We never saw her again. Six months later, we heard she had died of tuberculosis. My grandmother said the ghost had sucked away her blood. My mother believed that she died of a broken heart. The servants claimed that the girl's ghost haunted the tamarind tree and they never ventured near it despite the juicy tamarinds that ripened and fell to the ground.

Priya's ghost was different. It was a rich American ghost.

"You have to live here to know all the stories. She walks around at night, tending to the sick –"

Bansi was quick to interrupt her. "You sure, now, it's not Florence Nightingale?"

Priya blushed, but she stuck to her story even after Bansi had dismissed it.

Finally, she took us into the lobby. The tall, barred windows gave it the appearance of a cell. Priya told us that it used to have beautiful stained-glass windows, which the burglars had removed. "Imagine how lovely this place must have been!" she said.

We didn't say anything. I could see the light from the stolen stained-glass windows reflected in her eyes.

"That, over there," she pointed to a set of heavy folding doors at the end of the lounge. "That is the dining room – a ballroom, really. With mirrors on the walls. Imagine women in long evening gowns dancing with men in dark suits –"

"Silly, girlie stuff!" Bansi said. "You've been watching too many Bombay movies."

Bansi was a skeptic, but I saw it all. Candles and roses and burgundy shadows. A blur of pale faces, pearl-white shoulders, and velvet gowns swirling in the dusky mirrors. Priya promised to show us the mysterious room with mirrors and chandeliers one day. "You might even be able to see the lady in white," she said.

That day never came. All we ever saw were the ghosts of real life – single mothers, delinquent kids, and crazy men and women haunting the streets. Priya never ran out of her stock of stories. They multiplied faster than the cockroaches that she claimed to be swarming in their apartment.

"Cockroaches? In America? Impossible!" I said.

Priya dismissed my objection with a flick of her hand. "Nothing's impossible."

"You've seen them?"

"Scores of them, silly!" Priya's eyes were like polished mirrors reflecting shadows. "You have to come to our apartment and see for yourself. The roaches hold a carnival in the kitchen every night."

"You're kidding."

"I'm not. You step into the kitchen at night, turn on the light. And there they are – hordes of cockroaches crawling all over the counter, the floor, the oven." She shuddered. "You feel like you're in a sci-fi movie – like in the *X-Files* – where the insects have taken over the world. It's weird! Really, it is."

"But you can kill them with insecticides."

Priya shook her head, "No, you can't. These cockroaches are stubborn. They keep coming back. You kill one and ten spring up. Like the demon *Beejasur*, you know, the one who was blessed with immortality. From a drop of his blood a thousand demons would spring."

That was another thing about Priya. She knew many stories from Hindu mythology. She never lost an opportunity to use them to emphasize her interpretation of the world. It was only a year or so later, after she became friendly with Nellie and Chips, that she was to forget them all. The thought of thousands of cockroaches crawling on the kitchen floor was as nauseating as the thought of geckos, the house lizards, slithering on the walls of our rooms in India.

I had been terrified of the mud-gray creatures that crept along the walls, the ceilings, as they waited for the monsoon to bring mosquitoes and insects in its wake. At night, one could hear them clicking their tongues as they stalked their prey. Sometimes, a fat lizard would lose its grip and plop on the floor. And if it fell on someone, the whole house would be in an uproar as if a mad elephant had charged in. The dropping of a lizard portended death. Once it fell on my aunt while she was sleeping. Plop on her chest. She went crazy. Tearing off her sari and blouse, she ran screaming all over the house. Without a stitch on her body. But nobody dared touch her till Panditji, the priest, had been called in to perform rituals to ward off the evil.

Mercifully, there were no lizards in America. Only cockroaches in decaying apartments where rich and beautiful women with diamonds in their hair had once floated down the spiraling staircases. Or men got drunk and walked into lampposts. Or youngsters got high and threw up in the lobby. Or loonies went around hammering at the doors in the middle of the night. There was one who kicked at Chacha's door and shouted obscenities. "Go home. Go back, monkey chasers!" The loony cried in a cracked voice.

It was enough to send Shobha Chachi into a frenzy. "Why can't we move out? Why can't we buy a house of our own?" she complained.

"What do you want me to do?" Chacha would growl. "Put myself up for sale? Where can I get the money to buy a house?" And Priya would bury her head under the bedclothes, as if by doing so she could banish the horror of a crazy man kicking their door. Of disgruntled parents jabbering in the other room. Of cockroaches crawling in the kitchen.

She could never drown her mother's voice, though, which kept bouncing against the walls, asking, "Why did we come here? Why?" Nor could she block out her father's explosions when he tried to justify his decision. Sometimes, she too questioned her father's wisdom. If he had come for money or a better career, he had succeeded in finding neither. If it were for Priya, then he had made a mistake. Neither of the parents could agree on what they wanted for Priya. Shobha Chachi wanted to arrange her marriage with a doctor or a businessman, like Chachi's brother Suraj Mehta, so that Priya would have a comfortable life. "I don't want her to end up like me," she would tell Ma. "A slave at home and a slave at work." Chacha had different dreams. He wanted Priya to become a doctor or a lawyer. He was ready to send her to Harvard or Yale so that she could achieve what he hadn't. Priya, he dreamed now, could be his standard-bearer. If only she would take interest in her studies, America would fulfill all the dreams he had dreamed but which had gotten lost somewhere along the way.

Running a store in a neighborhood where someone painted graffiti on the walls or smashed his windows, working hard from morning till late in the evening, he would often stare at his nails, and ask himself, "Now why on earth did I come here?"

Perhaps it was the lure of an enchanted land where they said money flowed from the faucets and where janitors became CEOs that had brought Chacha to these shores. Or, perhaps, it was the desire to prove himself better than his brother-in-law, Suraj Mehta, who had come to America and had a thriving business, that had made him set out for the Promised Land. Papa said it was Jack who had encouraged him to take that leap. Jack was the owner of a construction company in America. He had loved India so much that he used to visit it every other year. It was during one of those visits that he met Chacha on the train from Agra to Delhi. Chacha invited him over to his house. He accepted. By the time Jack left to return to America, they had become friends. When he offered Chacha a job in his company and sponsored him and his family, Chacha saw the fulfillment of a dream, the realization of a myth about rich and generous Americans who befriended Indians and helped them emigrate to America.

Throwing caution to the winds, Chacha had tendered his resignation, sold his house, his car, his custom-made furniture within a week after he got his visa. To anyone who warned him against burning his boats, Chacha replied, "But that's what the Vikings did when they reached the New World. I'm following their example – making a clean cut with the past. Beginning a new life."

For two years after he reached America with his family, Chacha worked for Jack, who turned out to be everything Chacha had believed him to be. Kind, generous, and trustworthy. Perhaps things might have turned out better for Chacha had Jack's truck not skidded down a sloping road, one snowy evening, when he was returning from a late-night party. No one had discovered the accident till the next morning when Jack was found frozen to death in the upturned truck. For weeks after his friend and employer was gone, Chacha refused to believe that Jack was dead. Even after the company folded and Chacha lost his job, he couldn't forget Jack. He hung an enlarged picture of Jack's in his living room and told everyone who visited him, about Jack. I remember the big man in jeans, with long blond hair framing a ruddy face, holding a Coke in his hand and squinting at us from his high perch on the wall. It was when he had to file for unemployment that Chacha came out of his stupor. With a heart that seemed to have overturned in the snow with Jack's truck, Chacha started working with the township where he didn't make much money. His brother-in-law, in the meantime, was thriving and had bought a villa.

Chacha resigned from the township job. He sank all his savings into buying a convenience store. Taking risks, he believed, was part of becoming a millionaire. If Suraj Mehta could expand his small textile shop in India into a successful export business in America, he could prosper likewise. If Anthony Wong, who had begun with a small trash truck and now owned the largest trash-collection agency in the region, could become a millionaire, so could he. If Mukesh Patel could start out with a small motel and end up owning a chain of motels, Chacha believed, he too could own a franchise. Money and prosperity, he had dreamed, were just around the corner.

A couple of strides, and he could come up big. To the scores of success stories of immigrants in the American saga, there was no reason why he couldn't add one more – his own.

Now, after three years of running a store in a crumbling neighborhood, Chacha's dream of becoming a millionaire had begun to recede like the shoreline from a boat cut loose. He refused to go back to India with a sense of defeat. After all, he had put everything, all his life's savings, at stake when he came to America.

Shobha Chachi had found work stitching leather belts in a factory. She hated working there. She couldn't get the smell of leather out of her hands, her hair, and her breath despite the long showers she took after work. The whir of machines hounded her and gave her a constant migraine. Her nostalgia for her beautiful home in India, for her servants, for her friends, and the comforts she had left behind aggravated her unhappiness.

"This is not what I had imagined my life to be," she would complain, striking her forehead with her palm. "Who'd like to come to America to stitch belts?"

Papa didn't feel much sympathy for Chachi. He thought she whined too much. Since she didn't speak much English, the leather factory was one of the few places where she could get away without speaking English or without speaking at all. "America treats you fairly," he said, "provided you are ready to grit your teeth and work hard."

Chacha's store, which had begun to run at a loss, was a major object of contention between the husband and wife. Ma was convinced that Chacha wasn't cut out for business. Papa had vehemently disagreed with her at first, but when he saw the hours Chacha put into the store, and that without any returns, he advised Chacha to sell the store and take up a decent job with a corporation.

Chacha, however, remained inflexible. He refused to sell the store only because someone, black or white, didn't like him. "I am a free citizen of a free country – no different from anyone else who lives here. Why must I run away?"

I remember when Chacha said something about the store's not doing too well, one evening. He had come over with Shobha Chachi and Priya. It was after dinner, and they were about to leave when Papa said, "You could do ten times better doing what you have been trained for."

Chacha shook his head, cracked the fingers and replied. "It's my luck that is against me, Bipin. It's my fate. My destiny, you know, else why would Jack have died? We were going to be partners, he was like a brother, but fate had some other plans for me. And now look at my brother-in-law! There's a lucky man. His business is thriving. No, Sir! It's fate that stands as your arch enemy."

"Nonsense!" said Papa.

"You have no idea of its power," Chacha insisted. "You can fight against discrimination, tyranny, poverty, anything – but fate? No, Sir. It's ruthless. It waits to catch you and squashes you like a mosquito."

Papa tried to convince him to move to a better neighborhood and buy a house.

"Buy a house? Where's the money?" he asked.

"You can take a loan. Suppose you have ten or fifteen thousand saved –" Papa had pulled out a calculator.

"But I don't –"

"Let's suppose you did. You could."

They sat there playing tic-tac-toe. They added, subtracted, multiplied, divided, crossed out. One moment the numbers clicked. The next, they didn't. Finally Chacha threw up his hands in despair. "Forget it, Bipin. It's useless. If Shobha –"

"Don't!" Shobha Chachi, who had been sitting quietly, so far, screamed. "Don't! Don't you utter zmy name? I won't work overtime. I won't work overtime – not in that factory."

Chacha turned several shades of purple. "Am I asking you to work overtime?"

For a moment, it seemed, he was going to punch her in the face, or tear down the whole place, or go into an apoplectic fit. Then like a deflated balloon, he collapsed into a sullen silence. The furrows on his forehead deepened. His eyes hardened into chunks of granite. His salt and pepper hair stood on edge, like a troll's. Slapping his forehead, he said. "It's all written here. Remember Omar Khayyam? 'The moving finger writes and having writ moves on.' It's moved on and now nothing you do can wipe it off."

Ma, on her part, tried to pacify Shobha Chachi. "It's not that bad, you know. Your life –"

"Life? What life?" Shobha Chachi snapped her fingers. "This you call life? I lost two babies. My girl is growing up. Where will I find her a husband here? This thing you call life is nothing but – but," her voice faltered. Then gathering all her steam, she let out a big hiss. "Shit! I say shit! Life is shit! Shit! Shit!"

My mother, rarely at a loss for words, was tongue-tied.

"For god's sake–" Chacha began.

"Don't. Don't you say a word now," Shobha Chachi glared at him.

Chacha looked at Papa with eyes like that of a dying calf. "You see? You see this? This is what I get for slaving, for working my butts off."

"And what has that work brought you?" Shobha Chachi hissed. "Not even a decent house. Look at my brother! There's a successful man for you!"

That was enough to make Chacha go hopping mad – as if someone had dropped a hammer on his toe. He had been very close to his brother-in-law, Suraj Mehta, once, but now he couldn't forgive Suraj Mehta his beautiful villa, his butler Ganga Ram, his luxury cars, his money. In short, he couldn't forgive Suraj Mehta for being successful. Chacha accused him of having double standards. "He has one for Indians and another for white Americans. When he invites Indians to his house, he doesn't invite a single American ... and not one Indian to his parties for Americans," Chacha would say in a biting tone. "So high and mighty he is now ... in India, Suraj was a no-body. A hypocrite, that's what he is."

Shobha Chachi, in her turn, bore many grudges against her sister-in-law who had been her best friend at school. It was Shobha Chachi who had been the matchmaker in her brother's marriage to Gopi.

"Gopi must be quite a woman," my mother once remarked to Chachi.

"Pooh!" Shobha Chachi spat. "If I had that kind of money, I could throw parties too and better ones. I gave grand parties in India, no?" She looked at Chacha. "All you need is money. And my brother has made lots of money." She could never resist the temptation of singing litanies about the grandeur her brother lived in, "You haven't been there. You don't know what you have missed," she told my mother.

Accounts of the parties at the villa had filtered over to us through other sources too. It seemed that people from the Indian community would give anything to be invited to the villa. And once they received the invitation, women would pull out their heavy brocade saris from the closets and ponder the kind of jewelry they were going to wear. Then for days after the party, they would talk about nothing but Gopi's villa, Gopi's dress, Gopi's jewelry, Gopi's taste, and, of course, about Ganga Ram, Gopi's Indian chef and butler who had been with Gopi's since he was a boy. Ganga Ram, a widower, had gladly left his sons and grandchildren to come to America as soon as Suraj Mehta had sponsored him. My mother said every Indian woman dreamed of having someone like Ganga Ram to take care of their household chores. Shobha Chachi was convinced that Gopi didn't deserve the luxury of a housekeeper when she didn't even work or have any children. "Some people have all the luck," she grudged.

The Mehtas and their villa dominated my imagination so intensely that for days I could think of nothing else. For a while, I even forgot the girl who lived on Lincoln Avenue. Here was something more glamorous to dream about. Priya, on her part, had whetted my appetite with descriptions of gorgeous rooms, marble bathrooms, cast-iron balconies, crystal chandeliers, and so much more. "I tell you it's a fairy castle, straight out of the Magic Kingdom at Disneyland, you know." The first thing Chacha had done after coming to America, before Jack died, was to take Priya and Chachi to Disneyland.

My father was not the one to do so. "Disneyland? Why not the Smithsonian?" Left to Papa, we would never see anything but libraries and museums. That was fine with Bansi, Papa's copycat, but not with me. I wasn't cast in my father's image. I was more like my mother, who never hesitated to explore and to see something new, something different. I prayed for an invitation to the Mehta villa.

One day, it came.

The evening sky had turned bronze when we drove to the villa. The whole family had been invited, but Bansi had opted out. Papa would have been happy if Ma and I had done the same, but we didn't. We were determined to see the  villa and its mythical inhabitants, I – more than my mother. We drove along the riverside and I watched the play of light on the treetops, on the windshields of the cars, on the faces of joggers, on the river water. Evenings in America were beautiful. Even today, after having lived in this country for two decades, I am still mesmerized at the sight of steel-glass structures glowing in the light of the setting sun, of street lights floating like moons in the dusk, and of Canadian geese flying across the skies.

Soon, we were driving up a winding driveway. The villa sat atop a hill, surrounded with pine and spruce trees that shot high up into the sky, straight as needles, defying gravity. It was a huge mansion with tall columns and wrought-iron balconies. The windowpanes were aflame in the light of the setting sun. The mansion itself looked as if it had been dipped in gold. It was exactly as Priya had described, only more splendid.

"This should've been our house!" I sighed.

"Come now." Ma placed her arm lightly around my shoulder.

We walked towards the porch where a rather diminutive man in a safari suit was standing, welcoming his guests. He turned to us, one hand extended in greeting, the other pulling at his goatee. His eyes were hidden behind dark sunglasses, which he never took off that evening. Priya told me, later, that he was cross-eyed. I never found out if she had been right. I was disappointed to find that Suraj Mehta, the master of the villa, was a far cry from the knight with flashing dark eyes that I had imagined him to be.

If I felt let down by Suraj Mehta, I wasn't by his wife. Gopi Mehta was a big-boned woman with gray eyes set wide apart in a heart-shaped face. She wasn't like a film star, but there was something about the way she carried herself that made you want to keep looking at her. When she smiled, her face lit up with a fluid beauty and, when she laughed, you thought of electric cables vibrating in high wind. Dressed in a blue chiffon sari embroidered with sequins and threads of gold, she exuded the scent of riches. Opulence. A big star sapphire on her finger and starlets in her ears sent lightening flashes when she moved her head or tucked a thick reddish curl behind her ear. Shobha Chachi said she had had her black hair bleached and dyed a brownish red because she wanted to look like a white woman. "As if by dyeing hair you can dye your skin!" she had groused.

Whatever she did, Gopi Mehta was the unmistakable queen of the villa, and hence my heroine. Proudly, she showed us around. She took us four stories up and down, in the elevator, to the large rooms furnished with polished mirrors, gilt-framed paintings, oriental rugs, and crystal fixtures. The marble bathrooms were bigger than my room. I hadn't even heard of Jacuzzis till I saw them in the villa. The topmost floor, Gopi Mehta told us, was being remodeled for an astrologer who was coming to stay at the villa.

Then we stepped into the nursery. "But she doesn't have –"
I whispered to my mother who didn't let me complete my
sentence. "How wonderful!" she cut in as she squeezed my
hand so hard that I thought she would crush my fingers. "This
is the best part of the house." Gopi smiled and let out a small
sigh. The nursery was larger than the entire area of our house
on Brink Road. Its pastel green walls were painted with flying
unicorns, dancing bears, and leaping monkeys. The sun and
moon and stars smiled down at us from a sky-blue ceiling.
Wind chimes and dream-catchers swayed in the windows.

Gopi led us to the food court she had set up for the dinner
party, to the pushcarts piled up with food – from hot dogs
and ice cream to pizza and spaghetti to *puri* and *bhaji*. I met
Indian kids, but neither they nor I made any effort to be
friendly with each other. I watched them pile up their plates
with food and then trash them without consuming even half
the portion. They went in for more, and discarded more. My
grandmother would have been horrified by the waste. Never
would she allow anyone to throw away a morsel. Even
breadcrumbs or spilled sugar crystals had to go to the anthills
alongside the compound wall. Bansi called it recycling.

The dinner once over, we were sent to the second floor to
play games and watch TV. I did neither. Some of the kids knew
each other and had a lot to talk about. I sat there hearing the
pitter-patter of their conversation dribbling around me.

"Like I said …"

"… It pissed me of …"

"Hell no!"

"My Mom said …"

"I didn't …"

"You're nuts …"

"It sucks!"

"My dad …"

When I could stand their clamor no more, I went down
in search of my mother.

The grownups had finished their dinner and moved into a hall the size of a small auditorium which was carpeted wall-to-wall. Big cushions floated like islands on the floor, against which men and women sat half-reclined. A man in a silk shirt sat cross-legged on a raised platform, tuning the tanpura – a string instrument. Beside him sat a young man with long oily hair that fell all over his face every time he thumped a pair of drums – the tabla. I found my mother sitting not far from the raised platform. Happily, I huddled into the space she made for me near her. The women decked in gold and silk smiled at me. This was certainly better than being with those raucous kids, I thought.

Then the first notes of the string instrument began to congregate like monsoon clouds just before the rain. I remembered the sizzling sound as the first rain drops fell on the baked earth in Jaipur. The string instruments seemed to emulate that sound as the maestro began to play the tanpura. Slowly, his voice rose. It blotted out all sounds. He was singing a ghazal – a song of pain, of unrequited love, of longing. A hush had fallen on the audience. The lyric floated up in the air and time, like a jinni bottled and tossed into the sea, was swept away. Babies snuggled in their mothers' laps and fell asleep. Men's faces were transformed, softened, all lines dissolved as if by the wave of a magic wand. Gopi reclined against a cushion, gazing at nothing with misted eyes. I began to feel the charm. I dozed and woke up and dozed again. It was only when the singer began to put the instruments away that everybody stirred and came out of the trance into which they had fallen. In a flurry of activity, mothers gathered bottles and diaper bags, fathers picked up sleeping children. One by one, they got into their cars and drove away from Gopi's enchanted villa. So did we. With sleep-filled eyes, I looked at the fading mansion through the rear windshield as Papa drove us home.

I dreamed of the villa that night. I was running down the

spiral staircase to catch the school bus waiting for me at the foot of the driveway and Ganga Ram, the butler, was carrying my bag as servants of the rich children did in India. "You can go away now!" I commanded Ganga Ram, taking my school bag from his hand. Several pairs of eyes watched as he bowed and stepped back, bowed and stepped back. I was a princess from India. The moment I got on the bus, the kids started calling out to me. "Here! I've saved a place for you!"

"Come here!"

"No, here!"

"Near me!"

"Next to me!"

I heard them implore me. Beseech me. "Here! Juhi, come!"

"Juhi!" My mother was bending over me, shaking my shoulder. "It's time to get up!" The sun was shining outside my window. The villa had vanished and with it were gone Ganga Ram, the school bus, the children begging for my friendship.

I walked down Brink Road with flecks of last night's dream sticking to my eyes. The kids didn't even look at me when I boarded the bus. Their senseless chatter followed me as I slumped on the back seat.

"Like I said ..."

"It pissed me off ..."

"Hell no!"

"I want ..."

"I didn't ..."

"You're nuts ..."

"It sucks!"

The enthusiasm with which I had started school fizzled away within a week. In its wake it left nothing but misgivings, anxiety, and loneliness. At first the kids at school completely ignored me. They would walk past me as if I were thin air and they never talked to me. I had to pinch myself to make sure that I was real. My class teacher's efforts to team me up with buddies failed. Try as Miss Thompson might, no one cared to include me in their group except a girl named Tracy. She was a thin red-haired girl who wanted to become a soprano. New to the school, she was as much of an outcast as I was. Her father had recently moved from Idaho. The girls were especially cruel. "O La La La La!" They would sing the moment Tracy entered the class or the cafeteria. They would shove a rotten potato in her bag and whisper and giggle "Potato Head." Tracy tried to ignore them. "They're stupid," she would say, her pale nostrils quivering with anger. I was just getting to know Tracy when she left school. I never found out why, for she never told me or called me.

Then the crowd began to gang up on me, as if they wanted a substitute for Tracy. They blew bubble-gum balloons in my face, they called me Browny and Bookworm, they changed my name from Juhi to *Zoohee*, and they tossed my school bag into the trash can. Each day brought new trials, new ordeals.

"Your dress, your color, your hair, your accent, everything is so different. No wonder they make fun of you," Priya told me. "You have to mix with the crowd. You have to look cool."

Priya could say it because she was fair complexioned, almost white. She had short curly hair. She wore jeans and jumpers. She spoke English like Americans. I was different in more ways than one from her. I wore thick glasses, I had long straight hair, I spoke with an accent. Were looks all that important?

"Of course, they are," Priya said. "In America, you have to be good-looking. No one will even look at you if you are fat, or ugly, or dark."

I wasn't fat. I wasn't very fair, but I wasn't dark either. I did wear glasses, but my mother said I had lovely eyes. My grandmother said that I was her prettiest granddaughter. I did dress like others, except for wearing baggy trousers frayed at the knees. I did speak with an accent, but I got A's in my English class. Miss Thompson always commented on my vocabulary. Perhaps it was my long, dark, straight hair. While everyone wore theirs short, or permed, or dyed, I wore mine in two long plaits.

"Have it cut short," Priya suggested. "You'll look better."

I should have talked to my mother about it, but couldn't. Long hair had been nurtured in my family as if it were a living organism. The longer it grew, the prettier a woman was considered. Back home, mothers washed their daughters' hair with powdered herbs and pastes made of henna leaves and bitter amla – a green plum-like fruit. They rubbed scented oil into the scalp, combed, and braided their hair. Lustrous flowing hair was a gift from a mother to a daughter. A girl with dry, unkempt hair was believed to be in the keep of a stepmother. How I wished my grandmother were with us! She always knew how to resolve a problem. I couldn't even write to Dadi because her eyesight had weakened so much that she had to have my cousins read out her sacred books and letters to her. I could never bare my soul to my cousins. I clenched my teeth and bore the cruel jokes.

On the day when I found chewing gum in my hair, I went crazy. As soon as I got home, I picked up a pair of scissors and hacked off one fistful of my long hair after another till the bathroom floor was covered with dark tresses. I looked into the mirror. It wasn't my face that I saw. It was a pale face framed with wisps of spiky uneven short hair. The big brown eyes behind thick glasses looked bigger.

I had lost my face.

When my mother came back from the grocery store, she let the bags slip from her hands. They landed with a thud on the floor.

"By all the gods in heaven," she cried out. "What have you done to your hair?"

Even as I told her about the chewing gum in my hair, my voice rang false to my ears.

Ma's face flushed with anger. "And you couldn't wait for me, could you?" When roused, Ma could be worse than Papa.

"I –"

Ma didn't stop to hear my explanation. She went into the kitchen and came back with a dustpan into which she swept the mass of hair on the floor and threw the tresses unceremoniously into the trashcan. That hurt more than my bland face in the mirror. I had imagined she would want to save at least one curl. Cherish it. Wear it in a locket. She didn't. She washed her hands and that was it. Later, at night, when everyone was asleep, I retrieved the longest strands from the trashcan and put them in a small box in my bureau. Whenever I felt bad about my cropped hair, I would pull them out and marvel at their glossy length.

Papa's face turned red when he saw me. "Have you lost your

mind or what? Don't you see this is the first step to the loss of your identity? And when you lose your identity –"

His tirade on identity and self-image was to continue for a whole week. Bansi was even worse. He shook with laughter every time he saw me. "You look like a newly-shorn lamb," he said.

Only Priya comforted me. "They'll grow long again. What's the big deal?"

At school, the girls sniggered. They drew circles on their temples with their forefingers when they saw me. My first rite of passage hadn't brought any reprieve. If anything, it had given them more ammunition to tease me.

I was sitting in the school cafeteria one day when Marge, a red-haired, freckle-faced girl, who never let go of an opportunity to pester me, snatched my math book away from me.

"Hey!" she shouted to her friends, waving the book like a flag. "She's studying math at lunch! Can you beat that?"

"Booooo!" the gang cried.

"So?" She turned to me.

"Give me my book!" I said quietly.

"You want your book back?" Marge addressed this to me, then turned to the kids and said, "Schoolie wants her book back."

"Hey Schoolie? You want your book back?" the crowd jeered.

"Let's give it to her, shall we?" Marge said sweetly. "Come and get it, *Zoohee!*"

"*Zooohee! Zooohee!*" they sang.

Marge climbed on the top of a table and held the book high above her head. I leaped around her like a puppy. She tossed it to Tim, who tossed it to another kid. I fell and grazed my knee. Even though it hurt, I didn't even whimper. I was ready to cry when someone kicked it. No one kicked books in India. We had been taught to revere them. The first word that an Indian child wrote was the sacred *Om* and after that all books, all knowledge, was sacred. I glared at them.

The laughter grew wilder.

"Come and get it," Marge shouted.

"You can keep it," I hissed. More hurtful than the impact of the book hitting me on the shoulder was the pain of humiliation and helplessness that I felt. I whipped around and screamed at them. "Barbarians! You're all barbarians."

"Excuse me?" Marge's face had reddened.

"Barbarian! Barbarian!"

"Bookworm!" she retaliated.

"Bookworm! Bookworm!" The chorus picked up the chant and changed it into "Curry-eating bookworm!"

"Curried bookworm!"

"Fuck'n bookworm!"

The voices followed me wherever I went.

I felt sick. Disgusted. If only I could go back to St. Sophia, my school back home, in Jaipur. I missed the nuns whom all of us used to fear at school. They had been terrible, but they were preferable to these brats. They were like huge bats hanging in corners, for they were always watching and waiting in the shadows. One wrong move, and they would swoop down upon us. No matter what we did or said, they knew which way our minds trekked. Sister Mathilda, whom we called the tyrant, would stand at the classroom door every morning and size us up with laser eyes. She would inspect our nails, look behind our ears to see if we had washed properly, and check our hair to confiscate fancy ribbons or bobby pins. There was Sister Maria, the oldest and sweetest nun. She would sit smiling, sometimes, talking to herself or standing at the steps tending to flowers only she could smell and see. Everyone said she had lost her mind. We loved her unconditionally. But whether gentle or stern, smiling or scowling, the nuns made sure that we knew what we were supposed to do, or say, or think as clearly as we knew the school prayer or multiplication tables. Here, in this new country, school was chaos.

Bansi thought I was thankless and unappreciative of all the good things that America had given us. How could I not see and love the clean air, the vast playgrounds, the shining hallways, the free books that an American school offered? How could I not see the efforts people made to preserve the environment and the forests, to welcome strangers from other parts of the world, to keep dreams alive, and above all to give human beings dignity? "In this country you have the freedom to say what you want to say, to wear what you want to wear, to eat what you want to eat and to be what you want to be. Freedom is what America is all about, Sister Juhi. So stop being so difficult."

I couldn't.

My problems came to a head when Miss Thompson showed us a documentary on India in her Social Studies class. It wasn't the first time that she had shown us a film in class. We had seen documentaries on Africa, Mexico, and China before. They had been fun, but this time, something happened to me. The world went silent around me as images of thin, dark, hollow-eyed men and women living on sidewalks appeared on the screen. I didn't want to see dying cattle. I didn't want to see skinny children with runny noses, nor naked *sadhus* with ash-smeared bodies. Or stray cows. Or dogs. Or beggars. This wasn't the India I knew. And yet I couldn't move. I couldn't close my eyes or shut my ears. Ten minutes stretched into an eternity. When the film was over, I felt all eyes focused on me. I couldn't even hear what Miss Thompson was saying. Perhaps that is how one felt when sucked into a black hole.

Later, when we were waiting for the bus, Annie, another classmate of mine, called out, "Hey! Did you sleep on the pavement?"

She couldn't have asked me a worse question at an equally bad time. Is that what she thinks of me? I thought. Is that how they all see me? Is that how they view immigrants?

"Hey! Do you eat from garbage cans?" I mimicked her.

Her green eyes flipped open. "Shit!" she spat out. "Go to hell!"

"You go to hell!" I shouted back. Before a battle of words could ensue between us, the bus arrived. We looked at each other with smoldering eyes. I was determined to get even with her. With them.

Bansi defended Annie. Not because he knew her – he didn't – but because he believed in the principle of fairness. Bansi was incapable of savoring the delicious feeling of hurting and avenging a hurt.

"It was an innocent question," he said. "It only shows her ignorance. How can she know how you lived in India?"

"Why not? Do I look like a poor girl? A beggar who would live on the pavement?"

"It's not that. You need to look at it from their angle too."

"What angle?" I snapped at him. "There's no other angle."

"If I were you, I wouldn't make an issue of what they or anyone chooses to screen or not screen about India. India lives here," Bansi said, tapping his chest with his fist.

I couldn't feel India pulsating inside me, then. Years later, I was to understand what Bansi meant. It would be when I was shooting a film along the New Jersey beach and someone from the crew suddenly blew a conch shell. Swifter than the silver leap of a fish, I was back in Jaipur, a little girl, standing beside my grandmother in the temple. I could hear the priest blow the conch. I inhaled the incense of burning camphor. I felt the glow of oil lamps. I saw the rose petals strewn in front of the idol of Lord Shiva. In a second I had seen, and felt, and lived it all.

But that day, when Bansi talked about India breathing inside one's heart, I only got angrier. I told him he was a hypocrite. How could he love America and claim that India lived inside him? To me the two were irreconcilable. In those days I was convinced that I was the one chosen to defend India. If I didn't speak up, India was in danger of being swept off by an avalanche. Bansi hardly understood how painful it was to be hounded by one's peers.

Ma was more sympathetic. "I know it's difficult," she said. "But you don't have to be afraid of anything or anyone. God gave you a tongue to talk with. So talk back."

Papa was quick to dismiss Ma's advice. "What does your mother know about conflict resolution?" he scoffed. "Loud talk won't get you anywhere. Learn to reason with people. Logical argument is the key to success. Be clear, but be civil."

My parents seldom agreed on anything, anyway. If Papa cited Gandhi, Ma alluded to Lakshmi Bai, the queen of Jhansi, who had fought the British. If Papa talked about *dharma* – one's sacred duty, Ma was quick to mention *karma* – devotion to action. In any case, Papa's rational discourse didn't make much sense to me; Ma's open declaration of war did. Grandpa Miller endorsed it too.

By this time a quiet old man with a deeply furrowed face like a relief map in an atlas, Grandpa Miller reminded me of my own late grandfather who had loved birds and flowers as Grandpa Miller did, and who also used to take a snooze while sitting in front of the TV. I had loved my grandfather. I loved Grandpa Miller. Whenever we visited him, I would always wait for the moment when someone would change the channel or lower the volume and Grandpa Miller's eyes would fly open like a pair of blue poppies. He would frown and say in a peeved voice, "But I'm watching!"

During one of our visits to his house, when I told him about Annie and Marge and the way the girls made fun of me, Grandpa Miller brought his mouth close to my ear and whispered. "You know what?"

"What?"

"Give it back to them."

"That's what my mother said," I whispered back.

"Good! Take her advice. You should never take anything lying down. They're a bunch of bullies – all kids are. Once you've asserted yourself, they'll never bother you again."

"You think so?"

"I sure do." The wrinkles around his eyes deepened with laughter as he threw a punch in the air. "Sock them in the eye."

And that's what I did.

It was lunch break. Annie and Marge were riding their skate boards. I was standing near a flower bed pretending to be deeply interested in the tiny green shoots that had pushed their way up through the soil. I didn't even look up when Annie whooshed past me three times on her skating board. Finally, she halted near me.

"Hey!" she called out. "I saw something on TV last night. About India."

I looked up.

"You kill girl babies in India, right?"

Marge, who had joined us, sniggered, "What a savage practice!"

"Shocking! Imagine killing little babies!" Annie said, one foot on the skating board and the other poised on the ground, ready to take off again.

"Weird."

"Gruesome!"

"Uncivilized!"

"Brutes!"

The blood shot to my head. I took a step towards Annie and shook my fist in her face. "If you ever say that again, I'll show you what a true brute is," I said. "I'll – I'll cast a spell on you."

"That's what barbarians do!" she said.

I could hear the blood shooting in my veins, drumming in my ears, burning in my eyes. I spun around and stared at them. They stared back. I don't know how long we stood there trying to outstare each other. I think it was Annie's smirk that made me lose my cool. I threw a punch at her.

She wobbled even though I had missed her by inches, and lost her balance. It wasn't my fault if she fell into the flower bed. She shouldn't have been standing so close to the edge, anyway.

"You pushed her," Marge accused me, jumping to Annie's side.

"You did, you're a beast!" Annie cried holding Marge's hand and getting up. "If you say that again, I'll kill you," I said. "I swear I'll kill you."

The incident created a furor. I was looked upon as someone who practised black magic, who was a terrorist. Kids kept their distance from me. Annie and Marge's parents complained. Miss Thompson called Papa.

He was waiting for me, pacing the living room, when I returned from school. Ma wasn't home. "How could you do it? How could you even utter those words? How could you punch that girl? Do you understand the implications?" I was taken aback by the intensity of his attack. What had happened to his Gandhian tolerance?

I looked out of the window, at the children playing ice hockey on the street. They were waving their sticks like flags. Perhaps someone had scored a goal.

"Look at me!" he said.

I turned to him. "She said Indians were barbarians. She had no right to say that. I'm not a barbarian! We're not barbarians!"

Papa's voice softened. "But darling, you have to understand the context," he said. "Don't you think that killing babies is barbaric?" I kept staring at the hockey dance in the street. "And then, you can't threaten people. You can't be violent. The girl could have been badly hurt."

"She wasn't. She got only a couple of scratches. I wish I'd broken her teeth."

Papa winced as if a scorpion had stung him. To one deeply committed to Gandhi and to non-violence, such a statement from his eleven-year-old daughter was devastating. "What's gotten into you?" he asked.

I clamped my mouth shut.

"You'll have to apologize."

"Never!"

Papa grounded me. He said he wouldn't lift the embargo till I had apologized to the girls.

Bansi tried to persuade me to bend. "Why should I?" I snapped. "I haven't done anything wrong. And I'm not a saint like you."

My mother refused to take sides. "You have to sort it out with your father," she told me.

So, in the evenings and over the weekends, I sat at my window and watched the robins digging up worms in the backyard or Mrs. Mikulsky pinning her laundry to the clothesline. She never used a dryer to dry clothes. I could hear the McKinney boys playing basketball in their backyard. I wished we had never come to America.

I would sit dreaming of the flagstone backyard with rows of papaya, mango and guava trees, the flowering shrubs, and bougainvillea arches in Jaipur. I saw Shami, the washerwoman who came to do our laundry every morning, squatting near the water tap, rubbing soap into the clothes, and beating the dirt out of them with a wooden bat. Her thick copper nose-ring glinted in the morning sunlight as she turned her nut-brown face to smile at her baby lying under the neem tree. In hopes of a son, Shami had given birth to seven daughters, but she had never choked any of them. They were all living. How could people talk of killing daughters in India when Shami had seven of them, alive and healthy? They had it all wrong.

It was then that the idea of becoming a filmmaker took seed. I resolved that I would make films about India. The ones I would make would focus not on its lepers and beggars living in slums, or on maharajas and their gorgeous palaces, or beautiful women, wearing heavy makeup and gold and diamond jewelry, or rich business men standing in marble lounges, holding crystal glasses. I would make films about people like Shami. About simple, raven-eyed girls wearing flowers in their hair, singing and dancing during the Pooja days when Goddess Durga is supposed to visit Her father's home.

I dreamed of making a film about my grandmother spinning cotton, making mango and lime pickles, shelling peas, chopping vegetables, singing hymns, counting her prayer beads. I would focus on her as she sat reading us stories from the *Ramayana*, her face shining like crinkled silk, her eyes tender like warm molasses. I would zoom the camera on the mango and guava trees in her garden. On the jars of pickles and preserves in her pantry. On the fat cow in her backyard. On the large stone house with its doors always open to the monks and the *sadhus*, the poor and the hungry.

Then everybody would know that there was no hunger in India. No poverty. That there were no hollow-eyed children with protruding bellies and scrawny arms begging in streets. No women abused. And no infant girls choked to death.

I would reinvent India with my films.

One day!

I don't know how many scripts I might have gone on dreaming up, had Ma, tired of the tension in the house, not intervened. She confronted Papa at an hour when he was most at peace. It was after breakfast on a Sunday morning when he was in a good mood. He had just sat down with a thick bunch of newspapers and I was halfway up the stairs when Ma confronted him.

"So what if Juhi pushed the girl?" she asked Papa. "You can't punish the child for fighting back. No one has any right calling us barbarians." I crouched behind the banisters and looked on.

"Us?" Papa lowered the newspaper he was reading.

"Of course. Us!" she said. "It involves all of us."

"I can't allow a child of mine to behave like a barbarian."

"You think to stand up for one's rights is barbaric?"

"To lose one's temper is. Juhi has to learn to control her temper." Papa put aside the newspaper. He was prepared for her attack.

Ma stood, with her arms akimbo, ready to charge. They glared at each other. Suddenly, Ma dropped her voice. "You're a good man, Bipin, you're a teacher, a proud Indian yourself. You can't be unfair to the child."

Papa wasn't prepared for this sudden flip. He stared at her.

"I know you can't be unfair!" Ma's voice was dipped in rose water.

Papa opened his mouth to say something. Then gave in. Gingerly. Reluctantly. Almost grudgingly. "I don't want to hear any such complaints again," he warned. "Next time she misbehaves, she's out of that school."

Papa needn't have worried. The girls left me alone. I gained no friends, but the enemies were subdued. I was at peace, though still lonely.

Bansi philosophized that I shouldn't bother about feeling lonely. "Loneliness is a given. Accept it, and it will cease to bother you."

I didn't understand what he meant. Priya said she did, but she couldn't explain it. "You'll understand it when you grow up."

Growing up seemed such a remote prospect, then.

 It was one of those days in early
November when the sunlight dribbles
like warm honey and the trees turn to
gold when I went with Priya to the park
that lay at the end of Lincoln Avenue. I
had been reluctant to go there because
it was an extension of the wilderness we had stopped by when
Papa had first driven us to Brink Road, but Priya had assured
me that we wouldn't go in if I didn't like it. My fear evaporated
when I saw women pushing strollers or holding hands of
children entering the park. There was a low wall with a rickety
wooden gate over which anyone could have jumped if it were
closed. Once we were inside, I could see the sloping meadows
pegged in place by massive oaks and maples and pathways
weaving in and out of thickets. The park held neither shadows
nor lurking beasts, only geese that swam in a pond in the
hollow of the meadows.

Priya picked up a stick and flourishing it like a magic wand,
she declared. "I name it Panchvati." Panchvati was the forest
where Rama had lived in exile.

"And I'll call it Merlin's forest," I said. I had just finished
reading King Arthur's *Tales*.

So the park became our enchanted forest, our retreat. I
would wait for weekends when Chacha came to visit us with

Chachi and Priya. As soon as the greetings were over, Priya and I would rush to the park. Past the houses with crystal swimming pools and snaking driveways, past the houses on Lincoln Avenue, we flew as swiftly as our young feet could carry us. Women with children in strollers looked at us as we sped by. The wind whistled in our ears. Blew into our eyes. Stung our lips. Brushing back our hair, we zipped past a couple of elderly men dozing on cast iron benches under oak trees. They stared at us with bleary eyes. Sometimes, much to the chagrin of its owner, a dog on a leash would go wild. It yelped and strained after us.

In the park, we would lie under the huge oak tree around which Priya had drawn a circle – her *Lakshmana rekha*. She said it was to protect us from evil – like the circle Lakshmana had drawn around Sita to protect her from the demons in the *Ramayana*. There was so much to talk about. Our school. Our hopes. Our dreams. Our home. Our parents. It was Priya, though, who did most of the talking. Compared to her narratives, I had little to say.

Priya had a knack for spinning stories. She improvised as she went along, stories of ghosts in her building, of mugging and shooting in the streets, of teenagers pushing drugs in the alleys, and of girls throwing up in school toilets. Sometimes she talked about the difficulties at home, about Shobha Chachi's mood swings, about Chacha's frustrations. At home she was restrained, but once we were in the park, she would throw herself on the grass and laugh for no reason, or begin to sing, or dance. It was a strange dance. She would begin with a soft flutter of her arms, a pirouette, and then begin to leap and spin.

I still remember the day she pulled me up to join her. Dancing was something that made me feel awkward. Priya didn't let go of me. "Come on," she urged, "let your arms loose, like this, yes. Good." Priya was graceful, like a ballerina. She led me into a swirl. Then, before I knew, we were whirling around madly. I felt the trees and the earth and the sky join in the spin. Round and round we went. Laughter bubbled up and spurted out till our legs gave way and we sank down on the grass. The tree tops were still twirling, the earth was still trembling. I closed my eyes. Priya was giggling. Then, suddenly, she stopped.

"Juhi!" she whispered.

I didn't answer, for I was still dizzy.

"Look!" she shook me by the shoulder. "Look!"

I got up. She was on her knees, pointing towards the bushes. Her eyes were dilated with fear.

I spun around. The bush stirred.

"A ghost!" Priya whispered.

"Ghost?"

"Yes, of the man who died in my building."

I understood nothing. "A man died in my building," she said, her eyes huge like satellite dishes. "I saw them bringing him down yesterday. His eyes were open and fixed like stones – his face like dried up clay. It must be his ghost. Look!"

I looked again. This time I thought I saw a pair of eyes, staring at us from behind a dense shrub. There was no face, no body, just eyes, as if they were floating in the air. Then they disappeared.

A shiver ran down my spine as childhood fears of ghosts and evil spirits came rushing back. I remembered my grandmother's warning. "You should never walk under a tree after dusk."

"Let's go!" I tugged at Priya, and we ran without pause till we had reached Lincoln Avenue.

In the red-brick house, a garden party was in full swing. Girls and boys my age, or a little older, were lounging under a marquee, holding soda cans in their hands. They must have seen us come charging down the street, for they looked at us curiously. Then I saw the girl holding an ice bucket in her hands, also staring at us. Her dog was at her heel.

I must have looked dazed, for Priya nudged me, "Don't look as if you've seen a ghost!"

I whipped around and started walking away from the girl's house, away from her friends, and away from everything she had and I didn't. Priya had paused to tie her shoes.

"What's with that girl with the dog and that house?" she panted, when she caught up with me. "Why do you have to walk away without even waiting for me?"

I didn't answer.

She grumbled, "You see some stupid rich kids and your jaw drops. Why?"

I didn't say anything. I walked on till we reached Brink Road. And there they were – the small mute houses I hated, and the plain ordinary people who lived in them. Mrs. Wood was beating the dust out of a rug in her backyard. A bunch of kids were playing ice hockey on the street. Someone was hammering a fence into place. The strange woman whom everybody called "Crazy Jo" was sitting on the steps, knotting and unknotting yards of twine. Mr. Mikulsky was dozing on his porch. Brink Road was still as dull and plain as ever. To Priya, they would have been everyday sights, maybe even better than what she witnessed in her own neighborhood. But I wasn't going to be satisfied with where we were stranded, especially, when just three blocks down was what we could have, what we had to have.

It was our first Christmas in America. I watched the world transform itself into a fairyland as homes, bridges, lampposts, trees were contoured by strings of tiny lights. The leafless trees, defined by lights, assumed the fragility and beauty of blown glass. The malls and stores glittered with Christmas decorations, Christmas music, Christmas gifts, Christmas candies, Christmas dresses. Newspapers teased me with sale ads: Pre-Christmas Sale! Two-Day Sale! Buy Now-Pay Later Sale! Special Sale! Early-Bird Sale! Buy One, Get One Free, Sale! Our neighbors staggered home with bulging shopping bags, every day. Kids at school talked of nothing but shopping. Christmas, I realized, was the season for reckless shopping.

Everyone around us was caught up with Christmas preparations; only our house remained untouched by its joyous spirit. Perhaps Papa had forgotten that Christmas was around the corner. I needed to remind him, I thought.

"When are we going shopping, Papa?"

"What was that?" he asked, without taking his eyes off a sheet he had just retrieved from a file.

"Shopping, Papa!"

"Shopping?" He was startled, as if I had asked him about an expedition to the North Pole.

"For Christmas, Papa!"

"O, Christmas!" He sounded relieved. "But you know we don't celebrate Christmas."

"We did in India," I said. "You allowed me to celebrate it with the Sisters at my school. Why not here?"

Papa had always let us accompany the nuns when they went to the poor neighborhoods to distribute toys and sweets to children on Christmas Eve. He had never objected to our making nativity scenes or singing Christmas carols. I couldn't understand why he had become so indifferent now. America must do funny things to people.

"It was different in India," Papa said, picking up a folder. "The nuns taught you good things – generosity, forgiveness, and piety. It was quite different there. But here? Christmas means nothing but shopping and more shopping. I don't believe in this frenzy, this craze – this corruption of the spirit of Christmas."

"If –" I began.

"There are no ifs, Juhi."

"But Papa –"

"And no buts."

"You're a scrooge!" I blubbered in anguish.

"What?"

"Scrooge! Scrooge!" I stumbled out of the room. He heard the anger in my voice, but never saw the tears in my eyes.

To school, my classmates brought tales of Christmas bounty. I listened to their endless twitter about who was getting what and from whom for Christmas.

"And you? What about you?" they asked me. "Do you celebrate Christmas?"

"Of course," I lied, without a pause. "We do."

"And do you give gifts?"

"Yes. We do. We have a Christmas tree and we have Christmas dinner and we do everything you do."

They looked at me with eyes like newly-washed windows. I invented relatives. I made up lists of gifts for them. I didn't want to be considered an outcast. I didn't want them to look upon me as we used to look at the wandering gypsies in Jaipur who would appear outside our gate, as if the sky had dropped them.

I recalled the gypsies, now, with certain nostalgia. A family of four or five or six would strike a tiny camp on the curb outside our compound wall. From the safe distance of our veranda, we would watch them. The children – dark and lean like their parents – would sit under the *neem* tree waiting for the meal, which their mother prepared on an open fire. The lilt of a strange song would drift over to us as someone strummed an instrument and sang into the deepening dusk. The camel that pulled the cart would sit chewing the cud.

I always remembered the children sitting huddled around the fire, sleeping under the open sky. And I remembered their eyes, which appeared too big for their small somber faces pressed against the wrought-iron gate as they watched us cackling joyfully and showing off. They would stand outside. Their dark eyes growing darker with desire.

Then, one day, they would be gone as suddenly as they had arrived. They left behind nothing but half-burnt twigs and ashes and footprints of the camel on the sandy pavement.

I didn't want to be one of those gypsy children in America. I wanted to be inside the wrought-iron gate. Not watching, and not wanting, from outside.

On Christmas Eve, I prayed to Santa Clause to stop at my house. I hung a stocking at the foot of my bed and I left two Oreo cookies and a glass of milk on the table. I went to bed hoping for a Christmas miracle. I dreamed of Santa driving through the snow. I heard children dancing in the snow, singing, "Jingle Bells!"

I woke up to the sound of church bells ringing in the

distance. Tossing the bedclothes aside, I sprang out of bed. The stocking hung there, flat as if cut out of cardboard. The cookies and the milk lay untouched on the table. There was nothing to look forward to except another long day. Grandpa Miller called to wish us Merry Christmas. Grandma Miller said she was going to bring us her pies. Later, Mrs. Mikulsky brought us a plate of cookies. Ma baked a cake. But the day never lit up for me. What was Christmas without gifts?

"Cheer up, Miss Sad Face!" Bansi said, "We have our Diwali. We'll celebrate it, as they celebrate Christmas."

So I waited for Diwali.

As farmers wait for monsoons in India. Counting months. Weeks. Days. Hours. Minutes.

No one had heard of Diwali in America.

No one knew about the festival of lights that celebrated Rama's victory over the demon king Ravana, or about the triumph of good over evil. Of light over darkness. Grandpa and Grandma Miller, who lived in a small town in Lancaster County, and offered their hospitality to so many international students, were very keen to learn more about it. But for the rest of the world, Diwali didn't even exist.

Diwali, I realized, wasn't Christmas.

It wasn't Hannukah.

It wasn't Kwanza.

It wasn't marked on any American calendar. Inscribed on the tablets of our memory alone, it didn't exist for others.

Back home in Jaipur, we had counted the days to Diwali on our fingertips. Preparations for the celebration began months in advance of the festival. The house was cleaned and repainted. The hunch-backed tailor, who wore glasses that never stayed in place, would arrive to make new clothes for us. Bolts of colorful and printed cloth were ordered. Measurements taken. Patterns checked. Choices made. He would settle down in the veranda with his sewing machine. Cutting, stitching, sewing. And we would watch with eager eyes as he transformed a square piece of cloth into a frock, a blouse, a shirt, a pair of trousers. He was a magician who made us tiny rag dolls and exotic birds with multi-colored feathers, all conjured from the cuttings.

My grandmother was always the busiest person in the house around Diwali. A week before the actual event, she would gather all the women in the house to roll out *mathri* – small rounds of spiced dough – to be fried later. My aunts would munch betel nuts, and talk and laugh about things I didn't comprehend. It was their annual reunion. Grandmother would flit around like a moth, giving instructions to every one. There was so much to be done, so many arrangements to be made for the evening worship. No Diwali could be complete without marigold garlands, sweets, sugarcane, pomegranates, almonds and walnuts. The most important thing was to sketch an opulent scene that represented Diwali. That was a task that my grandmother never entrusted to any one. She would clean and whitewash a small square patch of wall which had acquired layer after layer of her artistic creation. On that patch, she would draw Goddess Lakshmi and Lord Ganesha. Fruit trays. Bags of wheat and rice. Gold coins. A house. A fountain. A pomegranate tree. A cow. A pen in an ink pot (she never reconciled herself to ball-point pens). Books. Children. The sun. The moon. The stars. The earth. These were the cardinal elements of my grandmother's universe, which she had to paint on the wall year after year, just so she could preserve them all for her family.

Sometimes, she would let us draw on her fresco wall. But after we had painted a cricket set, a doll, boxes of candies and chocolates, firecrackers, and a dog, Grandmother never surrendered her sacred wall to us again. "A dog next to the gods? What can you do with these modern children!" She had raged until Bansi effaced the dog with white paint. Even when arthritis had locked her joints, she persisted in transferring her dreams to that square patch herself. What if the lines were crooked and the colors smudged? "How will God know what I want unless I show Him the pictures?" she said to anyone who asked her to rest and not to bother about painting Diwali scenes all over again.

A day before Diwali, the potter woman came with a huge wicker basket filled with hundreds of clay lamps. She brought us clay toys, especially the ones made for Diwali. Blue and pink elephants with tiny clay lamps balanced on their trunks and heads. Red, blue and green birds, the likes of which we had never seen in our garden.

On Diwali.

Dressed in our new clothes, we arranged boxes full of fireworks in the order in which we would set them off. The sparklers came first; the most spectacular, which shot into the sky and burst like a fountain of fire, went last.

The celebration began in the evening with *pooja*, the ritual worship. The pundit would bathe the silver icons of Goddess Lakshmi and Lord Ganesha in milk, honey, and the holy Ganges water which always sat in a bottle in the fridge. Then he would cover them with sandalwood paste and offer flowers and sweets. The miniature human enactment was an offering to the gods. We would look at the eager skies and wait for the *pooja* to be over. But the pundit took his time chanting mantras, singing invocations, and showering blessings on everyone. Finally, it would be time to light up the oil lamps.

We squirmed. We wanted to go outside. But we had to suffer grandmother tell us the story of Diwali first.

"*Once upon a time there was a king. He had three queens ...*" Dadi would begin her narrative.

We would sit like prisoners. Our eyes fixed on the meteor showers in the sky. Our ears tuned to others' exploding firecrackers.

But my grandmother's narrative was like grandfather's old Austin, which still sat in the garage. Papa would start it now and then and take us out for a ride, but we never knew when the engine would die out and the car would begin to slide back instead of going forward. We were never sure when grandmother's narrative would similarly start sliding back. We preempted her. We knew all the twists and turns of her narrative, by heart. Dadi, however, refused to give in to our coaxing.

"*When Rama picked up his bow, the bow you remember was Lord Shiva's –*"

"Yes, we know," we interrupted and tried to hurry her up. "He shot the arrow –"

"Wait. Wait. Not so fast," Dadi would stop us. "*Rama didn't know that the source of Ravana's life lay in –*"

"We know –" we wailed.

"*He pulled the string and the arrow flew off.*" Dadi was unfazed by any interruptions. "*As soon as Rama cut off the demon's ten heads and arms, they sprang back into place –*"

By now the sky would be full of fireworks. And we were like sprinters, poised at the starting point, waiting for the gun that would not go off. Please, please, please stop, Dadi, we would whisper under our breath.

Finally, she came to the part where the demon king was killed. Nothing could stop us, thereafter. We took off. Rama had returned to his people, who had lit oil lamps to celebrate his victory. Now we were free to enact his return. We could hardly contain the joy, the excitement gushing inside us like a river in spate. The sky was bright with shooting stars. Tiny oil lamps flickered on parapets, in verandas, under trees, in windows, dispelling darkness, dispersing gloom, ignorance, and despair.

The houses on Brink Road remained plunged in darkness on our first Diwali in America. Ma and I waited for Papa and

Bansi to come home. It was late in the evening when we gathered in the kitchen and bowed our heads in prayer before the pictures of Ganesha and Lakshmi sitting on the shelf. Papa chanted invocations.

> *O Mighty God who dazzles with the light of a thousand*
> *suns! Let all my tasks be completed without impediments.*
> *Let me not falter in the completion of my obligations. O*
> *Lord! Bless this house. Bless your children!*
> *Om! Shantih! Shantih! Shantih!*

I waited to hear the boom of firecrackers. But the night remained tongue-tied. We called up Grandmother in India. She was happy to hear our voices. And she said she was going to send me a box of sweets with someone coming to America. In the background, thousands of miles away, I heard children laughing. I could see them cracking walnuts and popping pomegranate seeds with juice-stained fingers into their mouth. I could hear the clap of firecrackers in the background.

Bansi said I must have been dreaming. "Everyone's fast asleep at this time in India. You don't have firecrackers at five in the morning, do you?"

Papa turned off the lights and snuffed the candles burning in front of the gods. "Fire hazard," he said. "You can't leave anything burning in these houses." No. Not even an incense stick.

I kept a candle burning in my room so that the Goddess could find her way to our house.

"Careful now. Blow out the candle before you go to sleep," Ma said softly. She had entered my room to say goodnight. I knew she wasn't going to tell Papa.

Bansi ducked in. "Goodnight, Sleepy Head. Don't dream of firecrackers too much," he said.

"Good Night, Bansi."

The lights were out.

The street was quiet.

A lone candle burned in my room.

I lay in my bed, and I waited. My ears ready to catch each and every sound.

I waited for Lord Ganesha and for Goddess Lakshmi. My grandmother believed that they came at midnight. She had always kept an oil lamp burning and the front door unlocked to welcome them. Papa had, of course, objected to this ritual, for there had been instances of fire or of burglars entering the homes when people dozed off waiting for the gods. But my grandmother never exchanged the oil lamp for a simple electric lamp. The gods, she argued, hadn't gotten used to electricity. She would sit in her room, counting the prayer beads or singing a hymn and waiting for the midnight hour. Her oil lamps burnt out one by one.

I fell asleep watching the candle burn.

I dreamed that the houses along the street were decorated with strings of winking lights. And there were fireworks flowering in the sky. Then I saw them standing in our driveway. "Trick or treat?" They asked. I stared at them. Goddess Lakshmi had blond hair. And Lord Ganesha resembled an ET. Was I mixing Halloween with Diwali? They looked at me and began to fade.

"Wait!" I pleaded. "Don't go away! Wait! Please!"

I woke up. My room was dark. The candle had burned down. The house was quiet. Not a stair creaked. Not a night bird flapped its wings. Not a single meteor traversed across the dark skies of our neighborhood.

Diwali had come and gone.

For me, Rama was still in exile. Still wandering through the forest. Still fighting the demons.

"Don't look so sad," Bansi consoled me the next morning. "There'll be another Diwali."

But I knew it wouldn't be any different – never as it had been back home in Jaipur. Like so many other things, we had left Diwali behind too.

 Priya was becoming mysterious. First, she started wearing black or navy blue colors, then she had her curly hair straightened and cut short. She would start laughing in the middle of a conversation or go suddenly silent. I was convinced she was coming down with fever. Bansi thought she was hiding something.

When I could no longer bear the suspense, I asked her why she had been acting so strange. We had gone off to the park that day and were sitting under our usual oak tree. She didn't answer. She just continued pulling leaves of grass and shredding them to bits.

I waited.

Finally, she turned to me, and asked, "Can you keep a secret?"

"Of course, but can I tell Bansi?"

"If he asks." Her eyes were shining, but her face had grown pale.

"What is it, Priya?"

She hesitated, then said in a soft voice which barely rose above a whisper. "There's someone – I am in love."

"L-love?" I stammered. All I knew about love was what I had seen in Bombay movies – the heroine bursting into a song and dancing in the rain – or the passionate kissing in Hollywood movies.

She smiled and then she told me about Chip. He was a tall, handsome guy with long blond hair which he wore tied in a pony tail. She had met him at Nellie's. She had been seeing him secretly for over two months now.

"If you so much as breathe a word to anyone, I'll never ever talk to you," she warned me. She needn't have worried, for I was a good keeper of secrets. I couldn't hide it from Bansi though.

He lost no time in confronting Priya when she came to our house with her parents. We had gone up to Bansi's room to listen to some music.

"You don't even know him," he told her. "He may be a druggy, a criminal, a murderer, anything," he told her.

I had never seen Priya so uncompromising. "Why couldn't he be a prince or a scholar or a saint for that matter?" Priya asked him in a sharp voice. "Why must you draw negative conclusions? Do you know he is the first person who has given my life meaning, direction? I don't care what anyone thinks or says."

"Do you know what he does for a living?" Bansi persisted.

"Who cares!" she shrugged.

"You should tell Chacha." Bansi insisted.

Priya broke into a peal of laughter. "Are you kidding? Daddy would go crazy if he were to find out."

"Won't he, sooner or later?"

"Go crazy?"

"I meant find out?"

"I hope we'll be married by then."

"Has this man proposed marriage?"

"He will," she said. "The psychic said so."

"What's a psychic?" I asked.

"Hold it. Hold it." Bansi cut in. "You went to a psychic? What psychic? You must be out of your mind."

Priya jumped up and glared at Bansi. "What makes you think I am out of my mind? I am grown up enough to make my decisions, aren't I? Nobody calls Gopi crazy because she has an astrologer in her villa. What's wrong if I consult a psychic?"

"Nothing." Bansi turned away. "Do what you want."

Gopi's astrologer had finally arrived and settled in the newly constructed suite on the fourth floor of the villa. Swamiji was supposed to perform rituals to pacify the stars that prevented Gopi from bearing children. He had predicted that she was going to have not one, not two, but four children as soon as the angry stars could be appeased. What modern medicine hadn't succeeded in doing, Swamiji had assured Gopi and Suraj Mehta, he would accomplish for them.

Ganga Ram was so miserable after Swamiji's arrival that he sought Chacha's help. He was sure that Swamiji who had occasioned many changes in the villa, was a thug. He had put an end to the parties. He had advised Gopi to cook her own meals, so poor Ganga Ram lost his vocation. Suraj Mehta hadn't objected to any of the changes because he believed Swamiji had brought him good fortune. His business was doing so well that he had to go abroad almost every other week. Gopi no longer accompanied her husband on those trips because Swamiji had advised her against frequent crossings of the ocean. She was reported to follow the astrologer's counsel on everything – from the position of her bed and the colors of her dress to the nature of her meals. When he said it was auspicious to feed pigeons everyday, Gopi got a pair of pigeons and put them in a cage and fed them every day. Ganga Ram said with spite that they were a pair of mourning doves. At Swamiji's suggestion Gopi wore five rings with five different stones on her fingers – one for each of the five angry stars. Blue sapphire for Saturn, coral for Mars, ruby for sun, pearl for moon, and a yellow sapphire for Jupiter. Ganga Ram was sure that Swamiji had cast a spell on his mistress.

Chacha said with some pity, "The Swami is cashing in on her ignorance."

"She's not innocent!" Shobha Chachi was quick to denounce Gopi. Normally withdrawn, she always perked up at the mention of Gopi. "The woman's lucky. It's my brother who's a fool."

"So he is," Chacha chuckled. "All he can think of is making more money and that astrologer is making a fool of him."

Shobha Chachi's eyes grew foggy. "My brother's no fool. If he is, then why can't you be a fool too? Why can't you find an astrologer who would change our fortune?"

"Find an astrologer? In America?" Chacha bristled. "You're crazy."

"There are fortune tellers in America too," Shobha Chachi replied crossly. "After all, Nancy Reagan consulted one."

"Why don't you write to Nancy Reagan and ask her?" Chacha glared at her. "Women always want something. First she bugs me for a house and now it's an astrologer. Where do I find one, madam? This isn't India where you can find one under every pebble."

Chacha was right. There was no dearth of pundits and astrologers wandering in the streets and predicting births, marriages, deaths, jobs, layoffs, love life, litigation and suggesting remedies to ward off the undesirable. Wandering mendicants in saffron robes would stop you in the middle of the street and tell you how fortunate you were and how riches awaited you. Of course, we had been warned to stay away from them. Papa was averse to soothsayers. He said they were all impostors who lured children away to big cities and forced them to beg or steal or do worse things. There was, however, a shaggy old man who wore an eye-patch like a pirate and sat on the curbside with his parrot and a pile of worn-out and stained cards on the mat. Him we trusted. All we had to do was to pay him a rupee, tell him our name, and blurt our question.

"Come, my Mithwa," he would call out to his parrot. "Come, tell this little girl whose name is Juhi if she will pass her exam."

And the parrot would hop out of the cage, look around with its quick, unflapping eyes and pick out a card with its beak. The fortune-teller would read it out and announce, "You will pass your exam."

"Will I stand first in my class?" I would ask.

"First! First!" The parrot would shriek.

"Give me another rupee," the man would say. "You'll get first position."

We always thought that a first position in class was a question of a mere rupee. If you could afford a rupee, you could be ranked number one in class.

Dadi's astrologer was a wizened old man with a tuft knotted at the back of his shaved head. He wore a shawl with Ram printed all over. His forehead was always smeared with sandalwood paste, and we liked to see the hair-thin cracks appear in the paste when he wrinkled his forehead. His job was to allay my grandmother's fears if anyone was sick or about to go on a trip, to apprise her of the changing position of stars, and to advise her about what to do to prevent mishaps.

The idea of having my fortune told had been churning in my mind ever since Swamiji had come. From the moment Priya had mentioned her psychic and I had found out what a psychic was, I couldn't stop thinking of visiting Miss Lola, the psychic reader. I kept pestering Priya to take me with her when she went to see Miss Lola. After extracting another set of promises from me – I wasn't to tell even Bansi – Priya took me to Miss Lola.

She lived in a two-storied stucco house at the end of a street called Gypsy Lane. We saw a signboard nailed to the door of the house, which read: "Miss Lola. Psychic Reader. Fortune teller. Palm reader." It had a phone number printed at the bottom. The large front window facing the street was hung with signs of the Zodiac – Saturn, Leo, Cancer, Pisces – and a couple of plastic angels. There was something eerie about the place. I imagined a wizened old woman waiting for us behind the closed doors. I was afraid that as soon as we stepped in, she would bolt the door and trap us inside. My first impulse, when we got closer to the house, was to turn around and run. Sensing my fear, Priya put a hand on my arm and pushed me ahead, "Come on now! Don't be a chicken!"

We climbed the steps and rang the bell. No one answered. Maybe there was no one in, I thought, though a big card hanging on the door said, OPEN. I was ready to turn around and leave, when the door creaked open. A tall, thin woman with a pointed face and a big nose stared at us. She was wearing a shapeless long black dress. Her thick orange hair had escaped from the bright green bandana she had wrapped around her head. I peeked around to make sure there was no broom around.

"Yes?" Her left eye twitched.

Priya nudged me.

"Do you t-t-tell fortunes?" I asked.

A strange metallic voice repeated from inside the house, "Tell fortunes ... tell fortunes." I felt a chill in my bones.

"It's only a parrot," Priya whispered.

"Do you read palms?" I asked the woman. I could hear Priya's exasperated sigh. The woman wiped her hands with the corner of her dress and spoke in a nasal voice. "That's what I do, honey. Twenty dollars. Flat. A ten percent discount for first consultation."

Twenty dollars?

I stepped back. "I don't have that much!"

Suddenly, the woman descended upon me like a huge black bird with an orange-green plume. She grabbed my arm, and pulled me inside. "What do you have?" she asked me. The eye twitched again.

Priya was breathing heavily down my neck. The room smelled of licorice. A door leading into another room was slightly ajar. In the dim light, all I could make out was a rocking chair and a table. The woman was still holding my hand. I dug into my pocket and pulled out the money. Four crumpled dollar bills, some quarters and dimes. They fell to the floor. She swept them up and thrust them into the folds of her dress.

Then she pried my hand open and peered at my palm. "Aha! You're from a land far away – across the ocean. Right?"

I nodded.

"You're a good girl – you're lonely – I see no friends. Yes?"

"Yes, but what I want to know is – will I be rich?" I asked.

"Pictures," she murmured as if she hadn't heard me. "I see lots of pictures moving in your head –"

"I'm not crazy," I said, angrily.

"They're in your head. I see them."

"I'm not crazy," I said angrily. "All I want to know is when will my Papa have a big car and a big house and money –"

She laughed and sang in her nasal voice, "All in good time, little girl."

"And friends. What about friends? Will I have friends?"

She chortled. "Of course! You'll have many friends – boyfriends, do you want boyfriends?"

"No." I snatched my hand away. I wasn't interested in boyfriends. I hated the idea of giggling and making eyes at boys, the way girls did at school. Miss Lola had lost interest in me. My five dollars' worth of time was over. She turned to Priya who had pulled out a handful of dollar bills from her purse. The woman took the money and gave Priya a brooding look. "You were here before?"

"Yes, Miss Lola. I came with Nellie. You asked me to come again."

"Yes, yes, I remember now." She peered at Priya's upturned palm. "I see a handsome young man in your life. Tall, golden hair …"

"Yes! Yes! Go on!" Priya's eyes were sparkling.

"He will lead you into paths you've never been before – I also see –"

Just then something soft and furry brushed against my knee. The hair at the nape of my neck rose. "Priya! Let's go," I croaked.

"Your young man –" the psychic was droning.

In panic, I clutched Priya's hand and made a dash for the door.

"Stop it, Juhi!" Priya cried.

But I wouldn't, I couldn't listen. I raced down the steps dragging Priya along me.

"Wait!" The woman called to us. "Girls! Come back!"

"Run!" I pulled Priya by the hand.

I ran faster, bumping into people who looked at us with hostile eyes. I was afraid that the woman would get on her broomstick and fly after us.

"Are you crazy or what?" Priya pulled me to a halt. "First you want to have your palm read and then you run like demons were chasing you."

"What if she had turned us into a bat or a bird or a mouse? No one would've known where to look for us. Didn't you see there was a dungeon?"

"Dungeon?"

"A dungeon. I bet she has –"

"O, shut up! You're so silly. You didn't even let her finish."

"She knows nothing, Priya."

"Whether she does or not, I want my money's worth. I'm going back," she declared. "You can wait outside if you don't want to come in."

I had no choice but to follow Priya to the psychic's house. The woman was still standing at the door. I didn't look up to her. I didn't want to confront the twitching eye. She didn't say anything when she saw us. She let Priya in and closed the door.

When Priya came out a little later, I asked her. "What did she say?"

"A tall young man will take me away to a new world, and –"

"Did she give you his name?"

Priya laughed merrily. "She said it began with C. And she said I will have everything I want. Nellie was right. She's good."

We had started walking away when I remembered something. I stopped. "But you told us that Miss Lola had already told you that you will marry –"

"That was to shake off Bansi, Silly. I was sick of his quizzing."

"You lied?"

"So what?" Priya laughed. "Don't you? Don't we all?"

Something wasn't right with Priya. This wasn't the candid Priya I had known. She hadn't been devious.

In the coming weeks, I noticed more changes in Priya. She became obsessed with her looks. Whenever she visited us and she was in my room, Priya would turn to the mirror and examine herself from all angles. "How do I look?" she would ask me.

"Fine."

"What do you mean by fine? Am I growing fat?"

"No." She was, in fact, getting very skinny.

"Am I getting dark?"

I thought she was growing paler. She told me that Chip didn't like fat dark women.

Shobha Chachi complained to Ma about Priya not eating enough. "Who is going to marry her if she remains flat like a rail?" She nagged Chacha. "You have to start looking for a suitable match for Priya." Eighteen in Shobha Chachi's eyes was time for a girl to get married.

Chacha would nod his head, but say nothing.

"The groom isn't sitting at your doorstep, waiting for you to grab him. It may take two years to find one and by then she'll be twenty," she argued.

"I will. I will." Chacha said.

"I wish there were an astrologer you could consult!" she sighed.

"And make a fool of myself like your brother?"

"My brother is no fool. Look at the farm he is buying. Not everybody can do that."

Suraj Mehta had put the villa on sale and moved to a farm in New Jersey. The move had been necessitated when Swamiji mandated that Gopi should offer *roti* or pita bread to a cow everyday before she sat down to lunch. In India, it was customary to give the first *roti* to a cow. My grandmother never sat down to her midday meal without offering one to a cow, who appeared outside the wrought-iron gate everyday at noon. Besides, feeding a cow – or anyone for that matter – could never have been a problem in Jaipur. There were plenty of stray dogs and cows on the streets and pigeons perched on electric cables all the time. In America, you couldn't find a cow or a dog on the street. And because of the zoning laws, Gopi couldn't keep a cow in her backyard. After weeks of deliberation, Suraj Mehta had bought a farm.

"See the power of money?" Chacha said. "Now they can have not one cow but ten cows – and even donkeys and horses and what-not."

"I knew my brother would find a way out." Shobha Chachi let out a big sigh. "He's not like some who do nothing."

Soon after they moved to the farm, Ganga Ram was given leave to go visit his family in India. Peeved and heartbroken at the usurpation of his place, Ganga Ram told Chacha that he was never coming back as long as Swamiji was there. He was convinced that Swamiji would be the ruin of Gopi and Suraj Mehta, who had lost their mind and did whatever the man asked them to do.

After Ganga Ram left, there was no one to bring news of what was happening at the Mehta farm. Suraj and Gopi Mehta had faded from the scene. Sometimes, people reminisced about the parties, the villa, the musical evenings, but gradually, they were forgotten. Even Chacha and Shobha Chachi talked less and less of them.

It was a few months later, when Gopi Mehta's picture appeared in the newspapers that everyone's interest perked up in the couple. Gopi Mehta was reported missing and Suraj Mehta had announced an award of a hundred thousand dollars to anyone providing some information about his wife. Swamiji had left the villa after Gopi had given birth to a still-born baby. It was rumored that unable to take the two losses, Gopi had lost her mind. Some said Swamiji was a magician who had brainwashed her and used her. Chacha believed he was an imposter who had fooled everyone. Some thought Gopi had been kidnapped and Suraj Mehta would soon receive a note asking for a heavy ransom. After all, it was widely known that she was the wife of a rich man.

There were those too, who believed that Gopi had become a *sadhvi* – a nun – and followed Swamiji wherever he had gone.

"A nun?" Shobha Chachi cried. "Forget it. She's no more a nun than I am an angel!"

We never found out what happened to Gopi or to Suraj Mehta. Was Swamiji an imposter? A sorcerer? Did Suraj Mehta find his wife? The Mehta story remained an unsolved riddle. Perhaps even now Gopi Mehta's picture might be in a police file, marked "Unsolved."

I lost Priya to Chip and Bansi to the applications he was sending out to universities. He wanted to go in for graduate studies. I felt isolated and whenever I felt isolated, my thoughts turned to the girl who lived on Lincoln  Avenue. The woodpecker inside my chest went wild when I walked past her house, or saw her getting into a car, or playing with her dog. I was sure I would end up with a big hole in my heart some day. On my way back from the bus stop, I would keep my face averted from the house and my eyes fixed on the ground. What the eye couldn't see, the heart wouldn't miss.

It was a warm day. I had taken off my light jacket and had almost passed the red-brick house when I heard a growl and felt a tug at the jacket. I whipped around. The girl's dog had fastened its teeth on a sleeve. I tried to yank it out of his clenched teeth, but he growled even more. I was certain the sleeve would come off and it would have, had the girl not come running to my rescue. "I'm so s-s-sorry," she stammered, restraining the dog. "Peppy's a silly dog. Did he tear your jacket?"

I examined the holes where her Peppy's teeth had sunk in. "Never mind," I said.

"I'm so sorry. You shouldn't have been f-frightened. "

I shook my head as I made a mental note of her stammer. I told her I wasn't afraid of dogs. "I had one too."

"What happened to him?"

"Oh, well," I paused. "We left it behind – in India."

"India? My parents are from India too," she said. "But we were b-born here."

"Who's we?" I asked.

"My b-brother, my sister, and I."

"Do you speak Hindi?"

She shook her head.

"Not even at home?"

"Nope! We speak English."

So she was one of the America-born Indian kids I had seen at the Mehta villa. I looked at her again. She was a bit on the plump side. She wore green shorts and a lemon tee-shirt with a slice of melon painted on it. Her straight dark hair was tucked behind her ears. The braces on her teeth glinted when she smiled. She invited me in.

I hesitated.

"There's no one at home except me and Peppy," she said.

"Only for a few minutes," I said, folding my jacket and slinging my school bag over my shoulder. I followed her into the house.

Her name was Debyani, but she said I could call her Debby, for that was how everyone addressed her. She led me through a quiet hallway, past a living room with ivory walls and whipped-cream carpet, from the family room into a spotless, sun-filled kitchen. There were plants on the recessed windowsills, a row of brass pots on hooks, and a bowl of fruit on a glass-top table. So clean was the kitchen and so spotless the counters that it seemed as if fairies did the cooking when everyone was asleep. I thought of our kitchen with the raspberry wallpaper and turmeric-stained counters. Ma could never keep the kitchen uncluttered because whenever the impulse took her, she would go into a cooking mode and try out new variations of her favorite *bhajia*, deep-fried vegetable fritters. The cooking odors always hung in the air. Debby's kitchen smelled only of baked cookies and lemons.

Debby took out a pitcher of lemonade from the fridge and filled tall glasses. We sat around the glass-top table and sipped lemonade. Peppy had snuggled at her feet and dropped off to sleep. The house was quiet as a cathedral, as if the high ceiling and the thick walls had absorbed all sounds. Debby pushed a plate of cookies towards me and muttered something about Tina's making the best lemonade and the yummiest cookies in the world.

"Tina's your sister?" I asked.

She giggled, showing her braced teeth. "No, our m-m-maid!"

We ate cookies, drank Tina's lemonade, and talked. Rather, she talked, and I listened. Debby had so much to talk about – about the private school she went to, about her friends Liz and Connie, about her mother, who owned three video stores; about her father who played golf; about her brother, who was studying at Penn, and about her sister Mona, who had married an American.

"When Mona and Mike got married," she stuttered, "my mom had a huge m-marquee set up in the back lawn. It was like a carnival. Mom had special flowers flown in from Hawaii," she blinked.

"Special flowers?"

"Like birds-of-paradise and lilies and roses. You couldn't even dream of such flowers. And Mike wore a turban and silk *dhoti*. They looked so cute. My mom got a chef from India. You should have seen the party we had in the backyard –"

I saw it all. The carpets. The flower vases filled with birds-of-paradise and orchids. Women in silks and diamonds. Men in dark suits. Waiters walking around with snack-piled trays. Streams of music. A laughing bride. A handsome groom.

And I listened. Quietly. Hungry for details. Envious, too.

Finally, when she had run out of breath, Debby asked me. "And what about you?"

"What about me?"

"Well! T-t-ell me about yourself, now."

But what could I tell her?

There was nothing to match her exotic flowers flown from Hawaii, and her grand house and cars, her parties on the lawn, and a blue-eyed American brother-in-law. What yarn could I spin about my father, who taught at an area college? Or my mother, who dreamed of doing something, someday? Or my brother, who worked in a computer store, studied late into the night, and dreamed of searching for lost planets? Or Priya, who was on the ninth cloud with Chip? What could I tell her about myself? A gawky, skinny girl with short dark hair, who wore glasses, who went to a public school, and who lived in a twin house on a plain street? I could have told her about our house and my grandmother in India. I could have described the parrots in the guava trees and jasmine blooming in the garden in summer. I could have told her the stories that my grandmother had read from the *Ramayana* and the *Mahabharata*. But nothing I told her would have equaled her glamorous tales. I had neither birds-of-paradise nor orchids in my house, not even a dog bouncing at my feet. I kept drawing patterns on the frosted glass with my index finger.

"D-d-do you have friends?" she asked.

I got up. "I've got to go. My mother must be waiting for me."

"But you'll come again, won't you?"

"Yes, I will!"

The wind sang in my ears as I scooted home.

Ma was chopping onions in the kitchen. Bansi was ready to go out. He stepped aside as I barged in.

Dropping off my school bag on a chair, I pirouetted on a

toe. "I met her – the Indian girl who lives in that beautiful house on Lincoln Avenue? Her name is Debyani but everyone calls her Debby –"

"Very American!" Bansi sneered.

"She was born here and she has a dog called Peppy. Isn't that a beautiful name for a dog? Peppy?"

"It certainly rhymes with Debby!" Bansi chuckled.

"Her sister is married to an American and her brother studies at Penn, and she has a maid and her house is so beautiful that –"

Ma smiled. Not at me, at the onions. "Good, that's good. Very nice," she said.

"O boy! O boy! My sister has finally made friends with the rich Indian girl with an American name," Bansi laughed. "How wonderful! Now life is going to have some meaning for her!"

He kept chuckling even after he had closed the door behind him. I took out a bottle of milk from the fridge and poured some in a glass. "You can invite her over some day," Ma suggested.

"Here?" I spun around. "Invite Debby here?"

Ma had turned back to her onions.

"Here?" I asked again.

She tossed the chopped onions into a pan before answering. "Yes here. Why, what's wrong with this house? Grandma Miller thinks this is a beautiful house –" She wiped the onion tears from her eyes and blinked at me. The smell of onions mushroomed. I stared at the colorless floor tiles, the gray walls, and the stained counter top.

"Listen, Darling!" Ma said. "We can't change the house for your friend's sake, can we?" The onions were hissing in the pan.

I gulped down the milk and stormed out of the kitchen. "I'm not going to bring her here. Never!" I kicked the door shut behind me.

Mr. Mikulsky, the pink man, was sitting in his porch, reading a newspaper. He peered at me from above the rim of his glasses. "You bang doors too hard, kiddo," he said. "Not good for the house."

I ignored him. I couldn't understand why he had to be always sitting in the porch to keep account of how I shut my door. Papa said he was a good neighbor. They often sat down for a beer and talk about the cost of putting a new roof, or replacing gutters or repairing the driveway. Mr. Mikulsky was very fond of telling Papa about his life in Poland. He had been an engineer there. "When I came here, I was nothing," he would say. "I did not know no English, you see. It is difficult to get a job if you don't know English. How come you know English so good, huh?" he would ask Papa. Then without waiting for his answer he would continue, "I worked all my life in this factory here. But not my children – bless them – they did well."

"You okay?" he asked me, now, as I stood on the porch.

I didn't care to answer. He was a part of all that I despised on Brink Road. So was his wife. I watched her come out with a couple of magazines in her hand. She was a big woman with bleached hair. One of her arms was swollen like a huge link sausage. Ever since Ma told me that she had had one of her breasts removed, I could hardly look at Mrs. Mikulsky without seeing a big gaping hole where her breast must have been. She smiled at me as she lowered herself into a patio chair. I turned away before she could strike up a conversation with me.

The McKinney teenagers, in the third house from ours, were playing basketball. A stereo was hammering the golden evening into a flat gray sheet. On the pavement, children were buzzing back and forth, grating the concrete sidewalk with their plastic cars. Three houses down the street, someone was cutting down a tree. The snarling chain saw ripped the falling dusk into shreds.

I resolved I would never invite Debby to my house. And I didn't. It was she who insisted on my going to her house everyday.

There was always something happening there. Debby's mother, like Gopi Mehta, was very fond of giving parties. Mrs. Singh – I never knew her first name – was a tall woman with polished ivory skin, midnight-black hair, and slanting green eyes, lined with thick mascara. When Ma caught a glimpse of her as she was driving by in her car, she said Debby's mother reminded her of an aging Elizabeth Taylor as Cleopatra. A fair-skinned woman, she could have easily passed off for a white woman. The only thing that gave her away was her accent, her singsong voice.

"So you're the new friend Debby talks so much about," she said when Debby introduced me to her. "You're in her school, no?"

"No," I replied briefly.

"Then which school?"

I told her which.

"And you live where?"

"On Brink Road."

"I don't know Brink Road. Where is it?"

I told her where Brink Road was. She uttered a small "Ah!" The diamond earrings swung in her ears like a pair of lanterns. "And what is your father?" she asked.

"He's a professor."

"Ah, a teacher!"

"He's writing a book – a bestseller," I said, stressing the bestseller part.

She smiled. "And your mother?"

I hesitated. "She's a teacher," I lied. I don't know why I did that.

"Well," Debby's mother paused. "I could have been a teacher myself. But I wanted to make big money." She reached for a cookie from the plate on the side table. "And what you want to do? Teach like your parents?"

"No," I replied, watching the crumbs dribble on her lap. I could have told her about my dream of making films, but I couldn't bear it if she laughed.

"What then?"

"I don't know."

"Now, my children always knew what they wanted," she said, brushing away the crumbs. The gesture set off rays flashing from the big diamond ring on her finger. The gold bracelets jingled. "My Tony will be a corporate executive. My Mona wanted to go into finance. She did. And that's where she met Mike," she paused significantly. "Did you know she married an American – a real American?"

"I've t-told her all about him, Mom," Debby piped in before I could answer.

"You should have seen it! O Boy! So many people – the party starts at nine in the morning and it goes on till midnight. And Mike, I tell you," she paused, took a deep breath, then continued. "Mike was so good, such a nice man. He wore an Indian dress and went round the fire seven times. Straight, straight. He tried every dress I ordered for him. My brother, you know, is a big officer in India. All those clothes and things? He sent. Everything by airmail."

I could see airmailed parcels being delivered in special vans by liveried men in white tunics studded with golden buttons and handling each package carefully with white gloves.

When I told Priya about it, she laughed. "What else did she have flown in? An elephant? A palace? Water from the Ganges? Rich Indians can have the Taj Mahal transported."

I never understood when and why I became a confidante to Mrs. Singh. "Not a confidante," Priya corrected me. "A willing audience to her tooting her own horn." Priya was becoming cynical. It had to be Chip's influence, I decided.

Whatever the reason, I think I got more pleasure out of being with Mrs. Singh than with Debby, who had nothing new to tell me. Her mother, on the other hand, was always fizzing like soda emptied too quickly into a glass. She had started looking, then, for a bride for her son, Tony. Whatever time she could spare from her video store, her parties, her Mona and Mike, was devoted to answering letters from the parents of prospective brides. I often saw her sitting with pictures of young girls spread out on a table.

"Come! Come! They're beautiful, no?" she would say as soon as she saw me. "And from rich families too. Only the other day the big industrialist in Delhi? He called. His daughter is so beautiful. She's studying at Miranda College. All my Tony has to do is to say the word. Just say it, and I can get Miss India for him."

"But Tony is dating S-S-Susan these days, Mom!" Debby would remind her.

"Susan is pretty," she agreed. "But she doesn't have a good voice. Linda has a stunning face, but her eyes are small small. Tony, you know, has such big eyes. But I don't mind," she said with a rush of generosity. "I don't mind which one he chooses. They are all pure American. Tony will have such beautiful children. My grandchildren will have blue eyes – I don't mind green –"

Bansi could hardly control his laughter when I reported this to him. "Pure American? What's that supposed to mean? Besides why is she considering Indian brides if she's looking for a pure American?"

I didn't have any answer. Bansi kept chuckling even at dinner, and my parents couldn't hide their amusement, either. Priya, who had never met Mrs. Singh, but had taken a dislike to her, shrugged her shoulders, saying, "She's loopy."

"Loopy?"

"Crazy," she laughed.

Priya might have been right about Debby's mother to some

extent, especially when Mrs. Singh reminisced about the time when she and her husband first came to America. She would get quite agitated. "You see, we came to America twenty-eight years ago. It was a different country then. Very different. It was so clean. The old America is no more," she would say. "It's gone. And now? What do you see? So many colored people," she would glare at the walls with angry eyes and her face would turn red. "The real America's gone. Finished. The end!"

"Colored people, eh?" Papa ran his fingers through his hair. "What does she think she is?"

"What about the father?" Ma asked. "Doesn't he ever say anything?"

Debby's father was a quiet man with a vague smile pasted on his face. He hardly uttered a word more than was necessary. The look in his eyes, when his family or guests were around, was that of a moth that had lost its way in a brightly-lit room. Once he had stepped in when Debby's mother was holding court. He hesitated, then went into the kitchen, opened the fridge and took out a can of Diet Coke.

"No. No," his wife cried out. "Lemonade is fresh. Take some."

Obediently, he put back the can and poured himself a glass of lemonade, drank it, put down the glass, and left, saying, "I'm going to the golf club. Don't wait for me."

Mrs. Singh returned to her narrative.

The pile of the pictures of prospective brides and of letters from their parents grew higher by the week. Debby's mother knew little about Bianca Garcia, the girl Tony had started dating. Bianca was from Puerto Rico. She was a beautiful young woman, with skin the color of butterscotch pudding and eyes like sparkling cider. I couldn't take my eyes off her the first time I saw her. She was a Barbie come alive. Debby said Tony was crazy about her.

"Then why is he keeping it such a big secret from your mother?" I asked.

"He wants to give her a b-b-big surprise," she said.

Tony had decided to introduce Bianca to his mother at the Christmas party. Debby had invited me too. Mona and Mike were also coming. "You'll m-meet everybody," she said.

"Wait till she meets Bianca," Bansi predicted. "The color will fade so fast, she won't even know it."

"It sure will," Priya agreed.

"What paint?" I asked.

"Never mind," he said. "You'll see."

I don't know what really transpired at the Christmas party. I couldn't go. Debby reported to me that it had been a disaster. Mrs. Singh had taken one look at Bianca and blanched. Later, she had told Tony that she would never accept Bianca as a daughter-in-law. "You have offers from such well-known families, such beautiful girls – why this girl who isn't even white?" She had asked. That outraged Tony so much that, in the middle of the night, he got into the car and drove away with Bianca.

In the days that followed, the bustle in Debby's house ceased, as if a sudden power outage had hit them. Debby's father stayed away on business, her mother walked around with thunder in her face, and Tony stopped coming to the house. Debby's stammer grew more pronounced. Even Peppy looked subdued.

I felt sorry for Debby. Despite all her riches, all her friends and comforts, she was a lonely girl. For the first time, the twin-house on Brink Road superimposed itself on the red brick house on Lincoln Road. Later, when I was to make my first film, I would begin with a long shot of the twin house on Brink Road. For the first time, I realized that happiness, which I had taken to be such a simple affair, wasn't so simple, after all. Life was getting to be more like a complex algebraic problem with many equations and infinite relationships.

My belief was strengthened soon. One afternoon, we were playing Scrabble at Debby's house when the front door flew open and swung shut so hard that the pictures on the walls rattled. Debby trembled as her mother stormed into the room. She flung on the floor the bag she was carrying. The video cassettes in it scattered on the carpet. She didn't see them; she didn't notice us. She was sizzling like my mother's fritters in the wok.

"How dare he? How dare he?" She interrogated the walls. Her poise was gone. Her mascara was smudged. The usually-perfect hairdo had come loose and her hair fell in tired wisps around her face.

Debby and I froze in our seats. "I b-b-bet it's about Tony," she whispered.

Mrs. Singh slumped into the sofa. Her dark eyes shot around wildly. She kept repeating, "The bugger! Traitor! I should have known. I should have known!"

Finally, Debby asked in a small voice, "W-what's wrong, Mom?"

She spun around and looked at us sternly. "What's wrong?" She said. "Don't ask me. Ask your Dad. The traitor! That Tony – your brother – has announced his engagement in the papers. See!" She pulled out the area newspaper and threw it on the floor, ranting. "Without even asking me, he does this. Your father is behind this. But this is my house. Everything – everything will happen the way I want – okay?"

I thought she had lost her marbles the way Shobha Chachi sometimes did. "I had such dreams. Another grand marriage and dresses for the bride –"

That was when the door opened, slowly. Debby's father came in. He stood near the door, as usual, meek as a sacrificial lamb. Quiet as a dormouse.

"So there you are! You traitor!" Debby's mother screamed with renewed vigor.

The father was taken aback. But he didn't flinch. Quietly, he asked. "What happened?"

"What happened? Now hear this. Hear this. What happened, he asks. As if he doesn't know. Tell me you don't know about Tony's announcement in the newspaper." She thrust the paper under his nose. "Tell me. Slowly, slowly you have cheated me. Speak now!"

Mr. Singh paled for a moment. Then he cleared his throat and in a stronger voice, he said, "I don't see any harm. It makes no difference to me whom he marries. It's not as if this is happening for the first time in the family. Your daughter has already married an American. You've always encouraged Tony about his American dates. So what are you whining about now?"

That was the first time I had heard him speak so many words.

"Whining? Now listen to him," Mrs. Singh drew Debby and me into her circle. "He ruins my son, my only son –" she began to cry. Big tears rolled down her cheeks, and she didn't bother to brush them away.

Mr. Singh ventured a step closer to his wife. "How can you think he would have married an Indian girl? Haven't you always encouraged the kids to be more American than I ever wanted them to be? Isn't that what you have always wanted?"

There was a pause.

Then Mrs. Singh let out a big hiss – like steam escaping a boiler. "What do you know what I want? I ask you why this girl? She's no match for my Tony. She's dark – she's not pure American at all."

We stared at her in complete silence. She picked up a flower vase and hurled it at her husband. "It's because of you. Traitor!"

I had never thought Mr. Singh capable of the agility with which he skipped and dodged the flying vase and slipped out of the room. The vase crashed through the French windows, and fell with a thud on the deck. Peppy started barking furiously as Mrs. Singh picked up an ashtray, and then the videos lying scattered around her and sent them sailing through the window. Shobha Chachi could never have matched that frenzy. Debby's face blanched. Her lower lip began to tremble as her eyes began to brim with tears.

I didn't stop to see what would happen next.

My feet flew over the grass, sped to the curb, and carried me down the street to the twin house. I didn't stop till I had climbed the steps to the porch. For once, I was glad to see Mr. Mikulsky dozing in his chair. He opened a gray eye, looked at me as I sprinted up the steps.

"What's the matter, kiddo?" He asked in a sleepy voice. "Yellow jackets chasing you, or what?"

I swear I had never heard anything sweeter in my life.

After that evening's episode, I didn't have the heart to go to Debby's house. We switched to talking over the telephone. Perhaps Bansi was right. Mrs. Singh's outburst must have been embarrassing to her. Priya shrugged. "She won't be embarrassed for too long. She can't control her mother if she acts weird," she said. "My parents never agree over anything. I don't give a hoot any more."

A couple of months went by. Debby mentioned something about her mother's growing interest in President George Bush and his family. She wouldn't miss a single TV interview or news item about the First Family. Bansi was puzzled. "Maybe she plans to join the Republican Party! Maybe, she wants to go into politics!"

It remained a mystery till one day, when I was returning from the park with Priya. I heard a car brake beside us. A familiar voice called out.

"Long time no see!"

Mrs. Singh was grinning from behind the wheel. Debbie was sitting beside her. Before I could check my surprise,

Mrs. Singh announced. "Debby wants to tell you something. Tell her. Tell her. Don't be shy, Darling."

Debbie looked uncomfortable. She avoided looking at us as she stammered uncontrollably about a reception for Tony and Bianca.

"Grand reception, Yup!" Her mother interrupted. "Why not? It's going to be the biggest celebration you've ever seen."

"You mean –" I was going to say something about Bianca. She interrupted me.

"I tell you Bianca is so sweet. She'll wear a sari. She'll look like a *rani*, you know, a queen. I have ordered dozens from India."

"But –"

She continued. "You see we live in a multi-cultural society. Look, I have American son-in-law and now a Latina daughter-in-law – just like our President. We should be proud of diversity. My Debby will marry a –"

"P-P-Please Mom!" Debby interrupted with a flushed face. "We'll be l-late."

"Ya! Ya! We have to go now. So much to do! See ya!" And she drove off.

Priya was doubling up with laughter. "She had to translate *rani* for us. And that girl? I can't believe you were so gung-ho about her. I think she's quite dumb."

13

Grandpa Miller died in summer. His kidneys had been damaged by a dye-test. Thereafter, he would not submit himself to dialysis. He just took to bed, refusing all food and drink. The fight seemed to have gone out of his body. Grandma Miller called Papa. "May be, he'll listen to you," she sobbed. "He doesn't listen to anyone anymore." No one could dissuade Grandpa Miller. I remember him as he lay in bed at home when we visited him. He had looked a bit thinner, perhaps paler too, but his face had glowed as I had never seen it glow before. His eyes were as clear as the skies after a storm. He didn't talk much, just lay there smiling at us. Once, he winked at me. "Everything okay at school?"

I nodded.

"I told you, didn't I? Everything turns out all right in the end."

"Yes," I said, but I wondered if he was right this time.

Grandma Miller took Papa aside. "He's not eating anything," she sobbed. "I made him chicken corn soup and you know how he loves it, but he didn't take even a sip – you try, he always listens to you."

Grandma Miller's son shook his head at Papa, but Grandma Miller kept insisting.

From the fruit basket we had taken for him, Papa picked up a bunch of grapes, washed it, and stood with it beside his bed. Grandpa Miller opened his mouth like a baby and looked up at Papa with smiling eyes. He didn't eat it, he just held it there. I can still see the glistening green grape resting between his pale pink lips.

Two weeks after we returned, Grandpa Miller died in his sleep. Grandma Miller wanted us at the funeral because we were his family too. I will always remember Grandpa Miller lying in the coffin, dressed in his blue suit and red tie. His hair neatly combed, his eyes closed, and a shadow of a smile hovering on his lips. I was almost certain that he would open his eyes any moment, and say, "Now what are you all doing here?" He didn't. And Grandma Miller kept sobbing, "Sixty years together – sixty years – what'll I do now?"

When we were leaving, Ma and Papa made her promise that she would visit us soon. She nodded as tears still flowed from her puffed-up eyes. She looked so devastated that I was sure she would never step out of her house anymore.

She surprised me.

Christmas returned with its fanfare. Grandma Miller invited herself. Everyone was delighted. Papa rushed around sweeping cobwebs where none existed. My mother started ironing bed sheets, pillow covers, even towels – in preparation of Grandma Miller's visit. And Bansi made it his mission to polish every bit of wooden surface he could lay his hands on. Once he had buffed it, even the old banister began to glow like chestnuts.

I disliked the way Ma and Papa had begun readying the house for Grandma Miller's visit, as if she were an admiral coming for inspection. I hadn't taken to Grandma Miller. I still found her bossy. She talked too much, and she started sniffling at the slightest mention of Grandpa Miller. Why Papa had invited her over, especially when we didn't even celebrate Christmas, I failed to understand.

"Don't forget this is her first Christmas without Grandpa Miller," Bansi said, when I told him how I felt. "Imagine how miserable she'd be missing him, thinking of him all the time."

I couldn't imagine anything. All I could see was Grandpa Miller lying in his coffin and Grandma Miller crying noisily into the large handkerchief her son had handed her after she ran out of Kleenex.

"I can see nothing but a more dismal Christmas this time," I sighed.

"Nonsense," Bansi said. "This Christmas will be different."

I shrugged my shoulders and walked away. Fat chance of this being any different, I told myself. It was going to be the same story.

On the day before Christmas, the aroma of cardamom, cloves, burnt sugar and warm cider hung in the air like mist on mountaintops. Everyone was waiting for Grandma Miller to appear.

I knelt at the window and stared at the leafless trees outside. The snow had turned to ice and everything was still. The wind. The sky. The trees. Then I saw a small bird perched on an electric cable. It was motionless. Frozen. As if made of clay. Still as ice. Quiet as a word on a page.

A faint color in the throat glowed softly. I noticed the forked tail. I could hear Grandpa Miller saying softly, "See the forked tail? The color in the throat? That's a barn swallow." One summer he had taken us all to a bird sanctuary. We were standing on the deck around the sanctuary office when a bird flew out of the rafters. "I can't believe it," Grandpa Miller had whispered, "I just saw a swallow." There was wonder in his voice. "Make a wish, and it'll come true," he had chuckled, turning to me.

"Really? Can I ask for anything?" I had asked him.

"Yes, of course! But you see, you have to make a wish before the bird flies away. It's too late now."

Later, Bansi said that Grandpa Miller had been kidding. "Only a kingfisher can grant wishes. A swallow is not a kingfisher."

I didn't know who granted wishes. God? A barn swallow? A kingfisher? Santa Claus? Who? Flattening my face against the cold windowpane, I whispered, "Santa Claus! Stop at my house, please Santa Claus. I'll hang a stocking at the foot of my bed. I'll leave milk and cookies for you in the kitchen. Let me also wake up to the miracle of Christmas."

Then I remembered. Our house didn't have a chimney.

"Juhi!"

Ma was calling me. Obviously, Grandma Miller had arrived. I dragged myself away from the window.

And there she was, an oversized Cabbage-Patch doll standing in the middle of the sitting room. Her chunky face framed between puffs of silver hair gleamed pink. Her eyes shone like twin gray moons. She was talking breathlessly. "The roads weren't too bad although there were some icy spots but it took me so long to get off the turnpike you wouldn't know how heavy the traffic was till you got on it and Sara said I should ..."

She stopped in the middle of her sentence when she spotted me. "Look at you!" She fixed me with those slate-gray eyes of hers. "So thin! Just shooting up. We'll have to fatten this child," she said, turning to look at Ma and wrapping me in her arms.

I stood unyielding. I resented the way she had said "fatten this child" as if I were a calf or a sheep. She released me soon, for Bansi had staggered in with a huge box from her car. "Into the kitchen!" she said, following him, with all of us in tow.

"I'll have lunch ready soon. I've brought everything with me," she announced, planting herself in front of the stove. Brushing aside my parents' pleas to rest and have something to drink first, she began to pull out various containers and jars and bags from the box and to set them up on the counter. Her hands rummaged in the drawer for a spoon or a knife, matching the speed with which her words tumbled out. "I said to Susan I didn't want the curtains to hang limp – do you have a larger pan?" she asked Ma, holding out her hand like a surgeon at the operating table. My mother fluttered around her, handing her a knife, a cup, a spoon. Papa, who hardly ever peered into the kitchen, filled the doorway as he stood chatting with Grandma Miller about her children and grandchildren, about friends – some dead, some living, some gone.

"Of course, you know how Pop never liked to –" I held my breath. She was sure to burst into tears now that she had mentioned Grandpa Miller. But that day she carried on, swept by her own voice.

"You couldn't have forgotten that time when you came to stay over a weekend ... can you grate some cheese?" Grandma Miller asked, picking up a brick of cheese. I thought she was asking Ma. "You, Juhi. Come here. You can grate this," she said, handing me the cheese. "And Bansi, I want you to slice this bread," she unwrapped a huge loaf of bread.

"You can set the table," she told Ma.

I grated the cheese furiously. This was no Christmas. Grating cheese. Listening to the patchwork quilt of anecdotes. And working. Who wanted such a Christmas?

When we sat down to eat, there was steaming chicken soup on the table. Scalloped potatoes. Apricot sauce. Sweet corn that Grandma Miller had husked and frozen and had now cooked for us. Warm bread and butter. And rice pulav and *halwa* that Ma had specially made for her. Nothing tempted me, though. I thought of the array of cakes, pastries, cookies and candies I had seen in the stores.

"Now eat," Grandma Miller said, filling our plates. For a moment I was reminded of Dadi in India. She was tiny and fragile, but, at the dinner table, she would dish out food the same way as Grandma Miller was doing now, and say with the same authority: "Now eat!"

"It wasn't as if I didn't know what Suzy was doing at the church," Grandma Miller was saying, "You know our church has a new woman preacher but that old one was … Do you remember him?" she asked my father and, before he could reply, she turned to Bansi and asked. "Do you get Channel Thirteen here?"

Bansi nodded his head.

"We'll hear the Boston Pops tonight. It's a special presentation. But I was telling you about the preacher," and she resumed her grand narrative.

Later, when the table had been cleared and I was about to slink away to my room, she pounced upon Bansi and me, "Have you ever played Jenga?"

No. We hadn't.

She pulled out games from her box. Jenga. Password. Wacko. She ordered Ma and Papa to join in too.

We all sat around the dining table. I didn't play. I didn't hold my breath when the Jenga tower teetered. I didn't laugh when everyone got hysterical. I didn't scream. Nor groan. Nor shout when the tower collapsed.

Bansi nudged me, "Enjoy! It's fun."

They started on another game. And then another. Grandma Miller's words gurgled like a hot-water spring. "The woman wouldn't give the child what she wanted and that child howled so hard that I thought the windowpanes would shatter and David …" I began to feel a delicious lethargy steal over me, as if I were lying at the bottom of a warm ocean, being lulled by the song of mermaids.

When I opened my eyes, the faces around the table were blurred, for evening had cast its net. I heard Papa say, "Boston Pops at nine."

"Good!" Grandma Miller said, getting up from the table. "Let me start the dinner." Through sleep-filled eyes, I watched her waddle to the kitchen. Papa turned on the lights. Bansi was collecting the Jenga pieces into the box when the phone rang. It was for me. Priya wanted to talk about Chip. My mind had run a blank. "Are you there? Juhi?" she called.

I struggled out of my trance. "We have a guest. I really hate –" I stopped. I couldn't quite say it. So I said in a small voice, "I'm sorry, Priya, I'll call you later." And I hung up.

The house was still as a ship that had dropped anchor. It was so quiet that you could hear a glass clink. Somewhere a door shut. A clock struck. They were normal everyday sounds. So familiar, and yet, so strange.

I peeped into the kitchen, which seemed to glow like a jewel in a box. Ma was chopping onions. Bansi was taking out ice cubes from a tray. Even Papa had grabbed a towel to wipe a dripping dish. And there stood, Grandma Miller! A sorceress stirring a steaming pot, casting her magic spell. I heard the smile in Ma's voice as she talked to her. I saw the glow in Papa and Bansi's eyes as they listened to her. The aroma of warm bread and butter, of apples, cinnamon, and laughter swirled around them.

Only I was alone. Left out. Abandoned. I felt my eyes burn. My head hurt. I whipped around and walked to the window of the living room. The glass felt cold against my cheek. I don't know how long I stood there. Then I felt her standing near me, asking me, "You want to go to your cousin's house, don't you?"

I didn't reply.

"It's hard. Not being able to do what you want to do most," Grandma Miller whispered. "Especially on Christmas. Especially if you're stuck with an old woman like me."

Slowly, I turned to look at her. I saw the halo of silver hair framing the chunky face, the lavender shadows circling the squinting eyes, and the folds of loose skin hanging below the chin. My heart lurched.

"I have watched you the whole day. I know how you feel."

I said nothing. Could say nothing.

"Let me ask your father to take you to your cousin's," she said. Slowly, painfully, she started towards the kitchen.

"No. Wait!"

I took her by the arm as Papa and Bansi did when they helped her up or down the stairs. She leaned on me. Soft and warm and almost weightless. As I led her towards the kitchen, I glanced outside. The square of light from the window had thrown the leafless dogwood into relief. The tree shimmered like a beacon in the mist. Beads of frozen rain had caught the golden light. They glowed like stars.

I knew they would keep sparkling as the angels sang into the silent night. Holy Night.

Three days later, we watched Grandma Miller climb into her car. She kept talking to Papa as she fastened the seat belt. "Now you're going to bring the family to visit me. I told Sandy I was going to ..."

"Yes. We'll come over," Papa smiled at her. "Maybe at Easter!"

The gray eyes twinkled at us from behind the windshield. She waved. And then she sped into the liquid sunshine.

We couldn't visit her at Easter. Papa had too much work. It had to be after the semester was over, he told Grandma Miller who called us frequently. She enticed us with her plans for a picnic at the Hatchery. In the woods. By the river. At the bird sanctuary. She was waiting for us. Waiting.

The snow had melted and the crocuses had begun to open up on the sidewalks when the call came. Grandma Miller was gone. She had died. No one knew when. It was when she didn't turn up at her Bridge Party or answer her phone that her friends had called her daughter. She found Grandma Miller sitting in the sofa. She had been dead for two days. Or three days. Nobody knew how long.

Is that how old women died? I wondered. Is that how my

own grandmother would die? Alone? Unknown? No. My Dadi in India would never be alone, I said to myself. Even if my uncle and aunt weren't there, the servants would keep an eye on her. The neighbors would. The milkman would ring the bell furiously if he didn't see her. The gardener would stand outside her window with the flowers for her worship and call out to her. No one could die alone in India. Or lie undiscovered for days. It was only in America that people died alone. Bansi checked me. He said I was mistaken. "Don't jump to conclusions," he said. "Don't you remember how Grandpa Miller had been surrounded by his children and even great grandchildren?" he asked me.

Bansi had a point there.

Papa couldn't forgive himself for not visiting her. He moped for days after he and Ma came back from the funeral. I couldn't get Grandma Miller out of my mind either. She would suddenly appear from nowhere, her face a cobweb of lines, her hair a cloud of silver cotton candy, her eyes the color of sea under the sun. Curious. Laughing. Loving.

I saw her.

I saw her husking corn in the kitchen. Making chicken corn soup. Watering her African violets. Snipping dead leaves from her begonias. Eating chocolates. Talking over the phone. Reading. And I saw her, as she must have sat that day, reading a book. Or watching her *Judge Judy* show on TV.

Suddenly, that day, the shadow of death must have fallen. She must have looked up and seen it. A Halloween phantom swaying in the wind. A huge dark shadow planted in front of her. Would she have asked for time? Asked it to wait until she had called her daughter? Her son? Her grandson, who was going to visit her soon? Or did she just surrender?

No! No! Not Grandma Miller!

I was certain she would have looked at Death straight in the face with her clear gray eyes. So honest. So loving. So curious. So unafraid.

She must have said. "Okay! So it's my time. Let's go." And she would have walked out with Death. Maybe, even holding Its hand as she had held mine.

I wondered if she had placed a bookmark between the pages of the book she had been reading. Or if she had stopped to switch off the TV. To turn down the heat. To water her plants before she left with Death.

I knew one thing, for sure, though. Grandma Miller must have talked all the way. She must have talked about her church, her children, and her grandchildren. She must have talked about Susan, about Stella, about Tom. She must have talked all the way to wherever Death was taking her. And Death must have been dumbfounded.

14

I have often wondered what would have happened if Papa hadn't come down with pneumonia, that year, and if his fever hadn't returned two days after he started teaching again. It's quite likely that my mother would have stayed a housewife and Razia's Bhajia might have never come into existence. However, when Papa was forced to take medical leave for the whole semester, Ma started scanning "Help Wanted" ads. She brushed aside Papa's objections by saying, "Extra income can only help, and you can do without teaching all those extra courses."

"But Leela –"

Ma didn't let him say a word more. "The kids are grown up. I can easily work."

"But –"

"I can't sit at home and twiddle my thumbs. What would I do if something happened to you? We would be on the streets."

Papa must have been too feeble to argue anymore. In the days that followed, we watched Ma's transformation from a housewife into a soldier marching to the beat of an unseen drummer. Chin up. Shoulders thrown back. Arms swinging. Eyes shining. Face beaming. I was sure she could raise a storm on a still day with a mere flick of her wrist. She drove the car as if she were on the Grand Prix track. When she roared into the driveway, Papa would growl, "What does she think she's driving? A truck on an Indian highway? I tell you she's going to get killed in some accident!" Oddly enough, it wasn't Ma who had an accident, it was Papa who met with one. But that was later.

Eventually, Ma found a job with a small newspaper, a four-page rag one finds lying in the driveway. She dreamed of writing her own column and starting a food section for the newspaper within a few weeks.

"It's not *The New York Times*," Papa warned her. "Don't expect too much."

But once Ma got on a high horse, it was difficult to get her off. The woman who owned the newspaper and was the editor as well as the reporter had assured Ma that she would let her write feature articles. Weeks and months passed, but there was no invitation for Ma to write on anything. Her job remained what it had been the first day – typing invoices, making coffee, and delivering bundles of newspaper to carriers. "This is not what I was told I would be doing," she sizzled. "I didn't come to this country to sell newspapers."

Papa, who had fully recovered by now, was his old self again. "You're not a CEO of a corporation," he said with some sarcasm. "If you want to get a better job, you must retrain yourself. Go back to school. Earn an MBA. A master's degree in home science from an Indian university is not much good here."

Ma refused to go back to school. "Not at my age," she said. "I won't."

"Then quit the job or stop complaining!"

Ma did neither.

She went to work everyday. She typed invoices. Attended the phones. Made coffee. Delivered newspapers. And she rumbled like Mt. St. Helena about to erupt. The thunder in her face was unmistakable when she came home.

One day, however, she came back beaming. Papa was reading. Bansi was repairing a broken toaster. I was cutting pictures for my project on the American Frontier. She was smiling. Had she written an editorial? A column? We waited. She sat down, kicked off her shoes, and announced she had turned in her resignation.

"Good!" Papa said. "Now relax." He went back to reading.

"I'm done with working for others," she said in a bright voice. "But I'm not done working. I think I'll start a business of my own."

Papa stared at her. "Business?"

"What kind of business?" Bansi and I chorused.

"I have to think about that," she said, peeling off the knee-highs, rolling them into a ball, and tossing them aside. "I could, if I were a good seamstress like Shobha, start a clothes-line of my own like – like this K-Mart woman –"

"Jaclyn Smith," Bansi prompted.

"Yes – but I can't even hold a needle straight. If I had studied law, I could be like Johnny Cochran. I could go into politics, but I'm not familiar with the politics of this country. So –" She sighed. "What should I do?"

"Buy a video store," I suggested. "Like Debby's Mom. That would be fun."

"Nonsense!" Papa retorted. "Whoever heard of anyone going into business in our family?"

Ma paid no attention to Papa. She sat toying with ideas. She could sell jewelry. Or rugs. Maybe Indian dresses and Indian groceries. She was still deliberating over her choice of business when Shanti Masi called to ask if she could stop over on her way from California. She was Ma's sister who lived in London. Of course, Ma was delighted. Masi had two passions in her life – her personal appearance and a clean house. Ma could keep up with neither. A quick smudge of lipstick or an occasional dab of mascara was all that she allowed herself. As for a clean house, neither of my parents was very organized.

Once in a while Ma and Papa would decide to clean and organize the scattered books and papers. They always started out as a team, but soon fell out. Papa, always fastidious about his papers, stopped to read every scrap before he could bring himself to throw it away. Ma, on the other hand, was like a twister that would sweep everything off in the blink of an eye. Papa would keep retrieving papers that Ma had dumped into trash bags with a ferocity that matched hers. They quarreled and, finally, when they grew tired of fighting each other, they would put off the task for some other day.

Shanti Masi's impending visit sent my parents into a frenzy of house cleaning. Papa piled up his books and papers on a table in a corner. Ma stuffed everything else – clothes, shoes, bedsheets, towels, boxes, bottles, pictures – into drawers and closets. For a change, everything looked to be in apple-pie order when Shanti Masi arrived. She looked as if she had come from a beauty salon. Her hair shone black, her eyes were lined with mascara, the color of her lipstick matched her nail polish. She looked around carefully. Ma held her breath. "Nice!" Masi said. Ma sighed with relief.

For the first few days, everything went well. On the fourth day, however, the dam broke lose when Shanti Masi happened to open a closet which she wasn't actually supposed to get into. Before she knew what had hit her, Masi was buried under an avalanche of loosely folded sweaters, balls of socks, towels, bed linen and a hundred other items. She went crazy after that. She pulled open all the closets; and things kept tumbling out. "Why do you buy these things if you can't organize them? In my house in London, I would never dream of having such a clutter."

"In America you go to sales and you buy. So I bought. What's the problem?" Ma said.

"Problem? Do you see the junk? Why can't you throw away what you don't need?"

"Junk?" Ma was cut to the quick. "Throw away what I

bought with my hard-earned money? No way. If people don't like it, too bad!"

"You haven't given up the typical Indian habit of saving, hoarding, preserving, have you? Take to American ways, Leela."

"The American way is to buy, buy, buy," Ma replied in the same tone.

Shanti Masi refused to be outdone by Ma. "Of course not. Americans buy and throw away and then buy some more. If they didn't throw things away how could there be such huge landfills of garbage? You know nothing about the American way of life. I have lived in London for –"

"Huh!" Ma shrugged. "London is not America."

Shanti Masi blinked her mascaraed eyes. "We don't collect junk in London the way you do here! Look at the mess in your house!"

She was quite right. Gradually, all the books and papers that Papa had removed from the dining table had found their way back. "In my house in London, everything is organized. Not like in some people's house where you find socks in kitchen drawers and spoons in bedroom closets. Cleanliness is a sign of civilized life."

"I'm glad I'm not obsessed with cleanliness as some people are," Ma said.

Shanti Masi's face must have gone red under her make up. She didn't say a word after that, but her looks said all, and my mother was left with a feeling of remorse.

Two days later, on the morning when Masi was to leave, Ma got up early to make up for her rudeness. She was going to give her sister a special *bhajia* treat. Ma's *bhajia*, vegetable fritters, dipped in spicy batter of chickpea flour and fried to a crisp golden brown, were considered unbeatable even by my grandmother, who was never satisfied with anyone's cooking other than her own. Ma sliced onions into perfect rings and potatoes into thin discs. She julienned red and green peppers, cubed eggplant, chopped coriander. She spiced up the batter with salt, peppercorns, fennel seeds, and crushed mint. She had it all arranged on the counter and had started heating oil in the fryer, when I left for school. What transpired between the two sisters, we found out later.

Masi came downstairs dressed immaculately. Her hair coiffured, her nails freshly painted, she was all dolled up for her flight. She stood at the bottom step, sniffing the air spiked with onions and fennel. The rich aroma was wafting through the living and dining rooms. The moment Shanti Masi saw Ma's *bhajia* sizzling on the cooking range, she rushed to turn off the gas and cover the wok.

"But I'm making these for you?" Ma cried. "I want you to take some back with you to London."

"To London? In the plane?"

Ma nodded.

"You idiot!" Shanti Masi shuddered. "You mean I'll board the plane reeking of your stupid onion *bhajias*? No, thank you."

Ma's spirits dropped like geese shot in flight. She left everything where it was. Masi had to fix her own eggs and toast.

I have always wondered what the drive to the airport must have been. Masi must have rolled down the window even at the risk of ruining her hairdo. As soon as Ma returned from the airport, she started frying *bhajia* with a vengeance. Onion and *paneer bhajia*. Spinach and mushroom *bhajia*. Cauliflower and green peas *bhajia*. Potato *bhajia*. Egg plant *bhajia*. I could smell the aroma of fried fennel, mint, and onions in the street when I returned from school.

"But why so much, Ma?" I asked.

She didn't hear me. She heaped some on a plate and set it before me. "Here! Taste these and tell me what's wrong with them."

Her eyes filled up with freezing rain. "Thank God she went

back to her London. What does she know about making *bhajia*? I bet she can't even mix the batter. London's gone to her head. But what do I care? These – here – eat!" Ma's eyes welled up. She wiped them with a corner of her sari and pushed a plateful before Bansi who had just come in. "Calling me stupid was okay," she said. "But calling my *bhajia* stupid? I can't take it."

Ma remained angry and depressed. At dinner, she would sit toying with her food. Her gaze would dart out of the window, over the rooftops, and steal back to us. This continued for a week. On the eighth day, she pushed her plate aside and looked at us. "You know what!" She said. "I think I'll become a restaurateur."

"A restaurateur?" Papa put down his fork. "Impossible! You don't even understand what the business involves." He recounted a long list of regulations that she would have to follow. "Besides you need at least a hundred thousand dollars to begin with."

Ma's confidence had evaporated. "So I've become good for nothing here!"

Bansi was quick to console her. "You're the best cook in the world, Ma!"

"No one makes *bhajia* like yours," I added.

"*Bhajia*?"

That was the magic word that sent rainbow trouts leaping in my mother's eyes. Then the dikes broke.

"Of course! Why didn't I think of it? I could sell *bhajia*. I could take orders for *bhajia* and cater to parties and celebrations –"

She went into a litany of *bhajias*. "I know what I want to do. I'll start a *bhajia* chain – like McDonald's or Wendy's –"

"What nonsense!" Papa left the room.

Ma, however, was past caring by now. "A veggie response to Big Mac," she said. "I'll have a rainbow as logo instead of the golden arches. *Bhajia* superimposed on a rainbow.

Imagine Americans eating *bhajia* at home. On the road. In their cars. In the office. On the train." A golden light suffused her face.

"What'll you call them?" Bansi asked.

"*Bhajia*, of course. No wait. Let me think."

We waited.

"I know what!" She announced after a while. How about Razia's Bhajia?"

"What's the connection between Razia and *bhajia*?" Bansi said. "Why not Fiery Fritters? Americans know what fritters are. And your *bhajia* will be hot in more ways than one."

"No, No. That'll take away the poetry," Ma shook her head. "Razia's Bhajia, dear child, has a historical connotation. Razia Sultana was the first Muslim woman ruler of India who led armies into battles, her coins were minted with the inscription 'Pillar of Women.' My *bhajia*, named after her, will appeal to women, to feminists the world over."

The combination of history, cuisine, and feminism had become a bit too complex for me to digest. "But Ma," I interrupted. "Would *bhajias* sell in America?"

"Sell?" She looked at me as if I had asked her if the earth would turn. "Orders will pour in non-stop. Fax orders. Phone orders. And people will be waiting in lines. Americans are crazy about food. They'll love my crunchy munchy *bhajia* –" She paused to take a breath. "They'll love them like burrito and pizza and spring rolls. Wait till they taste my *bhajia*. I tell you, the American palate is never going to be the same after my *bhajias* appear."

Interestingly enough, Shobha Chachi took to Ma's *bhajia* scheme without a moment's hesitation. She was ready to exchange the smell of leather for the aroma of roasted fennel and mint.

It was inevitable that Ma's ballooning *bhajia* dream would invite Papa's wrath. "Sell *bhajia*? Are you joking? I can't see the daughter of a distinguished judge hawking *bhajias* like a common illiterate woman who has no talent and who –" Papa's sentences could run a marathon when he was angry.

"I don't see where my father or even you come in. I'm not setting up a food truck near your college entrance."

"Only a woman could come up with such a foolish idea."

"This is gender discrimination – worse than racism."

"O, so now I am guilty of discrimination! So what'll you do? Go to the court?" Papa's frustration had turned into a seething rage. "I didn't know I was courting such disaster when I brought my family here."

Ma tossed her head as a bull tosses its horns before charging. "Shobha is willing to help."

"Shobha?" Papa was taken aback. He looked dazed. "America does strange things to women. They see the Statue of Liberty and they think it means liberation from womanly duties. Instead of the demure Indian woman you thought you knew, you find a warrior ready to bite your head off."

Ma was past hearing, past caring. She was a runaway train. "I'll advertise Razia's Bhajia by a blimp. There'll be streamers! Flyers! TV ads too. Maybe, I can have a web page, something like bhajia.com."

We listened to her in awe.

"I could have a Grand Opening before Christmas. I could invite the Mayor for the ribbon-cutting ceremony – imagine my *bhajia* becoming famous like Aunty Anne's pretzels. And imagine people munching *bhajia* on Christmas Eve! And –" The rainbow trouts in her eyes went wild.

"But where's the money?" Papa asked her.

"Money?"

"Money!"

Ma pondered over it for a while. Then her face lit up like a two-hundred watt light bulb. "Loan – I'll take a loan. They say you apply for a loan in the morning and you get it in the afternoon in America. You go to a car dealer without a dime in your pocket and you come out driving a brand new car. In America anything is possible."

Papa chortled. "Even in America, you have to have a collateral to get a loan."

"Collateral?"

Papa seemed to be winning, after all. "Yes, a collateral! Hard cash to put down! But don't worry," he added. "I have a suggestion. You could put your *bhajia* in a basket and hawk them on the sidewalks – a *bhajia* vendor won't need a collateral or a loan."

My mother stared at him with something akin to hatred in her eyes. "The frontier men and women didn't have everything laid out for them when they came to this country," she said with much pride. "They worked with their bare hands. I can do the same." She was repeating exactly what Papa had told us all the time.

The next day she had put stick-ons with telephone numbers of banks and other agencies all over the strawberries and blueberries on the kitchen wall. Getting a loan was an arduous task which involved calling banks, filling in applications, and waiting. The rejections would have dampened anybody's spirits, but not my mother's. She drove to banks. She filed applications. She went to attend seminars on small businesses even though Papa would have none of it. My parents didn't say anything in front of us, but I could feel the tension in the air, thick like smog. They never spoke directly to each other. When papa moved out of the bedroom and started sleeping on the sofa, I was scared. I had heard kids at school talk about broken families. Tim, Melissa, Janet, Corey – they were all from one-parent households. Of course, they rarely complained, but I always felt they were like spare carriages, shunted from one track to another. There were so many complications, so much sadness. What if we too ended up their way?

Bansi dismissed my fears. "Nonsense! They're not going to divorce."

Priya added her own words of wisdom. "Indians seldom divorce, you know. They aren't honest like Americans." She had suddenly begun to see faults in Indians. "My parents are at each other's throat every day, but I can bet, they'll never ever separate."

I wasn't convinced by either and I would have written to my grandmother for help had the tension not subsided as quickly as it had arisen with the publication of Papa's book.

It came out that spring. Papa's mood changed as soon as the first copy arrived. He often smiled to himself. The creases in his forehead melted. In fact, he was lost in the copy sitting on his desk – glossy and smelling of fresh ink and new paper. It seemed Papa had unearthed a treasure. In a way so had I.

Every time I walked past the table, I would touch the book with awe, wonder, joy, pride, and great expectations. I waited for a windfall. The local newspaper had published a short review of the book. I had flaunted it before the girls. I bragged that his picture would soon appear in *The New York Times*. He was going to be interviewed on TV. He was sure to sell a million copies.

"Lucky you!" They said.

I waited for the phone calls, everyday. I waited for reporters and I waited to see Papa's name blazing across the pages of the *New York Times, the Philadelphia Inquirer* – in fact in all the newspapers.

Everyday, when I turned the corner of our street on my way back from school, I expected to see a TV van with Channel 6 written in bold blue letters, parked outside our house. I looked around for our neighbors gathered around the van, staring at our house with admiring eyes.

But no van came to our driveway. No faces in the porch. No crowds. No cameras.

I asked Bansi. "When will the TV people come?"

"For what?"

"For interviewing Papa."

He didn't understand what I was talking about.

"Writers get interviewed on TV," I explained. "They get money. Like Stephen King."

"I see!" He gave me a searching look.

"Well?" I waited for some assurance. Some explanation. Bansi placed his hand on my shoulder. "Papa's book is not that kind of book," he said. "It's a book on Indian philosophy."

"But it can sell."

"It can't sell like popular fiction. It's not about sex or politics." He picked up a copy of the book and flipped through the pages before putting it back. "It's a scholarly book, you see. It'll be on the reference shelves in libraries and –"

By then I had lost all interest in the book's future. Why did Papa have to write a book that wasn't going to sell or bring reporters and TV cameras to our door? Why couldn't he have written about murder? Politics? Sex? Why did he do *this* kind of writing and not *the other* kind? Bansi defended Papa, as usual. "Papa writes what he wants to write about. Who cares about million copies and TV interviews, anyway?"

"I do," I said.

Papa, oblivious of my thwarted hopes, appeared to be contented and at peace. When he thought that no one was watching him, he would walk over to the table, pick up a copy and run his hand over the smooth cover. He would open it gently, reverently, just as my grandmother opened her holy books. He would turn the pages, one by one, and read. I wondered how he could read his own writing over and over again. I always had a hard time even revising my essays. But Papa never tired of reading his book. Reading and marking and reading again. His face became the face of a Buddha at those moments. Nothing could upset his serenity, his composure, then. Not even the impending opening of Razia's Bhajia disturbed him.

My mother had, finally, secured a loan. She had leased a tiny counter wedged between Wendy's and Auntie Annie's Pretzels in the 30th Street Station food court. Of course, the Mayor didn't come for its opening nor were the media around with their flashing cameras as Ma had dreamed. Only Chacha's family and ours were at hand when Papa broke the ceremonial coconut and chanted an invocation to Lord Ganesha. Shobha Chachi had stitched white aprons, each with a dazzling rainbow and "Razia's Bhajia" embroidered on the front pocket. She wore one over her sari when she chopped vegetables. Ma also wore one over her tees and trousers as she mixed the batter. Soon the *bhajia* started sizzling and curious passersby stopped. Priya, Bansi and I passed around samples in paper plates with Chacha's commentary. He had come up with some exotic story of a princess' passion that was behind the origin of *bhajia*.

It was six months before Razia's Bhajia began to bring in some profit. Shobha Chachi was less bitter and less hot-tempered now that she was working with Ma. The business seemed to fare better than Papa's scholarly book. Razia's Bhajia got a good review in the food section of a city newspaper. Of course, it never became a franchise, but it was popular and she got big orders for parties. Ma opened a branch of Razia's Bhajia under Shobha Chachi's supervision in another part of the city. Shobha Chachi was seen to smile sometimes now. Chacha too had begun to think of selling his store and going back to his engineering job. They had decided to put a matrimonial ad for Priya in the newspaper. Once Priya was married and had settled down happily with a young man from India their worries would be over. They could spend the rest of their life living happily somewhere near Priya and playing with their grandchildren. It was a perfect picture of a perfect life, too perfect to be true. And none of us saw the cracks.

In the early hours of the morning, the telephone rang. It was Chacha was calling from the hospital. Priya had to be rushed to the Emergency because she had swallowed a whole bottle of Tylenol. Ma and Papa left for the hospital at  once. I was not allowed to see Priya till she was released from the hospital the next day and she came to stay with us for a few days. Ma thought that would help her heal.

The skinny, grim-faced girl with dull eyes and thin mouth set in a straight line was a shadow of the Priya I knew and the one who had taken us around the apartment building. This was her ghost. She spoke to no one, not even to me and Bansi. We didn't ask her any questions. My mother said the best thing would be to let her rest. I would take the things I wanted from my room, for that is where she was staying and slip away.

Three days later, Priya stopped me. "Why do you have to sneak in and out like a thief?"

I told her I didn't want to disturb her.

"Don't you want to know what happened?"

I didn't know what to say.

"Where's Bansi?" she said. "Ask him to come here. What sort of a brother is he to keep away?"

Bansi came. He sat in a chair, I at the foot of the bed. Priya leaned against the pillows and looked at us. "You guys want to know what happened, don't you?"

She didn't give us a chance to answer. She had already started telling her story. It had all begun with Chacha having seen her coming out of McDonald's with Chip. He was waiting for Priya when she came home. "Daddy was mad. Real mad," Priya told us. "Without giving me a chance to explain anything, he pounced upon me. He had already jumped to the conclusion that I had been sleeping with Chip. He shouted and called me names and shook his fist in my face."

"And Chachi? Where was she?" I asked.

"She was there, crying of course, as if someone had died."

It was only when Chacha slapped Priya that Shobha Chachi had flung herself between them, screaming. "Have you lost your mind? Are you crazy? How can you hit your grown-up daughter?"

Chacha had stood there as if he had turned into a stone while Shobha Chachi kept blubbering that they should have never come to America. "You were crazy to come here, now pay for it."

In his anger and confusion, Chacha had forgotten Priya and turned to his wife.

In panic, Priya had run to her room. "I could hear my mother crying and Daddy was shouting. I sat on my bed and the next thing I knew was the lady in white was standing there. Ghosts can walk through walls, you know."

Bansi snorted. "Stop making up stories."

"I swear she was there in my room – standing there as clearly as you two are sitting here. She was wearing diamond earrings shaped like tulips … and … and a diamond tiara … you know like the one Princess Di wore."

I couldn't hold back my excitement. "Was it Princess Di?"

"Don't be silly!" Bansi frowned. "It's a story good for the *National Inquirer*. You could be in the news if you told them this story," he said to Priya.

"I didn't say it was Princess Di," Priya grunted. "Only she looked like her. She held the bottle to me and said, 'I'd rather die than give up my love.' I took the bottle from her and swallowed three tablets at a time. I guess I must have passed out soon after that. When I woke up in the hospital, I thought I was in heaven. Someone was singing. I thought it was an angel. I opened my eyes and what do you think I saw?"

"The lady ghost?" I asked.

"No, Silly! My Daddy! He was sitting in a chair, crying. That's what coming down to earth means, I thought." Priya broke into helpless giggles.

Bansi wasn't amused. "It's not funny."

"Don't be so grim, Bansi. Like Chip says, 'Don't worry. Be happy.'"

"Bullshit!"

"Chip says we can make this world a utopia where everyone will be happy –"

"There's no such thing as utopia," Bansi cut in. "And I think this Chip of yours is a dopey."

Priya glared at him. "Chip is no dopey."

"How well do you know him?" Bansi asked.

"I don't want to know anything about him. I trust him."

"Your father –"

"I don't care about him," she cut in. "Some fucking faith he has in me!"

"Don't be vulgar."

"Fucking. Fucking. Fucking," she hissed at Bansi. "It's nobody's business what I do and how I speak and who I go out with. It's my fuckin' life and I'll live it the fuckin' way I want."

"Have it your way, then." Bansi shrugged. "You'll have only yourself to thank for and no one else."

After he was gone and Priya and I were alone, I was afraid to move or say anything, as if my doing so would break some thin layer of ice I was standing on. Priya recanted. "I shouldn't have said all that to Bansi. I'm so tired of everything. I want to go home."

I should have said something to comfort her, but I couldn't. All I could do was ask, "What'll you do now?"

Priya combed her entangled curls with her fingers. "I guess I'll move out. Live on my own. Work."

"Leave your mother and father?"

"Who cares!"

"But where will you live?"

She stared at the wall as if she could read something written there. "With my friend Nellie. She's promised to find me work. Or with Chip."

"Where?"

"Wherever," she shrugged. "I won't give him up. No way."

"You're not going to run away with Chip, are you?"

She didn't say anything.

"Are you?" I repeated.

A faint smile flickered at the corners of her mouth, like a sliver of sunlight touching an icicle.

"Forget it, will you?" she said. "Forget I said anything about Chip. I'm not going anywhere."

That was to be the biggest lie Priya had ever told me.

In less than a week after she went home, Priya disappeared. She left a note propped up on the TV, saying, "I'm going away." Chacha looked as if a bolt of lightening had hit him. Surprisingly, it was Shobha Chachi who showed more courage. It was she who called Papa and then informed the police. It was she who stayed dry-eyed and practical. Papa was amazed at her control. He thought she had proved to be the sane one, for Chacha had collapsed like a sandcastle at the punch of the first wave. After sitting there, saying nothing, he finally picked up his car and drove like crazy around the city for two days and two nights, stopping to stare at any girl who looked like Priya. Papa had to drag him home where he slept for days after the doctor had sedated him.

The police didn't do much. Perhaps they couldn't. They had no leads. Scores of kids and young women disappeared every day; how could they find each one of them? Besides, as Bansi pointed out, Priya wasn't a rich man's daughter. Who was interested in searching for an immigrant store-owner's daughter? She must have run away with a boyfriend, they said. Was there a boyfriend? Did Chacha suspect a foul play? Was there anyone he suspected? Was she on drugs? Chacha kept shaking his head like a dog trying to shake off fleas. The police did go looking for a girl named Nellie at Priya's school. There wasn't any girl by that name. Maybe Nellie was not Priya's schoolmate. Or maybe that was a fake name. The police assured Chacha that they had her picture on their files; they would do their best. All he could do was wait. He waited. And I waited too.

I dreamed of Priya all the time. I imagined what I would say to her when I met her and she laughed into my face, saying, "Don't look so surprised, Silly! Here I am."

"Where have you been?" I would ask her.

"Wait till I tell you all about it," she would say, sitting down beside me. Encircling her knees with her arms, she would look up at the sky, and tell me some implausible story that only Priya could tell, lacing it with allusions from Hindu mythology.

I would hold her hand, and make her promise that she would never go away. She would nod and laugh and be the Priya I had always known and loved.

I saw her everywhere. Walking down the street. Standing under a tree. Stepping out of the house. Sitting in the park. I heard her calling me even when I wasn't alone, even when I was in my class, or on the bus, or sitting at the dinner table. I often heard her footsteps behind me when I walked down the street. If I stopped and looked around, I found no one.

Sometimes, if I saw a slim form flitting across the street, I would call out her name only to find a startled stranger looking at me. Embarrassed and apologetic, I would turn away. It became such a frequent occurrence that I began to dread looking at anyone in the street.

I didn't stop that day even when I heard someone calling my name.

"Juhi! Don't you hear me?" The voice was sharp, this time. And it sounded like Priya's.

I stopped and wheeled around.

The girl was an apparition in a black tee shirt and tight pants with a blue beret perched on her head. She looked a little taller, a tad thinner, almost gaunt. It couldn't be Priya, for she had never dressed like that. I looked hard at her pale face. A smile hesitated on her lips, then froze. The eyes were Priya's; except that one was black as if someone had socked her. We stared at each other without saying a word, without moving an inch.

Finally, she said, "Don't gape at me, Silly! Say something."

"Priya!" I gasped. "So – so you're not dead?"

"Obviously." She gave me a wry smile which never reached her eyes.

"Why did you leave home?" I asked her. "Where do you live? Did you run away with Chip? Where –?"

"Listen!" She cut me short. "It's a long story. I can't talk much right now. Chip had to go away. He'll be back one of these days."

"Then –"

She remained silent. I didn't like her silence. I wanted her to say something. Anything. I wanted her to laugh and call me Silly. I tried to be funny. "Are you living with ghosts?"

She didn't laugh. "You could say that." She took me by the arm. "Don't stop. Keep walking. I live with a group of girls like me. Runaways, you know. We live together and – only –" she hesitated as a car slid to a stop at the other side of the street. I hadn't noticed it before.

"Why did you leave home, Priya?"

She shivered as if an Arctic wind had hit her. "Can't say. Maybe it was a mistake – maybe I was foolish – but, well, I did what I had to do." She spoke haltingly. "Is my mother all right?"

"Yes."

"Daddy?"

"All right." I stared at her pale face. "You're hurt. Did you have a fall, Priya?" I asked pointing to her eye.

"A fall? Yes, Yes! It was a fall. A fall," she said, then added abruptly. "Listen, Juhi. Don't stare at me like an owl. I'm in a hurry. I – I need some money."

"Are you living with Chip?"

She didn't answer my question. "Give me – whatever you have on you. Quickly. Please!"

She stretched out her palm. The gesture stabbed me straight to the heart. It reminded me of the beggars I had seen in the film on India in Miss Thompson's class. Skinny children. Their bellies swollen. Their scrawny arms sticking out like the limbs of trees blighted by drought. Their voices whining for money. It was as if Priya had become one of them. I couldn't bear it. Quickly, I emptied my coin purse into her hand without looking at her. Four dollar bills. Some quarters. A few dimes. Pennies. She closed her fist on the collection. "Remember Nellie? The girl I told you about?"

"You're living with her, aren't you?"

"I was ... she's dead. Killed in a –" She couldn't finish the sentence. The car honked. "Got to go now," she said quickening her steps.

"Priya, wait!" I stumbled after her. "What happened to Chip?"

She didn't answer. I asked again.

"I don't know. He's gone."

"Come back, Priya. Come home."

She shook her head and moved ahead.

"When will I see you again?"

She paused. "I don't know," she said, flinging the words over her shoulder.

Then, she changed her mind, turned around. "No, wait!" She said. "Meet me in the park. On Friday. Same time. Alone. Don't tell anyone."

"Priya!" My voice had grown hoarse. "Don't go away. Come back. Please!" I thought she'd turn around and return.

She didn't.

"Wait!" I called out.

She was already halfway across the street. The car door opened and swallowed her. She was gone. I stood there wondering if I had been dreaming. Maybe I had. Then I looked at the empty coin purse in my hand and at a penny that must have rolled out and fallen to the ground when I handed Priya the money. I picked it up and clutched it so hard that it dug into my palm. The pain stopped me from crying.

Lt. Townsend, the police detective, was a tall black woman with dazzling white teeth and a scar on her chin. She wouldn't stop asking questions. When did you meet her? Where? How did she look? What was she wearing? Did she look scared? Who was with her? What kind of a car was it? Who was inside it? What did she say? Why didn't you hold her back?

I repeated what I remembered, keeping my eyes fixed all the time on her cap with a gleaming badge pinned to it where she had put it on the table. The scar on her chin distracted me.

Finally, she said it was quite likely that Priya was involved with a girl gang.

"Girl gang?"

She explained to us that it was like any other gang of

runaways or kids on drugs. The black eye could have resulted from a fight or an initiation rite. "The gangs can be quite violent. And most probably Nellie was a nickname. Gang members usually adopt nicknames."

She got up, picked up her cap, and asked me. "Did she give you anything?"

"No. I gave her money."

"You were lucky. Another gang member might have tried to hurt you."

She warned me to stay away from Priya and from the park. "Never take anything from her. The gang might be using her to sell dope. Who knows!"

I couldn't keep away from the park, though. I had promised to wait for Priya. I was her friend. Her sister. I wasn't going to fail her.

Bansi consoled me. "She'll come back when she wants to," he said. "She might even call you."

She didn't.

Every Friday, I waited for Priya in the park. I was sure she would come back and we would go home and everything would be fine, after that. We would have a fairytale ending. I didn't know then that life had no fairytale endings. I had yet to learn that Cinderella remains a cinder maid, that the wolf eats up Red Riding Hood, that the Sleeping Beauty never wakes up, that Snow White dies from the poisoned apple.

Priya never came. Never called. And I waited, week after week, till the golden autumn began to brown at the edges and the trees to get bare. The park took on the quality of a sketch in brown. Brown leaves. Brown trees. Brown skies. Brown thoughts. The geese had flown away.

Sometimes, an elderly woman arrested by the sight of a girl sitting sadly by herself under a huge oak paused to look at me.

"Are you waiting for someone, child?" she would ask.

"My friend."

"I wouldn't stay here alone by myself," she would suggest in a kind voice. "Go home before it gets dark."

Many Fridays went by. My parents began to worry about me. They didn't want me going to the park any more. I promised them I wouldn't – except one last time. Either Priya would show up, or she could forget me.

The ground was wet and soaking from yesterday's storm when I went to the park. I sat down on the cast iron bench near the oak and waited for Priya. Memory replayed all the stories she had narrated, all the dances she had danced. I looked up sharply when I heard someone walking on the grass. There was no one there. The silence deepened, the shadows lengthened, I began to feel scared. Maybe, I should leave, I thought.

A voice startled me. "Waiting for someone, little girl?"

I looked up. He was dressed in a long black coat with a turned up collar that hid the lower half of his face. Dark sunglasses shielded his eyes. A faceless, colorless, shapeless apparition. Was he the ghost Priya and I had seen that day?

"I want to show you somethin'." His voice had the pungent sweetness of a cough syrup.

I jumped up, ready to flee, but his voice shackled my feet. "You're waitin' for your friend," he said. "I know where she is. I c'n take you to her."

"How's she?"

"She's hurt."

"Hurt?"

"There – behind those bushes, up over there. She's cryin'. Don't you hear her?" I heard something, but it could have been the wind. It could have been anything. I was reluctant to believe him, and yet, I was mesmerized. "You don't care for your friend, I see."

What if Priya was really waiting for me? I thought. What

if she was really hurt? I looked up at the knot of trees. "Where's she? I can't see anyone."

"There! She's waitin'. C'mon. I'll take you to her."

He was breathing down my neck. I started towards the trees. His heavy footsteps dogged me. I began to run. His voice stalked me. "Wait! I have somethin' for you, little girl –"

I scrambled up the slope, slipping on the wet leaves under my feet. Suddenly, he came upon me from behind and caught me by the shoulders. In the scuffle, I lost my glasses. His face blurred as did the trees, the shrubs, the sky around me. "I won't hurt you," he breathed heavily, blowing a stench of rotting teeth in my face. "I don' hurt li'l girls if they're nice to me. Tell me," he asked in a squeaky voice "Are you from Pakistan?"

"– In – In – India!" I stammered.

"Ha!" He laughed. "You know, little girl? I am the Emperor of India. I had a palace. A throne of gold with emeralds and rubies. Emperor! I had tigers. Elephants," he said, dragging me to a little clearing under a huge tree. I tried to scream, but he pressed his hand on my mouth. "I won't hurt you. I won't hurt my princess," he muttered. "Stay quiet and I'll do you no harm. I'll make you my queen."

He was insane.

I tried to wriggle out of his grip.

"Don't!" he hissed into my face.

I kicked and I screamed. A back-handed slap sent me sprawling on the wet ground. He fell on his knees beside me and thrust his hand under my sweater. It was cold and slimy like the lizards that clambered across the walls in Jaipur.

"Now – now –" he said in a guttural voice as he grabbed my hand and pressed it against his crotch. I screamed again. I kicked wildly. He pinned my knees between his, cupped my mouth with one hand, and explored my body with the other. The bile rose in my throat. It filled my mouth. It flowed into my nose. I threw up into his hand.

"Damn you!" He spluttered, springing back and wringing his hand. He gripped my right with the other hand. I turned my face and sank my teeth into it. He howled. He cursed, but I didn't let go, not even when he pulled me by the hair, not even when he pounded on my head with his fist. It was only when my mouth was filled with saliva and his blood that I unclenched my teeth.

"You bitch!" he screamed, wringing his hand.

I looked around desperately for something to hit him with before he pounced upon me again. My hand fell on a piece of rusted iron rod. I grabbed it.

"Don't. I'll kill you," I cried, tasting the tears that were running down my face.

He laughed as he approached me. His raincoat fluttered like the wings of a bat. He was a Dracula. A Devil. I rammed the rod into his stomach as he lunged at me.

He dropped like a felled tree.

I struggled to my feet. Had I killed him? I peered at him lying there curled up like a giant fetus. Then I bolted, crying in a hoarse voice. I thrashed at the twigs and the branches that stood in my way. I didn't care if my arms and face were lacerated, if my clothes were caught in the briars. The horror was pursuing me like a giant's shadow.

I kept running. Out of my body, out of my mind. Running. I heard someone calling me, but I didn't stop. My foot slipped and I went slithering down the slope, into the creek swollen with rain water. I thought I saw someone running towards me. Ma? Papa? Bansi? Priya? Who? I tried to keep my eyes open, but the water closed over me.

It was cold. It was dark. It was an annihilation of all sound. All thought. All fear.

When I surfaced, I was lying on the ground, shivering under a blanket someone had thrown over me. A hand touched me. I started thrashing at the blanket. Hands pinned me down. I kicked and screamed and I kept screaming till Ma cradled me in her arms and Papa held me tight against him, saying over and over again, "You're safe, darling. Safe."

Later, Lt. Townsend had a lot of questions again.

What were you doing there? How long were you there? How often did you go there? Did you always sit in the same spot? Had you ever seen this man before? I kept shaking my head till she asked, "Could this be Priya's partner or friend?"

"No, no. Priya wouldn't be friends with such an ugly man," I cried.

She suppressed a smile, then gently asked. "Did you see his face?"

"No."

"Can you describe the man?"

I couldn't.

How did one describe a faceless terror? All I remembered was the stench and the sight of a huge bat flying towards me. I didn't know if he was black or white, Hispanic or Oriental. The police did find a bum loitering in the park. He was old and shriveled up – simply a bundle of bones. He wasn't the demon who returned to stalk me in my nightmares, who chased me, breathed into my face, crushed me. I hated my body. The breast where the man had touched me burned. I was afraid it would turn cancerous; and it would have to be chopped off. It would leave me with a gaping hole like Mrs. Mikulsky's. I would often wake up crying. Ma would rock me in her arms, Bansi would clasp my hands in his and assure me it was all right, and Papa would tower over, guarding us like a huge Papa Bear.

The memory of that day bled like a wound that doesn't heal. I was always afraid of someone chasing me, staring at me, pressing down upon me. I didn't go to my new junior high when school started. That upset Papa so badly that despite his distrust of psychologists, he took me to one.

Of course, it never worked out. It wasn't meant to from day one when a tall woman with gray flyaway hair and gold-framed glasses stepped away from a big desk to meet us. We shook hands. She asked Papa to leave because she wanted to talk to me. I sat with my legs crossed and my hands in my lap.

"Joohi? Did I say your name right?" she asked me as she pulled out a yellow notepad.

"It's okay," I shrugged.

She jotted down some notes and took off her glasses.

"Now," she said. "We're going to work together. You should feel free to tell me anything."

"Yes."

"Do you want to tell me anything?"

"No."

"Something that bothers you or frightens you."

"No."

"Do you sleep well?"

"Yes."

"Do you dream?"

"Uh-h."

"Tell me about your dreams."

"I can't remember."

"Well! Tell me how you feel about school."

"I'm not going to school right now."

"Do you want to talk about it?"

"No!"

We never got anywhere though I saw her every week. Looking back, I think I was unfair and stubborn. I never gave her a chance. She must have been frustrated by my refusal to share anything with her. I don't know why I did that. Perhaps I didn't wish to be reminded of the man in the park, or of Priya and all the unpleasant experiences I had been through. I was relieved when the visits ended after a couple of months and Ma decided to take me with her to Razia's Bhajia, instead. "I know you can help me," she said.

It was in the 30th Street Station food court, sitting behind the Razia's Bhajia counter finally, that I began to heal. Razia's Bhajia hadn't exactly conquered the food court, but it was doing well considering the hours and days it remained open. Chacha, who had sold his store soon after Priya left, had taken up a job with the township, and moved to a modest house not far from ours. He came to sit by me at the counter, sometimes, when Shobha Chachi worked at her Razia's Bhajia branch in a suburban mall. She had begun to take catering orders for parties. Finally, she had found her vocation. She would pause in the middle of mixing the batter, look up, and sigh. "I wonder where she is!" Then go back to her work as if she had made her peace with the loss.

It was Chacha who remained despondent. He had aged within a few months. He never complained. He never talked about Priya. Once I asked him if he thought of her. "No," he said, refusing to look me in the eye. "No. She's lost."

He never laughed. He never cursed his fate. "We can't erase our *karma*," he would say philosophically. "So we have to bear it as best as we can."

He would sit beside me and tell me stories about railway stations in India and the train journeys he had taken, from Kashmir in the north to Kanya Kumari in the south. He told me stories of *fakirs* who could stand on one leg and meditate for years and he told me about old forts, citadels, temples and mosques he had seen and visited. But all his stories were connected with his railway journeys, which took me back to the journeys I had taken with my grandmother and grandfather. I lived it all – men haggling with coolies balancing piles of luggage on their heads, mothers struggling with children and tiffin carriers, engines blowing steam, puffing in and out of the station, hawkers selling sweet hot tea in clay cups, and spiced potatoes and *puri* wrapped in banana leaf. We used to love looking out of the window when the train curved and pulled our heads in only when coal grit blew into our eyes. Then my grandmother would blow into the corner of her sari and press the soft warm cloth, scented with her breath, to the hurting eye. This memory comforted as the other one had hurt.

Sometimes, when he wasn't in a mood to talk, Chacha and I would sit quietly and look at people scurrying in and out of the station. We heard the arrival and departure announcements; we felt the floors vibrate under our feet as the trains thundered underground. The station hummed like a beehive. Both of us forgot our personal pains. His soothing presence, the shared moments of watching the constant movement of men and women, the incessant rumble of trains, the perpetual sight of people eating, talking, laughing, running yanked me back into the round of everyday life. The trains, the lively train station, gave me back what I had lost in the tranquil park.

"Life is a railway station, anyway," Chacha would say in a sad voice. "People come and go. There's no stopping before the final destination."

He sounded somewhat like Papa, who had always told us that motion was the principle of life. "To stop is to die."

"Arrivals and departures," Chacha would say. "Joy and pain, having and losing – that's the name of the game."

Seated beside him, I watched the constant movement, the joy of arrivals, and the sadness of departure. I hoped there would be no more departures. Priya's going away had been enough. I didn't know that there was another waiting around the corner.

Once, when Bansi was assembling a miniature ship in his room, I had asked him what he thought was most important in life. He hadn't replied immediately, for he was gluing a tiny sail to a mast. After placing the boat carefully on the  shelf, he had smiled at me and said, "Having dreams. That's most important. If you don't dream, you die."

"Dreams?" How could Bansi talk about dreams when he had none? I thought. "What do you know about dreams, Bansi?" I asked him. "You never dream."

Bansi's eyes had darkened like Indian monsoon skies in July. His fingers had beaten a tattoo on the table. "Everyone dreams," he had laughed softly.

"Even you?"

"Even I. Why what's wrong with me?"

"But you are always so – so sort of practical. What can you dream of?"

He had looked at me with eyes like dark caverns. He had drifted so far away from me in the split of a moment that even though all I had to do was to stretch out my hand and touch him, I knew I couldn't reach him.

"What do I dream of?" He had mumbled, talking more to himself than to me.

I waited. And silence had ticked on.

"I dream of the suns and the moons and galaxies we know very little about – of the worlds that exist beyond our small planet – of the infinite spaces we've never entered and the vast oceans we've never crossed. Like Carl Sagan –"

I had lost him. I hadn't understood his dreams of suns and stars. I couldn't have imagined the infinite spaces he talked about, nor the vast seas he dreamed of. Dreams, for me, were tangible. Cast in concrete. Rock-solid. They were like a crystal globe, which you could hold in your hands and turn around. Bansi's dreams were fragile like a butterfly's wings. Evanescent like dew drops trembling on the tip of a leaf. I couldn't understand him. He was like a somnambulist talking to himself, an astronaut floating in space, beyond the reach of gravity.

Then he had wrenched himself free from his dreams. "Enough!" He had said, glancing at his watch. "Time to go to work."

A shaft of sunlight had stolen into the room. It had washed the boats on the shelf with a copper light.

"What will you do with all these ships, Bansi?" I had asked him.

"Why! Sail out into the open sea," he had laughed. "Like Columbus, conquer new worlds. Find lost kingdoms under the sea."

Standing there, jingling the car keys, and looking at the ships as if they were about to set sail, Bansi had looked very comical to me. I had never imagined how serious he was underneath.

They were sitting at the dining table as if they had lost their speech. No one looked up or said a word to me when I returned home from school. That was quite unusual. I looked from Bansi to Ma to Papa. Had some calamity overtaken my grandmother or Chacha? Had the house been burgled? Had Papa lost his job? Had they heard some bad news about Priya?

Finally, I asked. "Is something wrong?"

"Nothing," Papa said. "Come, sit down."

It felt strange being asked to join the adult group from which I was normally excluded. I pulled up a chair and sat down. Papa turned to Bansi. "So you've decided?"

"Yes, Papa. I have."

I thought Papa was referring to Bansi's decision about some graduate school.

"Which school?" I asked breathlessly. "Yale? Harvard? Which one, Bansi?"

Bansi shook his head.

"You didn't get rejected, did you?"

"I did get rejected at one, but it's not that."

"Then what is it?"

Papa rubbed his forehead with his fingertips as if he had a bad headache. "Your brother has joined the Navy – without consulting me or your Ma. Do you think it's right?"

I was surprised. Papa was asking me for my opinion? He must be terribly desperate to want my support. I turned to Bansi. "You mean you're not going to study? Are you dropping out of school?"

Papa could barely keep the disappointment out of his voice as he said, "Tell your sister what you've decided."

Something was definitely wrong. Very wrong. Why else would Papa give me so much importance? He had never sought my opinion before. If anything, he had always rejected it brusquely. I looked at Bansi.

He seemed to be brushing off invisible cobwebs from his eyes. "I'm not sure I'm giving up," he said slowly. "I'm just putting things on hold. I want to think about what I want to do with my life."

"I thought your heart was in research and in higher education!" Papa said slowly, weighing every word. "I had built my hopes upon you. Your mother –" He stopped to look at Ma, who was unusually quiet. "I brought you here, to

America, to give you the best education so that you would become something. Someone." Papa's voice was dry. He said something about how he had dreamed that Bansi would become a physicist, a space engineer, or a scientist who would do the world some good. Bansi's jaw tightened as he waited for Papa to finish.

"Why must every one be a physicist or a space engineer, Papa? There are other things one can do," he said calmly. "I need to think about what I want to do with my life. I may go to graduate school later –"

"Why not now? Why waste time?"

"I have to make my own decisions, Papa. I have to think of money."

Money? Bansi talking about the tabooed word? What was happening to my brother who had disdained material aspirations and who had believed in living a simple frugal life? I looked at Bansi again. His eyes were clear and honest as always, his face calm.

Papa sent the chair crashing as he got up. "To hell with money," he said, towering above us. His face had turned red. His eyebrows were arched and his nostrils flared. "Are we starving? Don't we have a roof over our heads? Didn't I tell you I would make all the arrangements? Who gave you the authority to make decisions?"

Bansi's lip twitched, but his voice was level when he spoke. "The Navy will give me more than I need. I can save for my education – and I can help you buy a house. We'll send Juhi to a good school. I will get time to map out the course of the rest of my life –"

"What course of your life? Hadn't we mapped it long ago? Didn't you always want to be a space engineer? A –"

"That's what you had wanted, Papa. It was your idea, your dream, not mine," Bansi said. "I don't know what I want. I have done nothing except working hard. I've never even dated while everyone –"

"I didn't stop you."

"You didn't, but I felt committed to your dream. Give me a break now. Let me discover the world on my own. I'll leave the Navy after three years – maybe sooner."

Nobody said anything for a while after that. Papa kept pacing the floor. He cleared his throat and ran his fingers through his graying hair. Finally, when he spoke, his voice cracked as if he had a sore throat.

"It'll be such a long time. You could get caught in the mad whirl of life so easily. Making money. Spending it. Making more. Spending more. It's a vicious circle." Papa shook his head sadly. "No, Son, you won't come back."

I wanted to tell Papa that he was wrong, that nothing could corrupt Bansi, that he would come back and be everything and do everything that Papa had dreamed for him. But I couldn't say a word to Papa. Instead, I asked Bansi, "What about your dreams of finding lost planets?"

"Dreams can be deferred."

I couldn't understand him. How did one square up conquering the world like Columbus and dreams of discovering unknown galaxies and planets with joining the Navy? Had he been planning to go away all this time? Had he given in to the lure of money? I was baffled, and, all of a sudden, scared. What did Bansi really want? What was going to become of him? My brother, my mother's *sadhu* – was he lost?

I looked at Ma, who hadn't spoken a word so far. Bansi was totally devoted to her. I knew he could never say no to her. She understood him. She would know how to bring him to his senses. What was she thinking of? Why didn't she say anything? Was she mulling over what had happened to her son, her monk who wanted nothing, who desired nothing? Ma's face gave me no clues. Her eyes were like the sea under a dense fog.

"You must reconsider. Ask for time. We can talk it over,"

Papa was pleading. He turned to Ma. "You tell him, Leela. Tell him he's headed the wrong way –"

Ma's gaze swept over Bansi's face and came to rest on Papa's. She looked into his eyes, sending some message that he alone understood. Her voice was steady. "He knows what he's doing," she said very gently. "He's not a kid. He's –"

"But don't you understand?" Papa's eyes were bewildered like a child's who tries to put the sand back in a broken hour glass.

"He's old enough to make his decisions. He must find his path. Let's leave it at that." The love in my mother's eyes, as she fixed them on Bansi's face, was thick like treacle.

The inquisition was over.

Bansi leaned back in his chair. In a voice that sounded like a cross between a laugh and a cry, he said, "Even Buddha had to go in search of truth."

"Buddha would have died if someone hadn't fed him," I mumbled, sounding more like Papa.

Bansi smiled at me. "There are many ways of dying, Miss Know-It-All." He turned to Papa. "I hope you'll forgive me, Papa."

Papa remained quiet. It was the still moment before a storm breaks. "Forgive you?" The anger in his voice was compressed thunder. "For what? For crushing my dreams? For letting me down? For choosing the easy way out?"

I saw the moisture in Papa's eyes. Suddenly, I wanted to put my arms around my father and protect him. I, who had resented him and hated him many times, now wanted to do something to wipe off the hurt from his face. Then my mother got up and went to Papa. It seemed so natural that she should take his hand in hers, look up into his face, and say, "Shush! Everything will be okay." It was as if she were soothing a frightened child.

Papa's face softened for a while, then he pulled his hand free of my mother's and shrugged his shoulders. "Have it your way."

Winter, that year, was the coldest we had ever known. Arctic winds froze the heavy snow into ice. In many neighborhoods electric cables snapped, water pipes froze. The city opened its shelters to the homeless. The roads were a hazard, especially after dark. While returning from a late-evening class one day, Papa lost control of his car. It slammed into an electric pole. Because of a dislocated right shoulder and a couple of fractures in his right leg, he was unable to drive for a couple of months, so Bansi drove us to the airport the day he was leaving. Ma was to drive us back. Chacha could have been a great help, but he and Chachi had gone to India for a few months.

Bansi had packed his bag long before the day of his departure. There wasn't much to pack, though, just a couple of pairs of pants, shirts, underclothes, some books, a sweater that Ma had knitted for him and the ship that grandfather had given him.

I pointed to the fleet on his shelf when he was ready to leave. "What about your ships? Aren't you taking them with you?"

"No," he said. "They're yours now. I'll be on a real one for a change."

"Where will you go?"

"I don't know," he said. "I guess wherever the ship takes me."

I felt disappointed. I had imagined him standing at the helm and steering the ship through a storm-tossed ocean to lands still waiting to be discovered. A young Columbus looking for places beyond the horizon. I looked at the tall thin young man who was becoming a stranger by the hour. The mop of unruly dark hair had been replaced by a crew cut which made his face thinner, his eyes larger.

It had started snowing before dawn the day Bansi left. We woke up to see houses and cars, roads and driveways lying under a thick white blanket. The fences and trees were latticed with snow. It was difficult to distinguish the road from the curb.

"Here we go again! Snow in April!" Mr. Mikulsky growled, pointing to the shuddering daffodils and tulips drooping under the white weight.

It took us a long time to shovel the snow and make a track to the car. Bansi had difficulty pulling out when it was time to leave for the airport. The engine roared, the tires spun only to settle deeper. We could hardly move till Joe and Bill, who lived across the street, ran up to clear the path. Mr. Mikulsky stood at the edge of the steps – directing, shouting instructions. "First push. Yes. Right. Now one, two, three. Go!" Finally, the car leaped clear of the trenches the tires had dug into the snow. It lurched onto the street like a tipsy sailor till we reached Lincoln Avenue, which had been partially ploughed.

Our drive to the airport was unusually quiet, as if we had all run out of words. I cleaned the frosted window with my gloved knuckles and looked at the bare brown trees beyond which the gray sky lay stretched out, now full, open, and limitless. I remembered the lush green trees and the blue sky that day when Papa had first driven us to the house on Brink Road. It seemed we had traveled light years away from that point. Time had, indeed, stepped out of the bottle like the fairytale jinni. If only I could lure it back into the bottle, seal it, and toss it into the sea. Then nothing would have to change. Bansi wouldn't go. Priya would come back. And we would keep dreaming dreams that would never fade away, never alter. In fact, we could start all over again. Now that we had traveled the road once, we wouldn't lose our way again. We knew every milestone, every turn. I found myself thinking of the home we had left behind in one country and the home we had made for ourselves in another. The distance between what we had left behind and what lay ahead seemed immeasurable. Bansi's going away made it seem immense. For a moment, I couldn't recognize the road, the sky, the landscape, the time. Where were we? Were we lost again? Then the sound of a plane descending behind the trees swung everything back into perspective.

"We've arrived." Bansi said.

The flights were slightly delayed because of the heavy snowfall. We sat facing the plate-glass windows and watched the huge snow-ploughs clearing the tarmac for takeoffs and landings. The sky had cleared.

When his flight was announced, Bansi slung his duffel bag over his shoulder, hugged us, and strode away. I watched the tall spare figure with thin arms and long legs moving with the crowd. At the door of the concourse, he stopped and turned around.

I saw his eyes, then.

They were not the eyes of my self-assured brother who knew everything, who had an answer for everything. They were opaque with fright – the eyes of a child about to climb a Giant Ferris Wheel for the first time in his life.

Instinctively, I took a step towards him and called out. "Bansi!"

He looked at me. Swiftly, the shutters came down. He smiled and waved, turned and went through the door.

We scuttled to the plate-glass windows that overlooked the tarmac. The sky had cleared up except for bits of clouds. The ruby-red sunlight, tinged with gold, had thrown a mesh over snow mounds. There were planes taxiing, taking off, landing. We followed Bansi's plane with our eyes as it pulled away from the terminal. It wheeled away. It taxied on the runway. It turned. It came back. It sped on the tarmac. We watched its windows catch the evening light. The steel wings blazed as it rose up into a sky splashed with crimson, as if a thousand flamingoes had taken wing. Soon it was no more than a distant star that twinkled and was gone from sight.

Ma was the first to move away from the window. "I'll get the car," she said.

Papa was still staring into the graying evening.

I shook his arm. "Papa! Papa!"

He started and looked at me as if he were noticing me for the first time.

"I'm going to get the car," Ma said.

"All right."

Ma asked me to stay with him. She was going to bring the car to the passenger pick-up area where we were to meet her.

After she left, Papa turned to the window. I followed his gaze. There was something very graceful about the planes as they taxied and took off or landed in the crimson evening. I don't know for how long we might have remained transfixed had not the commotion behind made us turn around. A plane must have arrived, for passengers were streaming into the lounge through a gate just opened. Their faces reflected the glow of arrival, of the end of a journey, or maybe, the beginning of another. I watched them hurry to the telephones, troop to the restrooms, and head for the baggage-claim area. A toddler with a shock of copper hair shook free of his mother's restraining hand and darted ahead with a chortle. The mother quickened her steps, tugging the carry-on and the stroller behind her, returning an elderly couple's smile with a short laugh. I placed my hand on Papa's arm and we let ourselves be carried forward by the surging humanity.

AND OTHER STORIES ...

In the City of Storks

"Let me take you around Alcala while we have some daylight left," Carmen says. "Let me show you my city."
"Of course! Let's go see your city." Ben disentangles his long legs and heaves himself out of the sofa. "Give me a minute."

He goes to the powder room down the hallway. Carmen and I collect the empty glasses and carry them into the kitchen. I rinse; she arranges them in the dishwasher.

"I like him," she says. "He's gentle, so full of life!"

"Thank you." I smile at the running water.

"You know what, Renu? You have changed since we met in France."

"Have I?" I wipe my hands on the kitchen towel she holds out to me.

"You were different – sort of sad, withdrawn. Now there's

color in your face and a smile in your voice. Happiness suits you."

I laugh. I want to tell her that happiness suits everyone, but I don't. She might consider it flippant.

"I'm ready." Ben calls out from the hallway.

We step out of the kitchen. Carmen grabs the red shawl she had taken off and hung on a peg in the hallway when we had come in. It's an intriguing shade of red which changes with the light, perhaps. In the dimly-lit hallway, it appears almost burgundy in color. "Let's go," she says, draping it around her shoulders.

And so we step out into the amber evening. We walk through a small field of poppies swaying in the slight breeze. Carmen's shawl merges with the color of the poppies, an intense red in the dying sunlight.

"It's beautiful!" I breathe in the open air and the beauty of the Spanish skies.

"Isn't it!" Carmen smiles. A few strands of chestnut hair held back with a red comb have come loose. They caress her high cheekbones. Her eyes are the color of orange-blossom honey. She seems to have put on a little weight since we met last, but it's becoming. She reminds me of a rich mellow wine which one never gulps down, but rolls on the tongue and savors the taste till it sets every nerve tingling.

I had met Carmen at a conference in France a couple of yeas ago. She was giving a paper on birth and death rituals in India, I on post-coloniality and Third-World women writers. A professor of anthropology at Alacala, she was glad to be able to talk about her research with someone of Indian origin. I was glad to break away from the endless discourse on critical theories, and to talk about something that was a part of my consciousness and not of what I had gleaned from books. Those few fleeting hours spent together had prompted me to write to her when I was invited to give a paper in Madrid.

"Of course, I remember you," Carmen had written back. "Alcala de Henares, where I live, is only twenty-five minutes by train from Madrid. You must visit me. I am so excited at the prospect of meeting you again."

I was in a bit of a quandary, at first, when Ben expressed his desire to accompany me. He wanted to take me to the Alhambra after the conference. I didn't know how to introduce Ben to Carmen. We had been living together for sometime now. Then I wrote to her. "He is a very special friend."

"But, of course!" she had e-mailed at once. "You're both coming to Alcala."

Skipping the last day of the conference we arrived in Alcala this morning. Two days of scholarly papers and discussions on post-colonialism and post-modernism have been enough for me. Tomorrow, we leave for Granada. Ben can hardly wait to get to the Alhambra. "I still remember the courtyards and gardens with latticed walls and fountains. You'll love the sheer poetry of the Moorish architecture," he had promised me when we were planning our itinerary. "I don't think it would have changed much since I was there some twenty years ago."

"With your wife?" I had asked, suppressing a spark of pain.

"Yes," he had said, without taking his eyes off my face. "But that's not the reason why I'm going there. I want to show it to you, to see it with you – through your eyes."

And so here we are, only a day away from the Alhambra.

Carmen leads us into the main square which is teeming with flowers. I recognize some – azalea, dahlia, begonia, primrose. The rest are a sweet confusion of colors and fragrances. I wish to linger a little longer, but dusk has begun to fall around us, and Carmen says that we must hurry if we want to see the Cervantes house. She steps lightly down the curb. We cross the darkening street.

"This is the old university – founded in the fifteenth

century," Carmen points to the adjacent facade which stands washed in a bronze light. She tells us about the polyglot Bible which was published here. She points out to the chapel which houses the tomb of Cardinal Cisneros, then, the Patio of the Three Languages. "Sorry you can't see the paraninfo – the old examination hall – it has a beautiful Mudejar ceiling –"

Ben and I listen quietly, like school children hanging upon every word of their teacher's. Between the walk from one building to another, she tells us about a Sri Lankan she has just started dating. He, like her, is an anthropologist.

"At the moment, he's away, visiting his family. You would have enjoyed meeting him," she tells Ben.

"Next time." Ben says.

"Yes, next time."

As we walk through the stone-paved streets, she talks about her two daughters, one planning to go into law, the other into art. "They're spending a week with their father who lives in Barcelona." She tells us about her late father, who had taught Spanish Literature in Madrid; her impetuous mother, who has a passion for travelling; and about her sister, who was once a Flamenco dancer. "And I have my dog, who hates to be left alone," she says with a short laugh. I remember the Siberian Husky she had locked up in a room upstairs. "He'll be sulking in a corner when I go back. He won't get up and come to me until I have hugged him."

"Lucky dog." Ben laughs.

His laughter has a rich sound, like a geyser spouting from the earth. Arresting. It's the same laughter which had gurgled around me in the museum restaurant in Philadelphia. I had turned around to find the source. It had emanated from a tall man, who had just come in and was bending, with his hand cupped to his ear, towards a waiter who must have said something amusing. The restaurant was crowded. Perhaps the man was looking for a table. He straightened up. I quickly looked away as his eyes reached mine.

I was scanning the Post-Impressionist catalogue I had bought when someone said, "May I?"

The man I had heard laugh had already pulled a chair and sat down.

"Sure," I said, gathering my pocketbook and getting up. "I was leaving, anyway."

"Please don't. How about joining me for another cup of coffee – or tea?"

I looked into a pair of gray-green eyes, clear like a child's. The salmon-pink tee-shirt he was wearing didn't add much color to his pale face which looked somewhat gaunt under a blue baseball cap – a size too big for his brow. I had no interest in sitting down and listening to some funny story that an elderly man might have to tell. I didn't like funny stories. I didn't enjoy laughter.

"I haven't offended you, have I?"

I paused. He was serious. He didn't look like one who would go around picking up women casually. I thought about my lonely apartment. About the papers that were waiting to be graded. About the lecture that had to be prepared. The lonely meal that had to be cooked and eaten. I hesitated. There was no hurry. There was no one waiting for me at home. No one was waiting for me anywhere. Why not? I told myself as I sat down.

"What'll you have?"

"Tea, please."

"With cream? Or lemon? Sugar or sweetener? Green or herbal –" He was listing the choices so earnestly that I couldn't help laughing. It was a sudden spontaneous laughter that made me feel much younger.

"Okay, let me guess," he said as he stopped running through the list. "A pot of Darjeeling tea with cream and sugar, right."

So we settled down to our tea and coffee and some talk of Monet and Van Gogh, of the Phillies, of the new mayor of the city, of the drought that summer. We didn't talk about ourselves. That was to come later. When I went to my apartment that night, I felt as if a big iceberg that had been sitting on my chest had begun to melt a little. I stood on my balcony and laughed at the traffic flowing fifteen stories below. I didn't care if someone watched me leaning over the rails and laughing to myself. I hadn't laughed for a long time. Years of living alone in self-exile, thousands of miles away from home after an annulled marriage, had left me dry.

"Was yours an arranged marriage?" a colleague had once asked me.

"Yes!" I had said shortly.

She had looked at me for more information, perhaps for a confession of anger against Hindu customs and traditions. I had said nothing, not a word about my ex-husband. Alok hadn't abused me, he hadn't demanded a dowry, he hadn't abandoned me. He still sent me New Year greetings. I had given my colleague no explanation of why I had walked out on him within two months of my marriage, just as I had justified nothing to my sisters-in-law. They had looked puzzled when I announced I had walked out on Alok. Their initial shock had been soon replaced by a sense of righteous indignation. They enlightened me about the duties of a good Hindu wife, the sacrifices and adjustments she must make for her husband and for her in-laws. In a fit of generosity, they had even offered to talk to my husband to clarify any misunderstanding that might have cropped up between us. Finally, disappointed at my reluctance, they dismissed me with a frown and withdrew.

Straightening the pleats of her sari, my elder sister-in-law had said to the younger one, "I'm going to get my nails done for the party next week. Want to come along? You can have your arms and legs waxed."

Neither had asked me if I would care to join them. Perhaps a woman separated from her husband had no need of waxing her arms and legs or having her nails done. She dwelt in an ambiguous zone where she was neither married, nor unmarried, nor widowed.

I hadn't contradicted my sisters-in-law during their sermon. Perhaps they were right. Perhaps I should have stayed with Alok. I should have waited, given him a chance, accepted his infatuation for the young man with gentle eyes and a soft mouth. I didn't hold a grudge against that sweet young man, but I wasn't ready to play the role of a Bollywood heroine who waits faithfully for the errant husband to come back to her, someday – repentant and reformed. I couldn't live a lie. I may have been understanding, but I wasn't forgiving.

"Does he beat you?" my innocent mother had asked me.

"No!"

"Does he have another woman?"

"No! Not a woman," I had said. Would she have understood if I had told her the truth?

"Tell me," she had begged. "Does your mother-in-law ill-treat you?"

"No, she's very nice."

"Then why?"

"You won't understand, Ma," I told her gently. "He and I don't connect."

"Connect?" she had looked bewildered. "I don't understand. What God ties together is connected for ever. A Hindu wife doesn't leave her husband even after his death. Don't you remember Savitri?"

I did. Like most Hindu women, I had grown up with stories of the dutiful, faithful, self-sacrificing wives. Savitri had followed Yama, the Lord of Death, all the way to the other world when he took her husband's life. She refused to comply with Yama's orders to go back. A Hindu woman's place, she had argued, was beside her husband. Finally, impressed by Savitri's steadfastness and devotion, Yama had returned Satyavan to life. That is how a Hindu woman was supposed to be – steadfast like the evening star.

"What will you do now?" My poor mother had looked at me despondently. "A woman's life is a steep mountain road, which she can't walk alone. You can't depend on your brothers. They have their lives and responsibilities and they'll soon begin to resent you."

Fortunately, before anyone could have started resenting me, I got a fellowship at an American university. As soon as the marriage annulment papers were signed, I left India, never to go back again, not even when my mother died. I had vowed to remain single, never to trust any man, never to be swayed by any.

"Watch your step!" Carmen puts her hand on my arm as a cab swerves by. I haul myself into the present.

"See that?" she pauses. "There, on the rooftop? Do you see?"

We look up.

"Sculpted birds?" Ben asks.

Carmen laughs. "No. They're real – storks."

"Storks?"

"Live storks."

We stare at the charcoal silhouettes against the darkening sky. A gust of wind ruffles their feathers.

"They used to fly away," Carmen explains, "and then return to the river every year. But now they don't go away at all. They live in the city all the year around. They nest here. See those?" She points to the dark smudges near the storks.

"Don't the nests fall off?" I ask.

"Oh no. The city sees to it that they're fastened by steel wires. So neither the wind nor the rain can blow them away. They're permanent."

Ben takes my hand. "How wonderful to have nests secured with steel wires!"

I return the pressure of his hand. I understand this longing for permanence in the face of remorseless transience without his uttering a word, as if our minds were connected by transparent skeins. That's how it was the first time, several weeks after we had met in the museum restaurant, when Ben had held my hand tightly in his and pressed it against his chest. It was a simple gesture. A primeval gesture. That is how the first man must have expressed his desire to the first woman. What would have been the first words spoken between them? None, I suppose. He couldn't have said as Ben did that evening, "Let me tell you about myself."

He had told me about his two sons and three grandchildren, about his dead wife, about the small firm for which he worked as a financial analyst, about the house he owned in Miami, and about the thing that would choke his life, one day. The doctors had given him two years, at best.

"I want to live till the last moment," he had said. "You may call it a financial analyst's instinct – this desire to take in as much of the life and beauty around me as I can."

I said nothing.

"Am I wrong?" he had asked me a bit anxiously. "Am I being selfish?"

"No!"

How could I pass a judgment? I hadn't loved any one, not since my mother had died. I didn't love life. Ever since that night in a hotel room in Ooty when Alok had put his head on my shoulder and begged forgiveness because he hadn't had the courage to tell his father about his sexual preferences, I had willfully locked out life. I had put a firm lid on desire. Stifled yearning. Stopped wanting. I didn't even know what Ben was talking about. Who was I to judge him?

"Look at me!" Ben had implored. He had pulled off his wig. His face held an expression halfway between a laugh and a cry. I had stared at his bald head without batting an eyelid, without averting my gaze. "Say something, Renu."

"You look like a new-born babe," I had said, at last.

His face had melted. He had fixed his wig and kissed me lightly on the lips. Later, he had taken me in his arms and helped me unlearn what I hadn't even fully learnt. I am still surprised that it was Ben – a stranger from another country, another culture, a man in his early sixties, dying slowly – who initiated me into the mysteries of love.

"And that is where Cervantes was born," Carmen points to a house which stands half hidden behind the trees and shrubs. "The house has been reconstructed, of course."

"I didn't know he was born in Alcala." Ben says.

I look at the shuttered windows, the pillars supporting the wooden gallery, the dark creepers clinging to the walls. I think of the manuscripts and copies of Don Quixote housed there. I have no mental picture of Cervantes, but I see Don Quixote. A lanky man with Ben's face, charging at the windmills. I hear him crying, "Fly not cowards and vile beings, for a single knight attacks you." I tighten my grasp over Ben's arm.

"Hungry?" he asks me.

"I'm sorry," Carmen apologizes. "I forgot you must be hungry. In Spain, we eat late."

"Are you hungry?" I ask Ben.

"Very."

I am happy when Ben says that. It means he is feeling fine.

"I have started hogging these days," I had heard him tell his son over the phone.

I don't know what his son had said, but Ben had laughed a happy laugh and said, "You bet, she is!" Ben has been very open about our relationship with his sons. They had asked him if we intended getting married. Ben had said we hadn't thought about that. In fact, we had, and in a very matter-of-fact way too. And both of us had decided, it was better not to.

Carmen has made reservations in an elegant restaurant where she sometimes treats herself to a lunch. She and Ben order roast suckling pig and paella. I have gazpacho and a special vegetarian dish that the chef has put together – baby spinach, snow peas, asparagus spears on a bed of saffron rice.

"Here's to friendship." Carmen toasts.

"To friendship."

Carmen looks beautiful in the soft light. The wine has added more color to her face and a luster to her eyes. If I were a painter, I would paint her just like that – a woman sitting with a glass of wine in her hand, her face flushed like the pre-dawn sky, the ruby-red shawl slipping down a rounded shoulder.

Like old friends meeting after a long separation, we talk about everything – the countries we have traveled to or not traveled, the foods we have tasted or not tasted, the books we have read or not read. The only thing we don't talk about is sickness. Or death.

After we've finished Cheese of La Mancha for desert and paid the bill, we get up. Suddenly, I am scared to leave the warm glow in which I have been basking. I wish I could secure this moment with steel wires so that neither the wind nor the rain would sweep it off. As if sensing my fears, Ben puts his hand lightly on my shoulder and steers me into the cool night. A gentle breeze stirs the leaves, tousles our clothes. Ben pulls his cap down on his head securely. Carmen walks us to our hotel.

As she bids us good-bye, Ben takes her hands in his. "You must visit us," he says.

"I will," Carmen kisses him on the cheek. She turns to me. We embrace. She kisses me on both cheeks. "I wish I could see you before you leave tomorrow, but I can't get away from an important meeting. I'll write to you. Take care!"

We stare at her receding figure, at the red shawl glowing like an ember in the light of the street lamp. She disappears at the bend in the street.

In our room, Ben and I stand by the open window. There's no need to turn on the air conditioner. It's cool here in May.

"Did you have a nice day?" Ben asks, putting his arm around me.

"Lovely. Did you?"

"Of course."

"Do you like Carmen?"

"Yes. She's warm like life itself."

I feel a strange pang of envy. I have never felt it before, not even when he talks about his dead wife, or his children. Why now?

We stand there – thinking our own thoughts. "I am still discovering life," I tell him after a while. "At this age."

"Lucky you!" Ben draws me closer to him. I detect a note of sadness in his voice.

"Are you all right, Ben?"

"I'm fine," he says, but his voice is subdued.

"What is it, Benya?" I Indianize his name when I am most concerned about him, and when I feel most intimate with him.

"The thought of life passing away," he says. "Of youth. Of so much left unseen. Untasted. Unlived. And yet –"

"And yet?"

"There's no quenching this thirst. There's no point at which one could say, I have had enough."

His voice is light now. I put my arm around him. I want to tell him, I have never had any craving for life the way he has. I wouldn't mind dying, at this very hour, standing beside him. If it were now to die, it were now to be most happy. Where had I read that? I can't remember. On the roof of a tall building across the street a stork stands contoured against the starry sky. Suddenly, it flaps its wings and flies straight at us. A dark shadow. Growing larger, and darker. We duck as if he was going to fly into the window glass. Then it's gone. I feel Ben shudder. I want to tell him that a stork portends life, but somehow, I can't.

In the middle of the night, I wake up at the sound of Ben gasping for breath. He flaps his arms as if he were choking. I give him his medication; I do all that the doctor has told me to do at such moments. When I see him grow paler, I call Carmen.

"I'll be there in five minutes," she assures me. "I'll call the ambulance."

I pack a few things into a bag – Ben's shaving kit, a change of clothes, his socks. I check his medical insurance card, his prescriptions. Carmen arrives with the paramedics. As they begin to take Ben downstairs, his wig comes askew. I fix it. "Please tell them not to remove his wig," I tell Carmen.

She says something in Spanish to the men. They nod at her. At me.

"Gracias!" I whisper the only word of Spanish I know.

Doctors have put Ben on oxygen. He lies sedated, hooked to a network of tubes. I touch his face, his hands. They're cold. I kiss him on the forehead. "Benya!" I call out. "We're going to Alhambra, Benya!"

He is already so far away from me. The doctor asks us to wait outside.

I sit in the lounge. I can think nothing. I can do nothing. I am glad that Carmen is taking care of everything. It is she who talks to the doctors. It is she who calls the airlines and cancels our flight. It is she who calls Ben's elder son. "He'll be here by noon tomorrow," she tells me.

Later, the doctor calls us into the room where Ben is lying. He says something in Spanish to Carmen. She nods. "He's sleeping. You can go to him," she tells me. "I'll be waiting in the lounge if you need me." She presses my trembling hand. "Wait," she says as I move away from her, "You're cold. Take this." She drapes her red shawl around my shoulders even as I protest. I feel some warmth flow into my body.

Ben lies with his eyes closed. His chest rises and falls softly with each breath that he draws through the tubes in his nose. I draw closer to his bed and stand looking at the face with a pointed chin, cliff-sharp jawbone, and a wrinkled brow that is distant in sleep, but familiar. He lets out a small sigh like puppies often do in sleep. I have a strong desire to collect him in my arms and shield him from the encroaching shadows. I wish I had the strength and the conviction of Savitri. I wish I could stand between him and the dark shadow and stoutly plead for his life. But all I do is sit down in a chair beside his bed and press his hand between my palms. A slight pressure of his fingers tells me that he is aware of my presence. I tighten my clasp. I know he will understand what I'm saying. It's not time to go away, Benya. Not yet.

TOUCHLINE

"Come with me," I plead with my mother every day. "Come and live with us, Ma."
My brother writes anxious letters from San Francisco. "Bring her back with you," he urges. "She shouldn't be left alone. I am scared at the thought of something happening to her."

Mother ignores our pleas. "But why must I go with you?" She asks. "Why?"

"Because we don't want you living alone. We worry about you."

"Then come back, come and live here."

I can hear the smile in her voice. "You know we can't. Because —" I fumble for words.

She looks me steadily in the eye. "You mean that I should leave everything and go to a strange country. Leave all this?"

She sweeps the silent walls with her pale palm. "My life swept up into corners, hung in the closets, stacked in the drawers –" Her voice trails off.

I see sadness spread its wings across her face. "Your father built this house for his children. And the children?" She looks around as if her children will troupe past her any moment, as they did years ago. "The children have moved to America, your father's gone, and the house is empty."

I don't know what to say. The house had seemed so small when we were growing up. Our bodies had needed infinite space to expand into. Now it is absurdly big – a fortress in which a frail old woman lives counting her beads, preserving her past.

Suddenly, she springs a question at me. "Remember your doll's wedding?"

She has this habit of catching me unawares and drawing me with her into the past.

"I remember the dress you made for my doll," I say, following her to the shores of my childhood. "Red satin –"

"Your father always felt so lost without me."

"Studded with sequins –"

"How could he go away without me? What happened?" she asks.

Blurred shapes begin to surface in my mind. I try to drag her back to my doll's wedding. "The tiny bead necklace you made was so pretty!"

She doesn't hear me. "There was never enough time then – the days have grown too long now," she mumbles.

And so we sit on the banks of the past like two fishermen casting their nets wide to catch flitting moments – slippery as little eels.

But after a while I pull away. I don't want to be drawn into mother's world – a world which she can gather in her net any time. Mine seems to have been swept away by the tides. I can bait it no more. But she sits patiently for hours beside the still waters. The rats scamper over her feet. My fists tighten as I see the radium glint of their eyes. Indifferent to my presence, they leap from the bed to the floor and to the top of a bureau. They don't bother her. She doesn't see the holes they have eaten into the doors, closets, bureaus– into everything. Nothing in this house seems whole to me.

It was quite unsettling the first day I arrived here, in Jaipur. Tired after my long flight from New York, I had barely settled down in a chair when the rats came bounding down the stairs. One would have thought that they were pets.

"How can you live with these monsters, Ma?" I had shrilled.

"What can I do? The house has always been open to them," Ma had said simply, her hands busy arranging tea cups in the tray.

"Why? Kill them. Ask the servant to get some rat poison."

Handing me a cup of tea, my mother had asked, "And what if they poison me instead?"

The absurdity of her remark I had attributed to mother's age and loneliness. A wizened old woman, fragile as the china cup in her hand, flaky as the homemade crackers she was offering me had earned the right to say what she pleased.

"Why should anyone want to poison you?" I had laughed.

"An old woman in a house by herself – easy!" She replied.

"But you are coming back with me," I had said, watching the rats slink away quietly like stray thoughts.

Ma had placed the bone china cup very carefully on the table and remarked, "Aren't these cups still as pretty as they were when your father was alive?" And I knew she had plunged back into her world.

The rats kept me awake for many nights. The sound of sharp teeth cutting into wood at night – as if someone were sawing off doors and windows, dismantling them – would wrench me out of my sleep. I would scan the windows for the lace curtains of my American bedroom and grope for the bedside lamp. But the faded heavy drapes and the bleary pictures on the walls would remind me that I was in my mother's house in Jaipur and I would slump on the pillows. The rats would steal back into the room. How I wished I was back in my neat house in the suburbs of Philadelphia where the spotless walls held no cobwebs, the carpeted floors no rats, where peace romped around me on padded feet.

Five years is a long time to have been away in another country. Father is dead, mother has yellowed like the pages of an old book, and the house is crumbling. The fragrance of *juhi* and *raat-ki-rani* still wafts through the nettled garden. But the walls are chipped, the paint has faded, the doors creak, the old neem tree has rotted away and the stones in the driveway have come loose. After having lived in America for some time, everything here looks shabby, worn out, different. I can't evoke any feelings for the past.

Mother, however, rarely notices the disappearing trees, the fading flowers, the shabby walls. She walks around the house searching for I don't know what, talking to I don't know whom. She never minds the rats scampering at her heels.

Often, I wake up to hear her opening and shutting doors, pulling out drawers, smoothing out the creases from father's suits hanging in the closet, and muttering to herself. In the long summer afternoons, she pulls out old dresses from the trunks. I watch her, then, as my daughter often watches me when I clean my closet. The smell of moth balls, the rustle of tissue paper, the flash of a dress make me want to run out into the open and take big gulps of fresh air. There's something about old dresses and musty smells that makes me nostalgic. And nostalgia scares me.

Unable to move, I watch her caress gossamer dresses.

Sometimes she pauses and turns her head as if she were listening to someone. I see her pinched mouth curve into a smile and her eyes glow. At such moments, I forget the neat house surrounded by maple trees in a far-off country. For I am once again a brown-eyed girl in pigtails holding out the hem of my frock to catch the raw fruit that my brother is throwing down from the mango tree. Father sits reading his newspapers in the veranda and –

"I was showing you your brother's baby clothes," Ma interrupts my reverie. She is holding a tiny blue frock.

"Why do you keep all these things?" I ask her. My voice is a bit unsteady. She ignores my question.

"The world," she says haltingly, weighing every word, "is a cruel place. Children grow up and go away, people die … What does one get in the end? An empty house – old clothes – a handful of memories?"

"Come with me," I chant the magical words, hoping they will open up a secret door of a cave. "Come and live with us, Ma. You'll like it there."

"My parrot!" She spins around. "Did I feed it today? My poor Mithu!" She goes to the cage. I have never seen such a sickly, pale gray parrot in my life. Her concern for the ugly bird amuses me. "I rescued it from the crows," she explains, "That was the day your father died. I have taken care of it since then. I can't leave it behind, can I?"

"You can't take it with you to America, Ma," I try to smile.

"Who's going to America?" She asks me. Her eyes remind me of my daughter's. "I'm not going any where," she declares. And I feel lost. Emptiness gathers around me like dusk on winter evenings.

"It bothers me – her living by herself," my brother says over the long distance call from San Francisco. "I can't leave my work and come back to India. The best thing would be for her to come here and live with us."

"But she won't leave the old house," I tell him.

"Try to make her see some sense," he says in a tired voice. "The house can be sold, rented, locked. But she shouldn't live by herself."

"I'm trying my best."

But no one can argue with mother. "It's you – you and your brother who left me alone," she complains when I press her too hard. I try to explain to her that I can't stay here for ever. Soon, it'll be time for me to go back to my family and settle back into familiar ways. So I plead, I argue, and I reason with her everyday. "The solution is to sever the past and go away," my brother has concluded. That's why he doesn't want to come visit her. And that's why I want to take her away.

We sit in the backyard watching the gnarled bougainvillea creeper – now a mere remembrance of a pink and white past. Mother turns to me and says coolly, as if she were commenting on the weather, "I think I should go with you."

"What? What did you say, mother?"

"I want to be with my grandchildren. I'll live there like so many other women my age do. After all you and your brother are the only people I have in this world," she says breathlessly, as if rehearsing a dialogue. "Make all the arrangements. Quickly," she says, getting excited just as my daughter gets excited at the prospects of going to the circus.

So the date is set and the flight booked. For the past few days Ma has been locking the trunks, stowing them deep under the beds and cleaning the closets. The rats look sad and disappointed. They tiptoe down the stairs, scramble silently in the drawers, stare foolishly around with their beady eyes. The parrot doesn't shriek for feed in the morning.

Mother, however, remains cheerful. She sits with her clothes piled around her arranging and rearranging her things in the suitcase. "Do you think I should take all these clothes?" She asks me, and then without waiting for my answer she begins to lay them out, her stiff hands caressing them, touching them almost reverently.

"Your father brought this from Kashmir when he went there for a meeting," she holds a sari as gently as if it were a new born babe. "And this one? Pure silk – you don't even get these today, he bought from Mysore." Her hands stray into the layers of the past and I know I'm forgotten, her trip is forgotten, the large empty house is forgotten. Her eyes sparkle, the wrinkles on her face melt away.

I envy her at such moments. I try to think about my life, my family, my short past in America. I don't find any Kashmir or Mysore silks rippling through my fingers. I look at the walls, the trees, the garden of my mother's house. Blurred patterns begin to appear again as if the walls were a child's magic painting book – a few strokes with a wet brush and the scene emerges clear. I am scared of making these strokes. I don't want the past to be brought back. I don't want to be tugged back, now that I have settled down in the States.

But mother's life is painted on these walls. She still wanders around at night touching the doors and windows, feeling the chipping walls and the falling plaster with her palms. "Fifty years," I hear her mutter, "fifty years in this house. Births, marriages, deaths –"

For two nights now, she hasn't slept. She goes around examining the iron bars the servant has put against the windows and doors that open on the balcony. She is afraid someone might break into the house during her absence.

My brother has been calling us almost every other day. Thrilled at the sound of his voice, Ma begins to list the things she's taking along with her.

"Seems to be working out fine," my brother says to me.

"Yes! Keep your fingers crossed."

She sits in the midst of piles of clothes. Her holy books, her gods, her praying beads go into the suitcase first. Then she stops. "Tell me," she asks. "Will my gods be happy there?"

"Why not?"

"It's a foreign land," she says.

"Your gods, mother, will be happy anywhere." I assure her.

She shakes her head and wraps the brass and silver icons tightly in a red silk scarf. "It's an alien place," she mumbles, "and it's so far away."

"But gods don't feel homesick Ma, or do they?" I try to joke.

"They do – just as we do," she insists. Suddenly, she whips around and asks me, "Don't you?" Her eyes drill holes into my soul.

Quickly, I say, "No, no, I don't. No, not at all. We – we just miss you."

"Don't you ever want to come back to your country? Your people?" She asks.

"We are happy there, Mother."

"Does this house, this land mean nothing to you?" She asks relentlessly. I feel the waters getting turbulent. "These trees – the fragrance of mango pollen, the sound of the temple bells in the morning – the feeling of being in one's own country, among one's people. Don't you miss all this?"

I can feel the powerful tug. I want to pull out my net before the past drags me down. "We love that country, Ma. It has given us so much. Money, comfort, confidence…" I keep my eyes fixed on the trees outside.

Ma turns her back on me and doesn't say a word after that.

Under the blossoming cherry and dogwood in my house in Philadelphia, mother sits turning her beads. Her eyes are my daughter's eyes – dark, innocent.

"What a beautiful house you have!" she says, speaking in my daughter's voice.

"What happened to your voice, Ma?" I ask.

"I lost it," her face distorts into a smile and she begins to rock back and forth as if she were riding a play-horse.

I wake up crying out. "Stop it, Ma!"

She is groaning in the bathroom.

I rush to her side. "What's wrong?"

"I think I've eaten rat poison," she says. I am shaken out of my dream. Then I remember we had never bought any rat poison.

"How? Why?" I ask.

"I found two rats dead in the bedroom," she says, retching again. I give her one of my travel sickness pills. She lies still for some time. "I'm too sick to go with you. My gods don't want me to go. Your father doesn't want me to leave this house," she says.

And I know she won't go to America.

Next morning, I make an overseas call to my brother. He grows very quiet at the other end of the line when I tell him about mother's condition. "What do I do now?" I ask him.

"Nothing. Come back. Mission failed," he says.

"But she's so fragile and alone!"

"Yup!" He replies, "So she is. But what can you do?"

I cancel her ticket. My husband calls me from Philadelphia. "Take it easy," he says from thousands of miles away. Suddenly, I want to go. I want to leave this house, the dead rats and my sick mother. I want to be where there are no rats, no smells, no sounds of someone throwing up in the bathroom.

But what if I don't get a booking for another month? What if mother doesn't get well? I feel my voice shaking and my dammed up frustration simply gushes forth.

"Why can't you take care of yourself? Why can't you come with me and give us peace? Why? Why?" I ask her.

Then I feel guilty. I feel sorry – for her, for myself, for my brother, for everyone. Sitting at the edge of her bed I begin to cry. Ma's fingers stray into my hair and I'm a little girl again crying for the butterflies I could never catch in the garden of my childhood. I don't know when I fall asleep next to her.

When I wake up the gods are back on the shelf and the rats have begun to scamper on the bare floors. The windows let in streams of sunlight. The parrot in the cage overturns the bowl of water and shrieks.

My bags have been loaded into the cab waiting in the porch. I turn around and look at the house. The curtains billow out of the windows. The creeper along the wall sways lightly in the wind. Mother's parrot scrutinizes me – its scrawny neck held to one side. Somewhere in the dark corners the rats are waiting for me to leave. Mother looks so small and fragile, so pale – almost transparent. As I hug her and hold her frail frame in my arms, I have this urge to pick her up and carry her as she must have carried me once.

"I'll come back soon, Ma," I manage to say. She pats me on the back and smiles a very twisted smile.

The cab splutters through the old gate arched with *juhi* flowers. The soft fragrance brushes me as we drive out. Through the rear window of the cab, I look back at the tiny figure in the porch. She raises her hand and says something. I can't hear her. She's already so far away. But her bewildered face reminds me of my daughter's the first day I left her at school. I can't stop now to console my mother, as I couldn't stop then to brush away the tears from my daughter's dimpled cheeks. The cab lurches out of the gate. I stare at the house, for I want to avoid the figure in the porch. But she's there – everywhere – looking out at me from every window, every balcony, every doorway.

MANNEQUINS

My teenage daughter doesn't want me
to go to the PTA meeting in a sari. "No
way," she said the other day. "You'll have
to dress differently, Ma. I haven't seen
anybody's mom in a sari at school."
"She's right," my son had interjected.
"You can't live in America and not dress like the Americans.
It looks so odd," he said.

"It does?" I asked them, trying to rub off the stubborn
turmeric spot from the kitchen counter. They nodded.

"You'd be more comfortable in a skirt or even a pair of
slacks, anyway," my daughter said after a while, pulling the
two sizes too big shirt over her shoulder. "You won't have to
wrap yards of material around you."

"Besides there's no point in being cons – cons –" my son
stammered.

"Conspicuous," his sister finished the sentence for him.

"We'll see," I said, glossing my frustration with a smile. I didn't want to admit to them that though I despised the idea of masquerading in an alien garb, I had begun to feel uncomfortable in a sari. I didn't tell them about my secret visits to a store in center city, outside which I have stood for long moments, drawing strength from the mannequins, poised behind the plate-glass windows. Huddled in tweeds or furs, supine in denims or cottons, languid in silks or chiffon's, they are like some exotic birds frozen in flight. The glazed smile never fades from their lips and their blue and emerald gaze never strays away from the steel structures across the street.

I have imagined myself going in and buying one of those dresses that hug their flawless figures and standing beside them in the show window. But always at the moment of stepping in, I have staggered at the door, suddenly reigned in by doubts. What if I can't walk? What if I trip and fall? What if I don't look elegant? And then, I have scurried home nursing yet another sense of failure.

Today I am determined to select a dress and take my family by surprise. I want to see the wonder on my children's faces and the admiration in my husband's eyes as I walk into the room and stand before them like a mannequin – slim, elegant, sophisticated – totally transformed. I want to show them that I too can cast off the old wrappings and become a brand-new person like my cousin, Mira.

"Look at Aunt Mira," my son had said last night. "She's new to this country, but she's gotten adjusted so quickly!"

And my daughter had whispered wistfully, "Wish you could dress like her, Ma! She looked so cool in that black skirt. And that new hair style suits her so well!"

Mira! The name sends my pulses racing and the blood rushing to my face. In ten months my cousin Mira has learnt more about the American way of life than I have in three years. After great coaxing Mira had come to visit her only daughter settled in the States. But once she was here, Mira decided to stay on and even found a part-time job in a store. Plain, mousy Mira, who had taken to wearing white saris, after she was widowed, flaunts all the colors of a peacock's plume now. The woman who hardly ever opened her mouth, chatters with the children about movies and basketball, even discusses stock market with Govind. She seems to savor each moment of her life, while I, a middle-aged mother of two, find myself still grappling with some obscure knots that never untangle. Teaching a course in world cultures to a group of adults here and there is all I have succeeded in doing, so far. I don't want to think about Mira. And yet, the face surfaces before my eyes – high cheekbones, eyes bright and quick like a bird's, and lips quivering with the hint of a smile.

Resolute, I turn to the revolving glass doors where the reflections of a busy American street and the colors inside the store spin into a waltz. I take a deep breath and make a plunge.

I don't know which way to turn. The place is teeming with women selecting clothes from the racks, holding them against their shoulders, their hips or their chest and gazing at their rosy reflections in the narrow mirrors that quarantine them from the rest of the world.

Skirts, blouses, sweaters, dresses, lingerie – where does one begin? Someone with an armful of clothes brushes past me with a brisk, "Excuse me!" I turn around and walk blindly into a section where a woman with mascaraed eyes and red fingernails stands holding a silk dress against her carefully groomed figure. Our eyes meet in the glass. She smiles vaguely and reaches out for another dress. A young mother with a baby strapped to a stroller and clucking a pacifier, pauses before a rack and picks up a salmon pink silk blouse. The baby stops sucking and looks at its mother as she presses the blouse against her body and smiles dreamily at her other self in the mirror. There is such a soft glow on her face that I wish I too was young and dreamy-eyed.

Caught by a sudden impulse, I grab a canary-yellow blouse.

I want to hold it against my body, and peer at my dusky reflection as I stand before the mirror with my head thrown back and my eyes admiring myself. But my sari, coiled around me, seems to cramp every movement. Even lifting my hand is an effort – like waking up at night and suddenly finding an arm gone numb. If only I could move and flow like those women! If only I could feel free and uninhibited! Carefully, I put it back and move away.

Wandering among the racks, I think of Govind. He has never asked me to give up wearing a sari. "You look nice in what you wear," he says, his eyes gentle, almost understanding behind those thick glasses. "Wear what you are comfortable in," has been his advice. I whip around to walk through the glass doors. Then I stop as another thought grips me. He too admires Mira, doesn't he?

Only the other night, when I was hanging his clothes in the closet, he had said casually, "Mira's quite a woman, isn't she? She seems to have adjusted so well to this part of the world." I had tried to read the expression in his eyes, but he was holding his reading glasses to the light and squinting at them.

"She doesn't have any responsibilities so she can spend all her money the way she likes and buy those expensive dresses and show off," I had said in one breath.

Govind had laughed and rubbed his glasses against his sleeve. "What she wears isn't important," he had observed. "It's how she responds to the world around her, how she carries herself that makes all the difference."

I had slammed the closet door shut and turned away, muttering, "Of course, she's the perfect woman. She can do no wrong." I couldn't forgive Govind for admiring Mira. For a long time that night, I lay awake, seething at Govind's obvious admiration of Mira. Finally, when I did doze off, it was only to wake up whimpering into Govind's shoulder. "Bad dream," I had muttered, and moved away.

As I pace the isles now, the dream comes back in quick flashes: I am standing behind the glass window among the mannequins. A pair of hands begins to strip me. My sari slips over my shoulder, slithers down my waist, my hips. Faces pressed to the glass window watch me intently. Laughing. Mocking. Jeering. The sari tumbles down. To my horror I find that I can't move.

Somewhere, a clock chimes three. I mustn't waste any more time, I think, walking away to the center of the section. Either I should buy something or quit the search and go home. Then I hold my breath. She's exquisite. My eyes travel from a pair of small feet wearing leather sandals, to the slim legs crossed like a ballerina's, up to the softly billowing dress around slender hips, caught in pleats at the narrow waist and swelling delicately again. The big beads twined around the swan-like neck make the pale face look smaller and the periwinkle-blue eyes, larger.

I stare at the mannequin and see my own face and my own body as it had gleamed back at me in the bathroom mirror this morning when I stepped out of the shower. Dark wet hair clinging to the shoulders, curling around a breast, and slithering down my waist had made me gaze at the reflection, first with curiosity, then with a growing interest. My hair is still dark, while Mira, I know, dyes hers. She doesn't have my curves. She is too thin, almost flat. I could accentuate my figure, wrap it in something more than a drab sari. I could –

"May I help you?" A crisp voice splinters the image. Startled, I gaze into the coolly appraising eyes of a store clerk.

"Oh! Yes," I stammer. "I was looking for a dress – for – for myself."

"What kind of a dress do you have in mind?" The question is direct, the voice detached, and the eyes unsmiling.

"Something sober – something in blue or gray, something –" I stammer helplessly, wishing the young woman would go away.

"What size, Miss?"

I don't answer her. The girl repeats the question.

"I don't know," I say, my ears beginning to burn. "You see, I'm buying a dress for the first time." I begin to fumble with my pocket book.

"Well, let's see," the girl says. "Perhaps twelve or fourteen would do. You could try these," she says, pointing to a rack. "The fitting rooms are over there."

"Thank you," I mumble, grabbing a few dresses and rushing to the fitting room as if all eyes in the store were turned on me.

Through the swinging partitions in the cubicles, I catch a dazzle of pink and white bodies in slips – pulling dresses over their heads or up their waists. God! How shall I change here? Gingerly, I step into a cubicle at the farthest end, tugging the curtain into place very carefully. I don't want anyone to see me. I have never undressed in a public place. What if someone walked in accidentally? I feel my ears burning as I begin to take off my sari and blouse. I realize I am not wearing a slip. One doesn't with a sari. Quickly, I pull a beige dress over my head and glance at the stranger in the mirror. I strip it off and slip into a brown skirt and a pale blouse, then a blue dress. I change one dress after another as if demons were chasing me. The mirror becomes smudged with blobs of color. Finally, I pull on a burgundy dress, very much like the one a mannequin in the shop window is wearing.

The store seems to have gone dead silent. As if everyone was breathlessly waiting, watching, listening. I turn to the woman in the mirror. My eyes take some time to focus on the apparition in burgundy. But the woman who stands there is small, fragile and scared. Who's she? Straight dark hair knotted at the nape of her neck. Dark, uncomprehending eyes in a pinched face, stare back at me. Who's this plain woman, anyway? She is neither tall, nor sleek, nor sophisticated. The dress bulges slightly around her hips and falls a little below her knees, over legs like Ikea chairs. She looks almost squat. The sari at her feet, the dresses on the pegs, the reflection in the long gilt-framed mirror – everything seems so out of place.

Then memory bursts like a firecracker. "What Mira wears isn't important," Govind had said. "It's the ease with which she carries herself. Confidence in yourself, that's what you want, more confidence." Of course, I am confident, am I not? I can carry myself with ease too, I say to myself as I scrutinize a pair of frightened eyes in the mirror. I have come this far, one step more and I could be like Mira. Like Nancy. Like Sue. Like Kathy. Like thousands of women who at this very instant are walking down the streets, sitting in cafeterias and sipping coffee, working in offices, or watching soap operas at home – perfectly at ease with themselves. Do they ever worry about what they are wearing and whether they are becoming strangers to themselves? Why do I have to be different and isolated? I pull off the dress without another look at myself and wrap on my sari again, and dash out as if fleeing from the stranger in the mirror.

All around me, I feel the buzz of activity – feet shuffling, voices asking questions. The sounds outside the store are muted by the glass windows. Cars and buses drone by in the dull afternoon haze. For a moment, and for reasons I don't understand, I panic. I wish to abandon the dress and bolt out of the store

"That's a good selection," someone says. It's the young woman wheeling away dresses on a rack. "Lovely color!" She smiles. I mumble something. My feet carry me to the cash register.

Without raising her eyes, the woman at the counter asks, "Cash or charge?" I am still grappling with myself.

"Cash or charge, please?" The cashier is getting impatient and tapping her blood-red nails on the register keys.

Someone behind me sighs. "Cash, please," I whisper. "If I

bring –" I try to say, but the metallic whir of the machine silences me. Quietly, I put the money down on the counter.

The glass doors swing open as I walk into the waning afternoon. People surge past me, almost sweeping me along with the tide. I brace myself and glance up at the mannequins. They stand with their faces turned away, their eyes glassy, their smiles frozen. I clutch the bag and begin to flow with the crowd.

After dinner, I wait till Govind and the children have settled down to watch the baseball game. Then I go into the bedroom to change. All eyes are intent on the TV, when I step into the family room. For a moment, I too watch figures sprinting and leaping and diving for the precious ball. The camera focuses on one of the coaches who is chewing and spitting and hammering his fist into his hand. Then I cough and clear my throat. No one looks up.

"How do I look?" I ask in a voice that hardly sounds like my own.

No one seems to hear me.

The commentator's excited voice rises above the roar of the crowd. "What a catch! What a great catch! The team –"

"Look at my dress."

"What a game! O boy! Let's go to Bob for –"

"Look at me!" I cut into the commentary, and turn down the volume.

They jerk bolt upright, and three pairs of uncomprehending eyes stare at me though they are still focused on the game. No one utters a word.

"Say something now. Here I am in a new dress," I smile. "Well?"

My daughter is the first to break the silence. "When did you buy this?" she asks, pointing at the dress?

"You mean the dress? Today."

"– Beautiful," she says, haltingly. It's quiet, once again.

After a while, without taking his eyes off the TV, my son mumbles, "You look, ah – fine –"

I seek Govind and look straight into his eyes.

He takes off his glasses, rubs them on his sleeve, and puts them on before saying, "Of course, you look great."

"You do," my daughter affirms, avoiding my eye.

"Well, thanks," I say, sinking next to Govind on the sofa. I cross my legs as I have seen Mira do and I throw back my head and laugh, the way Mira often does. In complete silence, we continue to watch the TV flashing images like lightning in a dark sky, till someone remembers to turn up the volume.

HOME

As soon as the train plunges into the suburban landscape spattered with evergreens, I pull myself away from the receding glow of the city and settle against the backrest. The young woman in the poster on the carriage wall, twirls a glass of Dubonnet, and looks straight at me over the heads of men and women scanning newspapers and magazines. I turn away from the gleam of her tawny eyes vying with the liquid in the stem glass and stare at the charcoal-gray evening.

Something brushes against my shoulder.

I look up into a pair of startled gray eyes in an oval face. A tentative smile hovers around her thin mouth. Clutching a coat and a bright red scarf with one hand and a worn out brown leather bag with the other, she lurches into the seat opposite mine.

"I am – so – sorry," she says haltingly.

I allow myself a brief smile. A few years ago, I would have started a conversation with her. I had always wanted to talk to people then. But now, I turn my face away and flip the pages of a book I have been dragging along with me for months. It is one of those romance novels you pick up at random at the bookstalls and finish reading at one sitting. In spite of my daily long commutes between the suburb where I live and the city where I work, I haven't been able to get beyond the first few pages. "*A saga of flaming passion –*" it says on the cover.

I had felt embarrassed when Manish had picked it up, the other day, and regarded me with puzzled eyes. Then with something that sounded like a cross between a groan and a chuckle, he had put it down on the table. I had felt rebuffed by his silence, for I had expected him to ask me, "You never read this stuff before. What's the matter now?" But not a word passed between us as we stood there avoiding each other's eye.

Now, the book falls open on a dog-eared page while my eyes stray to the wintry sky outside the speeding train. I try to find some pattern. I don't. It's empty darkness and darkness alone that meets the eye. My novel slides down and falls on the floor with a thud.

"Your book. It is fallen down," the woman with the red scarf says. She picks up the book and hands it over to me. I look at her squarish, work-worn hands and then at her face which has the clean scrubbed look of a new comer in a new country. I too must have looked somewhat like her, when we first came to America.

"Thanks," I mumble as my gaze falls on the book she is clasping. The face on the worn-out cover is familiar.

"Dostoevsky?" I ask in a flat voice.

Her eyes suddenly light up, as if someone had flashed a powerful light behind frosted glass windows.

"You know Russian?" The lilt in her voice is unmistakable.

"No," I say. "I've read Dostoevsky in English translation."

"Oh," the lights go out, and her face settles into grim lines.

Something in the droop of her shoulders touches me, so I ask a trifle gently, "Are you from Russia?"

She nods. "You see. I read Russian books when – when I am feeling nostalgic for home."

Nostalgic? Home? The words strike a gong in the empty halls of my soul. They have been shut for a long time now.

"You see – we have come here – we came here six months ago," she explains.

"Oh, did you!" I say.

"Yes," she says, turning to the window. Her tiny ear drops glint in the light. I notice the red-brown hair tied neatly in a bun at the nape of her neck and the somewhat crumpled collar of her shirt gleaming white against the dark green sweater. Once again, I see myself in her place. Then I firmly push the image out of my mind and return to my book and read: *"His dark eyes rested on her face with a hunger that seemed to consume her very soul. Her lips parted as she –"* But my mind dodges the words and goes racing ahead to a big empty house awaiting me.

With the children away in schools and Manish busy teaching his evening classes, the house will be silent and empty, as usual. Only Toby, my half-blind dog would be sitting patiently at the foot of the stairs, waiting for me. Often, when I insert the key in the lock and push the door open into the silent darkness, I feel as if I were sneaking into a stranger's house. I stand still, waiting for the owner to appear in some doorway and look at me questioningly. Then with the thump of his tail and a happy growl, Toby restores the house to me. I go from room to room, switching on the lights and reclaiming my possessions. It is a relief to see a couple of dirty dishes in the sink, a potato peel curling on the floor and a half-eaten piece of toast on the kitchen table.

"I hate coming back to an empty house," I had mentioned casually to Manish one day while I was ironing clothes and he was sitting with a book. Without removing his eyes from what he was reading, he had said, "You don't have to."

"What do you mean?"

"If you don't go out to work, you don't return to an empty house," he said.

"Then I am in an empty house all the time," I had replied, bringing the iron down on the shirt with a thud.

"But don't we live in emptiness all the time?"

"I don't want any philosophical answers," I had said in exasperation.

"Sorry. Well, I could – if you were at home – change my schedule," he was weighing the words very carefully.

"You never did all these years."

"I couldn't, could I? I had to establish myself," he said.

"Well, then it's my turn now," I replied, fuming. Manish didn't say a word and I went on steaming the wrinkles out of the clothes as if the act would iron out the creases from our lives.

When Manish spoke a little later, his voice was gentle. "You know, Anu, there's no need for you to work." His eyes were fixed upon me with a tenderness I hadn't seen for quite some time. A hard knot that had formed inside me began to dissolve. If only I could explain to him this strange feeling of not belonging anywhere! If only I could tell him how lonely I was! But I couldn't move. The tenderness in his eyes, I thought, was a trick of the firelight. So I went on ironing fiercely – as if that was all that mattered then. I wonder what would have happened if I had gone up to him and taken his hand in mine and said, "Yes let's live our life together." But I couldn't.

"Ah, excuse me, please, but this is Jenkintown?"

The question, asked in a soft voice, shatters the illusion.

The train has stopped and some passengers are getting off. I shake my head.

"No. Not so soon. Three more stops to go."

"I thought so. I thank you very much," she says, and settles back with a sigh. I look past her at the street lamps glowing quietly in the still evening. The dark silhouettes of houses with lighted windows loom mutely against a starless sky. The headlights of a car in the street across the railroad tracks throw the bare trees into relief, for a moment. Then the train begins to pull out of the station. I notice some snow flurries shimmering in the light.

"It's begun to snow," I remark.

My companion whips around.

"Snow? You said snow? Where is snow?"

I point to the window and say, "See the flurries? It's beginning to snow. They predict three inches tonight."

She laughs without mirth. "You call this snow? These drops?" She waves the red scarf at the flurries. Words begin to flow without much difficulty although her speech is halting. "When it was snow in my country, the ground – it was this thick with snow. White, all was white – everywhere. It was a very beautiful. We ski-ed down the slopes, you see, with our teeth chattering and – Tanya's cheeks? They were like red apples. At home, then, in front of the warm stove – we sit and drink tea. But here, it's so closed, no air." She clutches her throat as if she can't breathe, then lets her hand fall into her lap. I can hardly take my eyes off her animated face.

"I am sorry," she says, reddening. "I get carried away – when I think of my snow."

Unwittingly, she has set something astir in me. As I watch the glimmering flurries go slanting past the window, memory surfaces.

"Will it never stop snowing here?" I had asked Manish. It was our first winter in the United States and I had never seen snow before.

"Isn't it beautiful?" he had murmured pulling on his gloves, getting ready to join the children in the backyard. From the window, I had watched them pack fistfuls of snow into tight balls and throw them at each other. A yearning for the warm sands and the clear blue skies of my country had twisted me.

"Look at the snow in Daddy's hair," my daughter had cried rushing in.

"And look at the snow flakes on your eye lashes," my son had teased. With red cheeks and glowing eyes they had stomped in, leaving small puddles of melted snow everywhere on the floor. I hated their cheer, I hated the cold and I hated the snow. For weeks, that winter, I hadn't dared step out of the house. The hem of my sari would become soggy and the cold wind would sometimes balloon it into a parachute. It was so embarrassing to be confined by the dress you wore. So painful to see my American counterparts, snug in jeans and boots, shoveling snow while children laughed and tumbled around them.

Then over the years, I changed. I learned to wear snow boots and elegant tweed skirts when I went out. I learned to sit in front of the fireplace and sip cider when it snowed. I even helped Manish shovel the snow. The warm skies ceased to haunt me except in dreams which I usually forgot in the morning.

Something now compels me to turn to my companion and confess, "I hated the snow when we came here. You see, I had never seen snow before."

"It was snow for six months in my country," she whispers.

"I was always cold," I shiver.

"There was no central heating in Russia but – you see – the old stove was enough."

"When it was very cold we had big braziers in our house in India, blazing in the evenings –" I stretch out my hands, as if I were trying to warm them on an imaginary fire. We look at each other for a moment, then she asks, "You are from India?"

"Yes."

"I have seen pictures of India. It is a very beautiful country," she smiles. I feel a desire to talk to her, so I ask, "Do you have family here?"

"Yes. I have my daughter and my husband."

"Do they like it here?"

"Yes," she hesitates, "but we are lonely. We – we miss our home and relatives –"

I listen to her, mesmerized by the images of home she creates. "Back in Russia, we had family. Uncle Sasha, he was very fond of Tanya. He teach – taught – her how to dance. In the kitchen in front of big stove –" She goes on. Some dim shapes begin to emerge in my mind too. From the vaults of time, my memory pulls out some images. Faces half forgotten. Sites half remembered. Suddenly, I ask her, "Why did you come here?"

Her eyes darken with memory. After a moment's pause, she says, "My husband – his family is here. Life was hard in Russia –"

And why did we come here? I ask myself. Life wasn't hard for us back home. There wasn't any family here, either. Then why? Wondering, I gaze out of the window at the snowflakes sailing past the window. It's all so strange. I don't know for a few minutes who this woman is, what this place is, or where we are going.

"Excuse me. This train – it is late, no?" She asks. "My husband. He waits for me." She tells me how he gets off early from work and waits for her at the station everyday to walk home together.

My husband! Would he be waiting for me? I turn my face away. Manish is normally teaching an evening class or studying in the library when I get home. "What should I do in an empty house?" he asks, when I complain.

We work different hours. Manish is still in bed when I rush out early in the morning – first, to navigate for a parking spot at the railroad station and then to catch the train which always scuttles in as I am parking the car or pushing the coins in the parking meter. I barely manage to catch it to Center City where I work. When the day is over, I juggle my way to the railroad station in the milling evening crowd and come back to a dark house. I am almost asleep when Manish returns. A few words about the children pass between us and then the day is over.

I can hardly complain because this was my choice. Manish had never asked me to work. But I got so tired of letting my life revolve around his after the children had gone away. I so wanted to be like other women with a career that I grabbed the position of a medical writer when I was offered one. The first few months in my small office on the 11th floor overlooking the Center Square were very satisfying. Sitting there and writing about new breakthroughs in treating schizophrenia, cancer, or kidney transplant and looking down at the toy world, I felt detached, almost like some god in heaven. The height and the storm windows held the earthly noises at bay. But now that very distance makes me feel like a disembodied spirit floating in thin air. I crave to be in the hum of life.

"I am very lucky. You see, I found a good job." My companion tells me. I come back to the present. I look at her glowing face and search for my own. Where have I lost it? What has happened to me? I stare at my book. *"He tightened his arms around her, swearing he would never let her go –"*

Torn by an almost physical pain, I snap the book shut. A few days ago when Manish had stretched his arms to pull me close, why had I flinched?

"What's the matter?" He had asked, burying his face in my shoulder.

"Nothing, just tired. It was a rough day." I had said, conscious of the sudden stiffening of my body.

"Let me relax you," he had said rubbing the back of my neck. I didn't say anything but the tautness must have given him the message.

We lay side by side for a long time, without moving, without touching each other, without exchanging a single word. Ever since that night, Manish sleeps on his side of the bed, careful not to touch me. Even when I woke up from a bad dream last night, all he did was to pat my shoulder and say, "Go back to sleep," as if I were a little girl. I had wanted to move close to him, to feel the warmth and assurance of his body, but I couldn't. I lay rigid, staring into nothingness while my mind kept ticking furiously like a time bomb, repeating to itself, "This shouldn't be happening to us. This shouldn't be happening to us. No – no."

This woman has her husband waiting for her as Manish might have waited for me an infinity ago. What's happened now? Envy digs its claws into me as I stare at her. She has about her the glow and serenity of a woman loved. I too had that glow, once. Do all newcomers have it in the beginning and do they all lose it after a while? What will happen to her, to her Tanya, to them, after a few years? I ask myself. Will they still miss Uncle Sasha? Will they still miss the snows? Crave for the open air? Or will they become like us? Going round and round in unending circles? Will she still arch her neck to spot out her waiting husband? Will he still wait for her? I wish I could talk to her. I want to. My lips begin to frame words.

"Jenkintown! Jenkintown!" The conductor shouts.

My companion leaps up. An apple falls out of her bag and rolls on the floor as she ties her scarf and shuffles into the coat. I retrieve it and hold it out to her. She smiles at me. I want to ask her name, but she hastens down the aisle.

From the carriage window, I watch her stride away – a small figure in a shapeless coat and a red scarf. She pauses and stands looking around her uncertainly. Then a man, whose face I can't see, detaches himself from the shadow of the wall and steps forward. A sliver of light slides down the curve of her cheek as she turns to him. He puts his arm lightly around her shoulders, and they walk away into the dancing snow flakes. The train begins to pull out.

The image of a man and a woman walking away together from a dimly-lit railroad station singes my eyes. No matter where I look, I see them. I put my hand to my brow as a certain hollowness and a terrible hunger twists my insides. I want to call Manish. I want to ask him to meet me at the station. I don't want to drive home in this cold snow. I don't want to be by myself. I don't want to exchange one emptiness for another. I want to regain something we have lost. And yet! I know happiness is not an apple that had rolled under a seat and could be retrieved. I let out a sigh, then quickly look around. No one is looking at me. The two men in my row, across the isle, are still holding the stale newspapers before their faces. I look straight ahead of me. The young woman in the Dubonnet poster glows at me. The golden-brown wine of her eyes sparkles. The train goes hurtling through the snowing darkness.

GREENWICH LINE

I

We shall soon land at the Heathrow airport and wind our way through strange streets to some unknown apartment Jeevan has rented for a few days. We shall stumble into unfamiliar rooms, cross the floor, throw a window open on some back alley, and breathe in the sounds and smells of London. I know that the walls, the light switches, the bureau – nothing will be familiar to us. The bed we shall sleep in won't have taken on the contours of our bodies. And by the time the place begins to lose its strangeness, it'll be time for us to leave, to return to our separate homes where switches in the accustomed places and beds contoured to the shape of our bodies await us. This stay in London will become a memory too – of moments netted in the endless flow of time. And I'll wait for the returning tide to haul us out of the swamp

of our dull marriages and carry us away to distant shores –
for a few days.

But is this how we are going to live out the rest of our lives?
Cheating our spouses, bluffing ourselves? I ask myself. Is this –?

"What're you thinking?" Jeevan's voice breaks into my
reverie.

"Nothing," I turn to him. The roughness of his jacket
brushes my cheek and the faint smell of his after-shave fills
my breath.

"You looked lost, so far away," he says. Then glancing at
his watch, he adds, "We'll be landing very soon." I smile at
the decisive movements of his strong hands. They had
fascinated me the first time I saw Jeevan at the gathering of
the Indian community in Philadelphia. I think I fell in love
with his hands instantly. They were the hands of a sculptor,
sinewy and strong. They had moved, during his speech, as if
they had a life of their own. I had felt an inexplicable desire
to feel them on my shoulders.

"Something bothering you?" He folds my hand in his. The
warmth of his body flows into mine.

"I was thinking about us."

"And what about us?" His dark eyes are intense. Spheres
burning in the depths of a forest. After his hands, it was his
eyes that had mesmerized me.

I look at his graying hair, at his sharp cheek bones, at his
starched shirt, his navy-blue jacket and burgundy tie.
Everything about Jeevan is so well-coordinated. He is always
carefully dressed – not one bit like Sohan, my husband, who
always pulls out any shirt and whichever tie from the closet a
minute before he is to step out of the house. "It'll do, it'll do,"
he used to grumble when I tried to give him the right one. I
don't do so any more. We have learnt to keep out of each
other's way.

"Gauri?" Jeevan is waiting.

"I was thinking," I begin slowly. "I was thinking about how

we hop from one plane to another, go from one place to another, as if we were always on the run. Is this how we're going to live?"

Jeevan gazes at the shimmering blankness outside the window. After a moment of absolute stillness, he turns to me, and says, "Enjoy this moment, darling, this being together. Let's discuss the future later."

Later? But when is later? And where is later? "At some point we'll have to decide."

"Yes, I know," he says. Shadows speckle his eyes. I can't bear to see him sad. Quickly, I ask him, "What're your plans in London?" The shadows dissolve.

"You mean *our* plans," he smiles. "We'll go around London. Maybe, we can push off to Edinburgh for a day or two. I just want us to be together."

"That sounds lovely," I say.

"Good. I want you to enjoy the trip. You'll enjoy London," he says.

This has become the pattern of our lives now – ever since that evening when I found Jeevan waiting for me in the college parking lot. My life split up into two halves like a ripe pomegranate. It's never been whole again. I exist in two hemispheres now. One with Sohan; the other with Jeevan. Forcing away thoughts of my split life, I lean against the backrest and breathe in the peace that Jeevan's nearness always brings. No feelings of sin, or guilt, or remorse torment me. They come later, when I'm away from Jeevan, when I'm with Sohan, and when I turn away from him.

The plane begins to descend.

II

We met seven years ago. Jeevan was the speaker at a meeting of the Association of Indians in America. Sohan, who never compelled me to accompany him to those meetings, refused to go without me that evening. "Come, come. I have paid thirty five dollars for each of us. It would be a disaster to let that be wasted," he had said.

So we went to the rented gymnasium of a high school swarming with people I hardly knew. Men chatting in small groups, women flitting around in shimmering silk and brocade saris – the diamonds in their ears and the laughter in their eyes vying with the twinkling lights strung across the ceiling. By comparison, in my plain salmon pink silk sari and a string of rice pearls around my neck, I must have looked a poor relative. Feeling a little self-conscious and somewhat lost in that gathering, I stood in odd corners, catching bits of conversation about thousand-dollar *lachka*, Meenu's priceless carpets, Surana's promotion as VP of a corporation, Mehta's farm house with twenty rooms, and Joseph's booming textile business. Sohan beamed at me whenever he caught my eye. He was always at his happiest amidst the Indian community.

And then I saw him. His face molded from burnished bronze. Eyes like burnt stars. Our eyes met briefly, as he bent to say something to a short man clawing at his sleeve.

I turned away to look for Sohan. I needed him by my side. But he was at the other end of the room. Someone introduced the speaker: Dr. Jeevan Mehta, a well-known businessman, philanthropist, visionary, a man with progressive ideas, *et cetera*. I can still hear the boom of Jeevan's voice as he tried to enthuse the Indian community into taking new initiatives and giving up old beliefs which had no relevance to their existence in America. I was hypnotized by the orchestration of his hands and wondered how they would feel around my face. The whole evening, after that, was a muddle. Sohan, who was sitting next to me, had dozed off and his head rolled on to my shoulder for a split second before he collected himself and straightened up. "Ah! Good talk," he said joining the applause, for Jeevan had finished his speech. Over the uproar, Jeevan's eyes sought mine. I averted my face. Some instinct warned me to stay away from him. I wanted to slip away quietly, but Sohan dragged me with him to where Jeevan was standing surrounded by a group of people, discussing the role of the Indian community in America.

"– The desire to change is the first step towards growth and spiritual –" he was saying.

"Change doesn't happen as easily as you seem to suggest," Sohan interrupted him in his usual brusque manner.

Jeevan had smiled, "You're right, but Mr. –"

"Sohan Kumar. You can call me Sohan, I don't mind that."

"Yes, Sohan," he had said, "but we can't hold on to defunct social codes while –"

"Change is painful. It destroys so much. Specially values." Sohan would never let anyone finish a sentence. But Jeevan was patient, almost indulgent, as he listened to Sohan.

I couldn't hear anything anyone said, for my mind had stopped ticking. I wanted to be as far away from the tenor of Jeevan's voice as I could. It ruffled me as the wind ruffles a field of golden wheat. I stepped over to where a woman in a gold-fringed peacock blue sari was standing – a little away from the crowd – detached, somewhat bored and isolated. She had a childlike face. Soft, round, pretty, though almost expressionless. I distinctly remember the dark red of her lipstick and the movement of her kohl-rimmed eyes – like a pair of black birds trapped in a pale face.

"That was a very impressive speech," I said to her.

"Ah, yes," she replied, looking away. "Of course. He's always like that."

"This is my first time at this meeting. Do you come here often?"

"As many times as he speaks."

"You must admire him very much," I had laughed.

She directed the midnight darkness of her gaze at me, and said in a flat voice, "He's my husband."

"He's very good. Congratulations!" I faltered.

"On being his wife?" Dark flames leaped up in those otherwise listless eyes. The impassive face had a smoldering fire inside. I searched for something to say. But her eyes had already pulled the shutters down and were fixed at a point above my head.

"I must go," I muttered, turning around abruptly and barely missing the person into whose path I had stepped. It was Jeevan. "I'm sorry," I gasped, rooted to the spot. He broke the spell. "Hello!" He said, "We haven't met before, have we?"

Before I could reply, Sohan was at my side, saying, "No, no, no, no. She's come to this gathering for the first time. Meet my wife, Gauri. She's –" Sohan would have gone on had someone not stepped up to Jeevan. "Excuse me!" Jeevan said, his eyes still holding mine.

I urged Sohan for us to leave. "Leave the delicious food we've paid for? Thirty-five dollars, Gauri, and all you can eat. No way." Sohan could never understand any other hunger than the one for food. I was conscious of Jeevan the whole evening. Even to this day, I can't believe how I, a woman from a small town in India, raised in an orthodox Hindu family, married to a successful engineer, could have allowed a total stranger to make the rivers go mad in my veins. I listened to Sohan's commentary on the food attentively, I tried to make small conversation too, but the sensation of a pair of eyes following me never left me. I could hardly swallow a mouthful. Once we bumped into Jeevan's wife standing with an almost empty plate. "Oh here you are. Take this," Sohan said, and before she could come out of her trance, he had placed two *puris* on her plate and was offering her some pickles. "Eat, eat. This is good," he coaxed. Surprisingly, she started eating and did not mind Sohan at all. "You see you must eat when you are at such places. You've paid for it, so why not eat? We work hard to earn these dollars, okay?"

"We didn't pay," she replied with her mouth full. "We were invited."

"Aha! Lucky you. That's even better," Sohan laughed. And she smiled too, a very sweet innocent smile, which took away the passivity from her face for a while. As we were leaving, Jeevan said, "We must meet again."

"Of course, of course," Sohan replied with great enthusiasm.

"Hema and I would be very happy to have you over for dinner," he looked at his wife, whose face held no invitation.

"Hema*ji* doesn't have to bother," Sohan had said. "Gauri is a good cook, and I myself do a good job too. We'll invite you. Don't worry. Good bye now."

Driving home, Sohan kept analyzing Jeevan and his speech. "He's very intelligent, of course. But the man is phony. I tell you –" I stared at the lights blinking upon the dark heart of the river along the Kelly Drive. I never wanted to meet Jeevan again. But as chance would have it, we met. Again and again and again.

III

Our first morning in London.

I wake up in an unfamiliar room and lie still for some time, waiting for memory to return. For I think I am back in my bed in Philadelphia, in my study that I have converted into a bedroom. "I read late into the night," I had told Sohan when I moved out of our bedroom. "And you have to get up early to go to work."

"I know, I know," he had grumbled. Not even once did he ask me why I hadn't thought of it all these years. Not even once did he try to dissuade me.

Now, the sound of Jeevan's regular breathing and the pressure of his arm is reassuring. After a while, I slip out of the bed and creep up to the window. On a balcony, across the street, an elderly couple sits in white cane chairs, sipping tea. The early morning sunshine has haloed their silver heads. I cannot see their faces, but I watch the man hold out a plate to the woman who takes it in one hand and brushes his shoulder with the other. Her fingers stray to the back of his neck and linger there for a moment. The gesture, so simple and so spontaneous, fills me with hollowness – a strange sense of longing. Watching them, I am, once again, reminded of Sohan. Why couldn't we in all these years ever sit down together and enjoy a moment of intimacy? In the early days of our marriage, when I had just come from India, Sohan used to bring me lilac blossoms sometimes. "Here, take these. Remind you of home, don't they?" He would say. There used to be tenderness in his brusque manner. I was a different person then. Perhaps, so was he. Lilacs, we didn't know then, couldn't bloom for ever.

"Did you sleep well?" Jeevan puts his arms around me. "What do you want to do today?" He asks.

"You decide," I reply.

His body is strong and warm. Sohan, though slightly younger than Jeevan, has a soft body, almost like a woman's. Lately, he has gained weight. And why wouldn't he? He has developed such a passion for fried potatoes that every weekend, his mission is to fry potatoes – whole or mashed balls dipped in a batter, or plain French fries – and eat them.

"Why do you do this to your body?" I had asked Sohan one day.

With a sad laugh, he had pulled a bowl of fried potatoes towards him. "What difference does it make? Who cares?" He had said, stuffing a greasy whole potato into his mouth.

I had wanted to tell him, "I do." But I couldn't lie. Not even to reassure him. I know Sohan still wants to believe that all is fine between us. I don't feel any tenderness for him. We don't share anything. Sohan is an electrical engineer even in his sleep. He can never talk, or think, poetry. When he comes home from his job with the Township, he is mostly tired and hungry or full of stories about hydraulic engines and troubleshooting, which do not interest me. When I was still a bride and quite new to America, I used to take interest in his work. Then everything changed. After three years of marriage, when we couldn't have children, I went back to school to earn a Ph.D. degree. Our drifting away from each other was like the movement of the earth – unseen, but certain. When I started teaching, I began to feel embarrassed at his stock jokes, at his abrupt ways, at his sloppy appearance. At parties, I was never sure at what point Sohan was going to come up with a shocking remark that would upset or amuse my colleagues. I think Sohan considered them his adversaries. He was always pitched for a battle. My Don Quixote!

And I? Didn't I try to be a good Indian wife? Demure? Undemanding? Giving? I did. For quite a while. I even learned to ask him the right questions about hydraulic engines and troubleshooting. But, to use Sohan's terminology, our circuits couldn't always connect. Certainly never after the day when Jeevan and Hema came for dinner.

I had not wanted Jeevan to sense the gulf between Sohan and me. I had been very tender and loving to Sohan that day. Against my better judgment, I had fried for him a bowl of crisp golden-brown potatoes. I was determined to project to Jeevan the image of a happy couple, for I had sensed a dangerous, an almost helpless attraction for him. I even tried to coax the torpid rivers to rise when Sohan touched me. He seemed to be happy too, till Jeevan began to show me small courtesies like clearing off the center table when I brought in the hors d'oeuvres and holding my chair as we were sitting down to dinner.

How could I remain immune to Jeevan's attention? My face must have reflected my happiness. As the evening matured, Sohan grew quieter. To avoid tension, I kept a steady flow of conversation, moving from the Chagall exhibition to mugging on the subways, to Sohan's favorite Indian music. It was a mistake, for the more we talked, the gloomier Sohan became. Jeevan's wife, who seemed to have taken a vow of silence, was no help. She sat eating quietly or smiling to herself, never lifting her eyes from her plate, not even once. She didn't cheer up even when the conversation shifted to India.

"Haven't been there for eight years now," she said in a gloomy voice. The only time she perked up was when Sohan knocked over a glass of water. "O! O! The tablecloth! Quick! Give me a towel!" With great alacrity, she had removed the dishes and mopped the water. But as soon as we had settled down, she ducked into herself.

The evening dragged like a sack of cotton drenched in rain. I wanted it to be over soon. Sohan didn't even wait for the dessert before he rushed into the kitchen and started doing the dishes. I whispered to him, "I'll do the dishes later. Let's have dessert first."

In a voice that spluttered like fritters on a hot griddle, he had said, "Ya, ya, why would you want to miss a chance to show off and talk your heart out?" I knew Jeevan was listening. Hema was smiling at the tablecloth.

I had swallowed the tears and turned on the dishwasher. I did not look at Jeevan for the rest of the evening, for my face would have melted under his gaze.

Next day, after my classes, I had just stepped into the gently falling snow when I saw Jeevan. Even if the snow flakes had turned into a blizzard, I couldn't have turned away. I remember my frozen smile, and I remember him opening the car door for me, and I remember the snow blowing against the windshield as we drove away. I asked no questions, he offered no explanations. We drove in silence to a remote country restaurant. And then he spoke to me for the first time, "What time do you have to be home?"

"Not for some time."

"Good," he had said and held out his hand across the small table at which we sat. I didn't care what the waitress thought, and I didn't care who might be looking. I had let my hand rest in his till the waitress brought our orders. Then we slipped our hands below the table and held on to each other as if an earthquake might tear us apart any moment.

"I am sorry about last night," he said.

I kept staring at the slightly drooping carnations in the vase on the table.

"I know how you feel," he said. "I too have embarrassing moments with Hema. She —"

"Please!" I stopped him. "You don't have to tell me anything."

"I want to," he had cleared his throat and continued. "Were it not for the children, we might have separated long ago. Hema's never forgiven me for bringing her here. She refuses to change — she was never meant for this country. But —" he had shrugged. Then, after a pause, he had added, "I've never discussed my life with anyone, I don't know why I'm telling you all this."

But I knew. He was trying to ease my hurt by sharing his pain. Later, in the car, it was this very pain that I tried to rub off with mine. Inside the lambent dome the snow had created around us, I began to feel the rivers stir and then rush. In retrospect, it appears strange that it was I who cradled his head on my shoulder and tried to smooth the grief from his face the first time we were together, although Jeevan was the stronger one.

When I went home that night, I had no feeling of guilt or sin. I looked at my glowing face in the mirror and I ran my hand gently over the mouth Jeevan had kissed. I could have kissed Sohan that night — I could have even let him make love to me, so pure and so renewed did I feel. But he was asleep the moment dinner was over. I lay awake a long time, reliving the evening.

That was the beginning.

Now, Jeevan and I take off to places away from home. We pretend we are married to each other for those three or four or five days we are together in strange apartments with windows opening on clueless streets in cities faraway. I don't know how much his wife knows about us. I don't know how much Sohan suspects. Sometimes, I think he knows, but is reluctant to admit it. He might even be scared to admit it. He has accepted my frequent trips to conferences or to libraries abroad where he believes I go to collect material for my research. That's what I am supposed to be doing in London now. What Sohan doesn't know is that Jeevan is with me. Or, maybe, he does.

IV

London is like a heady wine. I have never felt so fulfilled anywhere. Together, Jeevan and I have lit candles in the cathedrals, we have walked along the Serpentine, we have stretched ourselves under the trees on the soft grass in a lonely meadow and watched the clouds, we have sat amidst the blaze of colors and fragrances in Kew Gardens, and we have skidded up and down the Thames and come back exhausted and made love, oblivious of the noise of the traffic that never stops, unmindful of the alley cats screeching and snarling in the dead of the night. I don't want to go back to Philadelphia.

But today is our last day in London. We have just returned from Greenwich Park. We settle down for a cup of tea in this wayside restaurant. I am peeked out after the steep climb to the Old Royal Observatory where the world's prime meridian runs through the courtyard. I had imagined something like a bolt of lightening slicing through time and space. But what I saw was a thin metal line running across a small patch of grassy land astride which people stood laughing and posing for photographs.

"Here's your prime meridian. Go, stand there," Jeevan had said, giving me a gentle push. Laughing, I had walked up to the line, planted my feet on either side of it, thrown back my head and looked at Jeevan.

"You're straddling two worlds now," he laughed. The wind had tousled his hair and turned up the collar of his T-shirt. At that moment, I felt as if he was standing at the other side of an ocean. It seemed to me as if we were separated from each other by half the length of the globe. Something happened to me then. The sun grew mercilessly bright. The wind dropped. The sound of laughter and voices around me ceased. Straddling two worlds. Belonging to none. Did I have to come this far to realize it? I stood there with my feet planted on either side of the line for what seemed like an eternity. The laughter died on my lips. A crowd of Japanese visitors stood waiting. I stepped aside.

"What's the matter? You look pale," Jeevan said, as we started back.

"Tired," was all I could say.

Now, arranging the crumbs of a buttered scone in a circle with my finger, I ask him, "Will it always be like this, Jeevan?"

"It?" His hands reach out for mine over the table.

"This existing in two worlds?"

"Let's go," he says abruptly, and gets up, pays the bill, and we stride off, not saying a word to each other.

Once inside the apartment, we hold on to each other as if some catastrophe were going to wrench us apart. The ferocity of our lovemaking frightens me. Later, much later, lying in the crook of his shoulder, I ask again, "Will it always be like this?"

"I don't know." He sighs.

I can't stand it. I can't bear his not knowing. He, who is so strong, so confident, and so sane, how can he not know?

If Sohan says, he doesn't know, I wouldn't mind, for I don't expect him to know. But when Jeevan says, he doesn't know, my rivers get stalled. How can he not know? He was the one who sensed my pain and loneliness, who stood there in the snow waiting for me to finish my classes, who held me in his arms with infinite tenderness in that small motel the first time we lied to our spouses and got away. How can he not know? I switch on the light. It falls on a gaunt face – tired and gray.

"I can't walk out and let the family crumble," he says with a tremor in his voice. For a moment, I feel knocked out – struck by a hurricane which will soon sweep everything into primal darkness.

Then I cry out. "What about me? Your wife, your children mean everything to you. Am I nothing?" I fling the covers aside and leap out of the bed. He sits up quietly and looks at me across the expanse of the tumbled bedsheets.

"What am I? A whore who steals away from her husband every now and then and goes back to live a lie? This is not how I visualize my life – a sneaky affair lived out in strange apartments – no way." I can say nothing further. I pull a suitcase and start throwing my clothes into it. I try to snap it shut, but the clothes are spilling out. I subside on the floor. Jeevan rocks me against him, saying, "Don't, don't cry. Please, darling. I love you too much to see you unhappy. Do you want us to stop meeting?"

"Do you?"

"If you want to," he says in a voice that seems to be coming from inside an empty tin can.

I say nothing.

He clears his throat and says, "It's nothing but pity that I feel for Hema. You know, you must know there's no love between her and me. We haven't slept in the same room for years now. But I have a responsibility to her, to the children – can't just abandon her – She's crazy. Sick. You're strong, you're sane," he pauses.

"And I must pay for being sane, for being strong." I feel the bitterness of poison ivy in my mouth.

"You are the only love in my life. But how do I walk up to Hema and tell her I want to divorce her? Can you ask Sohan for a divorce?"

"Can't I?" I ask myself. Sohan emerges from some dark corner of my mind, doddering around the house with a grumpy face, sulking like a neglected child, stuffing himself with fried potatoes.

"Tell me," Jeevan's voice is soaked with sadness. "Would you be able to live with the guilt if I divorced her? Would you?"

"Of course I can," I want to say. And yet, I can't.

For the first time, I understand the predicament of my life. I am not whole when I am with Sohan. I am fragmented when I am with Jeevan. "So this is how it will go on. Till the day we die?" I squeak, as if a boulder lay on my chest, clogging the free flow of rivers in my veins.

In his eyes is gathered all the darkness of a moonless night. "Perhaps yes, unless we decide to walk out on our marriages."

I know we won't. Even after all these years of living in America, after changing our citizenship, after altering our ways of walking and talking and thinking, and after making all the tall claims that we usually do, we're still shackled to some rusty moral code that may not have relevance even in a small town in India. The fight, the anger, the bitterness subside and give way to a tired despair. We sit staring into the darkness for a long time, saying not a word to each other. Finally, he says, "We have to catch the morning flight. Sleep, my darling." His voice doesn't touch me. It comes from a far off space. I hear the sound of a lone car passing. Footsteps hurry from somewhere to somewhere. The fragment of a sentence drifts in the night air. The cats snarl in the alleys. I lie awake, till the darkness turns a pearl gray.

V

It's time to leave London.

Jeevan has carried our bags down. The taxi will be here soon to take us to the airport. My rivers are quiet now. My sand castles have been swept away by the receding tides. I take one last look at the apartment. One more remembrance to be hung on the crowded walls of memory. I glance outside the window. The balcony across the street is empty today. Were they too visitors like us? Gone? I wish they were there. The sight of a man and a woman sitting on the balcony on a summer morning, drinking tea, growing old together in harmony, love, and peace would be reassuring. I wait. A taxi honks. Jeevan calls me. I wrench myself away from the window and run downstairs. The door swings shut behind us as we step out into the damp London air. The promise of sunshine has turned into a threat of rain. I look up. The chairs in the balcony remain empty.

DISTANCES

Jasmine and *bela* bloom in the backyard of my father's house. I collect handfuls of swirling fragrance while my mother sits with her back to me, turning her rosary beads.

"Ma, please pack this fragrance in a box too," I call out to her. "I'll take it with me to America."

She doesn't move. She doesn't respond.

"Quick Ma! It won't last long."

And even as I utter these words, the fragrance vaporizes. My hands are empty.

"It's gone! I want my fragrance back."

The sound of my whimpering wakes me up. Manish is fast asleep beside me. It takes me a while to realize that I am not in my father's house in India. I am in my bedroom in the suburbs of a strange American city, but my hands are still damp with the fragrance of jasmine and *bela*. In the light of the digital clock-radio, I see patterns forming and dissolving. I rock back and forth between a sun-splashed backyard and a smoky-gray bedroom. Then the alarm goes off. Released, I slip out of the bed.

The effort of waking up Samir and Mini blows away the flecks of my dream. I whirl about, handing Samir his clothes, brushing Mini's dark curls, packing their lunch boxes, bundling them up in their coats and pushing them out into the frozen street just as the yellow school bus snails around the corner. Once my son and daughter have disappeared into the bus and I have closed the door with chill-roughened hands, the dream begins to pound in my veins. As I wait for the kettle to boil, I turn on the radio, ready to hear the notes of a morning *raga*.

"And now for the weather –" The crisp and clear voice of the announcer jolts me into the present. "It's going to be bright and sunny –"

The kettle whistles. I switch off the radio.

Manish is still asleep when I place his tea on the bedside table.

"Wake up, you'll be late," I whisper, letting my fingers stray to his face, tracing the curve of his jaw. He turns his face away. I jerk my hand away, compose my face and voice, and ask briskly, "What time do you have to go?"

"What's the time?"

"Eight."

"Eight? O, my God!"

In a moment the covers go flying and he is gulping down his scalding tea. I want to steady his hand and tell him, "At least drink your tea in peace." But the words remain smothered somewhere.

Manish slams his mug on the table and rushes to the bathroom. "My blue suit – please Anu – and a fresh shirt."

I put away my tea, resisting the impulse to hurl the cup against the closed bathroom door. Manish breezes in, a little later, smelling of soap and after-shave lotion.

"No time for breakfast – I'll take something with me for

lunch," he mutters, his eyes intent on the pair of socks in his hands.

"Aren't you coming home for lunch?"

"No. Two meetings in a row," he answers, lacing his shoes. He addresses these words not to me, but to his shoes, to the floor.

I press the lunch bag in his hands as he rushes out of the door. He pauses. My face tingles as I surge toward him.

"My notepad – I forgot it on the table –"

He swoops for his notepad. For a brief second his arm brushes my shoulder and then he's gone.

For a long time, I stand behind the storm door, staring at a brown leaf that lies frozen in the snow and remembering our first snow when Manish had held me close to him and said, "It's only a change of place, Anu. Nothing has changed. Nothing ever will."

We had watched the snowflakes alight and settle down on the grass and fences like tiny butterflies.

Now, four years later, I want to ask him, "Nothing? Has nothing really changed?"

But I stay the impulse because I know his response.

"Still thinking of the past?" he will ask. And I won't be able to tell him that past is like the lingering fragrance of sachets in the closets – faint as a whisper and delicate as a mist. No matter where you go, it clings to you. It follows you as it has followed me to this land, across the seas.

I close the door and step into the kitchen. The smell of the dish-washing soap begins to curl around me as I do the dishes. A sliver of sunlight steals in from the window and lights up my brass flower pot. The past comes cascading in, flooding the mind with so many images – sunlight rollicking on the flag-stoned garden path, clothes bobbing on the line, father shuffling his newspaper under the bougainvillea arch, mother turning her rosary, jasmine and *bela* flowers lying sheeted on the grass, and fragrant winds blowing into the house through the open windows.

Then the fumes of dish-washing soap haul me back into my neat American kitchen. How I wish I could sheet rock the past, plaster it, paint it, so that it wouldn't gape at me! How I wish I could celebrate what I have and block out that which is gone! But I can't. For outside the window, it is still winter and the snow on the ground lies dead. Somewhere far away, there are saffron fields, fragrant and endless, streaming in the sun. But here it's cold, dead winter. The clumps of snow outside the window are muddy gray. What is this place? Why am I here? What am I –?

The phone begins to ring.

The last button on Mini's dress stitched, I snip off the thread and look out. The elderly lady next door walks past with her dog. We smile when we catch each other's eye. But today the window pane is frosted. I hear the mailman push the letters through the slit in the door. I know there aren't any from home. Who is there to write, anyway? Father is dead and mother has turned her back on the world. Father used to write to us regularly. His letters had been full of questions: "Have you bought a car? What model? When will you buy a house? Are you taking care of the children? Do they have enough warm clothes? Has it snowed yet?" Letters full of information: "Your friend has moved to another city. The neighbor's dog was run over by a car. The neighbors' house was burgled again. They shouldn't have put the jewelry in the locker." Letters full of love and tenderness: "I miss you all. I cry when I feed Samir's fish. I miss Mini's prattle. I can't bring myself to eat without you all at the table. I'm growing old. Your mother misses you. I wonder if I'll ever see you again." And then – he was gone. The heart that yearned for us clocked out as he sat under his bougainvillea arch. He was there no more to inform us about the abundant fruit that the mango tree yielded that year. If only we hadn't moved. If only I had stayed back. If only – but remorse couldn't bring him back.

While I mourned for Father, Manish threw himself into his work with a fury that frightened me. We moved from the apartment to a large house. We had everything we could want. I felt there wasn't any need for him to work that hard. I tried to convey this to Manish, one day. He flipped through the pages of the book in his hand and replied, "Yes, we have enough to live comfortably, but I want to buy a bigger house – one with a swimming pool and a tennis court. And send the children to the best schools."

"But we'll be going home very soon," I smiled, my mind leaping.

He looked at me and said quietly, "We're not going back, Anu."

I winced as the words hit me. I had feared his speaking them. I had dreamed his speaking them a million times. He had never yearned for the fragrances and colors we had left behind. For him, the past was dead. And yet, foolishly, I had been blowing at the cold ashes in the hope of finding a spark somewhere. Now they blew into my face.

"But why?" I cried.

He snapped the book shut and stared at the wall. I repeated my question. He turned to me calmly and said, "Because there's nothing to go back to. Nothing. Your father's gone, I don't have much by way of a family, what's there to go back to?"

"But –"

"We'd be misfits there, anyway."

"We're aliens here."

"Better to be aliens here than strangers in your own country."

"But this loneliness? This – this sense of always living on the periphery? It hurts," I said. "Doesn't it hurt you?"

He considered my question. Then in a flat tone he answered, "No. It doesn't. Not any more. I've reached a point where I don't feel lonely anywhere."

"But what about me? I'm lonely. I'm miserable. Doesn't that matter?"

Manish gazed at me with opaque eyes. "You create your own loneliness, Anu. You refuse to let go of the past. Forget it and you'll find your peace."

I looked around, searching for something to say.

"What about the children?"

Surely, he would reconsider his decision if I mentioned the children. But he merely laughed, as if I had said something very funny, very childish. Jasmine and *bela* flowers swam before my eyes, the sunlight broke into a thousand shards, and I heard the peacock cry. I snatched the book from Manish's hands and hurled it against the wall. He quietly picked it up and dusted it with his sleeve. Without a word, without a glance, he turned away.

Samir and Mini are back from school. They sit munching cookies.

"Anything new?" I ask Samir.

He shakes his head, "Nothing."

I turn to my daughter and ask, "How was your English class today?" She smiles vaguely, then bubbles forth, "You know Ma, Amy is in the school play." Then she turns to her brother and begins to tell him about the play. Samir laughs. I glance at their glowing faces and turn away. They have already forgotten me.

The bleached sunshine merges with the evening shadows. I slip a cassette into the cassette-player. The pure notes of an evening *raga* on the sitar fall on my ears like a gentle rain. The crevices begin to fill up. Faces emerge and fade away. Father and Mother at the airport – their faces like those of two children lost in a fair. Eyes glazed and smiles frozen. They had finally glimpsed the monstrous loneliness they would be left with, once we were gone. It wasn't as if after a romp in the open we would return to the fold. We did not.

Their faces dissolve into endless space even as I stretch out my hand to touch them. The record has stopped. I hear Manish's car in the driveway. The key turns in the lock and he is home.

I study the droop of his shoulders, the lines around his mouth and the sagging gait as he stands near the table, scanning the day's mail. I want to touch him, hold him, soothe him. My hands flutter towards him. He turns his head slightly and asks, "How was the day?"

I open my mouth to reply, but he is opening letters, reading them. My hands fall limp at my sides.

"Want tea?"

"No," he answers with his back still turned to me.

I want him to look at me, to turn around and hold my hand, to say, "I've had a tiring day. Come, let's sit down for a while." But his hands keep tearing letters open.

I go into the kitchen and chop vegetables as if my life depended on how finely they were chopped.

A little later, the silence is broken by splinters of laughter. In the living room, the scene has changed. Samir is eagerly narrating something about his baseball game to Manish. Mini pipes in, "You know Daddy, I spelt all the words right today."

Manish pinches her little nose and says, "Really?"

She puts her small arms around his neck and hums, "I love my Daddy." Manish and Samir smile at each other over her head. And I observe the haloed scene through a frosted pane – a stranger on a wintry night, gazing in through a window at the circle of beaming faces around a bright fire. I wish to be included in the magic circle, but if I went in now, the children would slink away to their room and Manish would turn to the TV.

When we sit down to dinner, Samir makes faces at *dal* and potatoes.

"The same stuff," he grimaces. "I don't like this food."

"You can't have hamburgers everyday," I admonish him.

"But Ma –" Samir protests.

"How about if we went to McDonald's this weekend?" Manish intervenes quickly.

"Hooray!" the children shout.

Left out of the circle once again, I blubber, "Why do you have to shout so much?"

"O Ma!" Samir mutters. Manish avoids looking at me and turns on the TV.

Bits of news fall into my ears. Fear of nuclear war. Increasing rate of unemployment. Cases of mugging and rape. Cyanide in Tylenol. Acid rain. AIDS. Drugs. A child killed in a crossfire shooting. The food turns to sand. The walls of the room begin to cave in. What are we doing here? This is not the land we had dreamed about. What if something happened to the children? To Manish? What if there's a war? What if the food we are eating is poisoned? What if –? I swivel toward Manish. If only he would extend his hand, calm my fears, tell me everything is fine. But, he sits eating his dinner. Unperturbed.

Supper over, dishes done, children in their room, I crumple in the big chair and flip through the pages of a book where words are hieroglyphs I can't decipher. Manish sits scribbling on a pad.

"What're you doing?" I ask him.

"Preparing tomorrow's lecture," he replies, without lifting his head, without stopping the flow of his hand on the notepad.

I stare at his hand, at the sharp angle of his jaw, the stoop of his shoulders, the shadow of his head on the wall. If I stretched out my hand I could smooth away the hair fallen over his forehead. He's so near. And yet, so far away.

"Nothing has changed," he had said that winter, "Nothing ever will."

"If nothing has changed then what is this vacuum? What is this distance?" I want to ask him. But I can't.

The book slips from my fingers and falls on the carpet with a soft thud. I look at my hands – so clean, so empty. What happened to the fragrances I wanted to hold? What's happened to me, to us? How much have we gained or lost, created or destroyed, understood or rejected? Questions swamp me from all sides. Days have slipped by like milestones on a road, like the pages of a book ruffled by the wind. I wish I could hold something in the hollow of my hand and show it to Manish and say, "Look! This is what I created today." But there isn't the slightest trace of a fragrance, neither color nor song, anywhere. So clean and yet –

"Tired?"

The question is asked in a gentle voice. I tremble out of my stupor as Manish cups my face in his hand.

"Coming for a walk?"

"Your work –" I stammer.

"It can wait. Come on," and he pulls me to my feet. For a moment I can smell the flowers beneath our feet. Then, we move to the closet to get our coats.

The trees stand quietly wrapped in mists and the street lamps float over our heads as we walk past them. Manish whistles a long forgotten song. My feet carry me effortlessly along.

Perhaps, I have brought the fragrance along with me, after all.

Perhaps it is somewhere in a box I forgot to unpack. Perhaps it's sitting in the attic or in the basement, listening to the sound of my footsteps as I hurry back and forth.

We have reached the bend in the road from where Manish always begins his brisk walk. The fog thickens around me. Any moment now, he will turn to me and say, "A bit faster, Anu. You hardly walk," and propel me forward.

Any moment now, he'll increase his pace and shoot ahead and call over his shoulder, "Don't lag too far behind, Anu. Walk faster."

And I know that even as I'll implore him to slow down, ask him to walk beside me, the wind will blow my words away and I'll watch the distance between us increasing. But he hasn't said a word so far, nor has he hastened a step ahead. I tremble towards the next bend in the road.

SMOKE SCREEN

"Marmalade?" I ask Manish at breakfast.
"Can't find my car keys," he says, searching in his pockets. I spread some marmalade on an English muffin and set it before him. He picks it up and,  without taking his eyes off the newspaper, begins to munch on it. I pretend to sip my juice for a while. The silence becomes unbearable.

"Mini needs a new winter coat," I mumble.

"Ha! We're in for more terrorist attacks," he says, as if it was news.

"Samir, you know, didn't drink his milk."

"These power maniacs are going to destroy the world," he says.

"He eats junk food," I say.

"My goodness! Magic is HIV positive!"

"At the next PTA meeting I want –"

"Gosh No! Not another scandal about the President!" Manish bangs his hand on the table. Words carom back and forth between us and fall neatly into their slots. For months, it seems to me, we have let this smoke screen of words rise between us, smothering tremulous emotion.

"The children want to go to the movies this evening –" I venture again.

"I'll have to stay after classes – the conference, you know," Manish folds the newspaper and glances at his watch. "Must rush. Grace'll be waiting for me."

I watch him grab his coat and briefcase and dash out of the house. I look around as if trying to search for something, some mirth that used to hover around, but has disappeared now. Never in the past two years that we have been here have I felt the futility of words so intensely. And never before have I felt words blow away like soap bubbles. Even weekends have become a routine we must play out.

In those first few months of our arrival here, every Sunday we used to drive along the Schuylkill River and race with the canoes that went slicing through the amber waters, rowed by demigods whose bronze bodies rippled in the evening light. The children would squeal with delight as we drove past. Later, we would spread out our picnic basket under the maple trees and the children would toss bread crumbs and popcorn to the ducks that paddled up to us from the little island in the river. They could have been swans. As the sun dipped behind the weeping willows, both Manish and I would slip quietly into the mango groves we had left behind in that small town in India. Neither the cars that roared by nor the planes that droned overhead disturbed our tranquility.

"Remember the parrots swinging on the branches?" Manish would ask.

"And the peacocks crying in the morning –" I murmured.

"And the half-eaten fruit scattered on the ground –"

"And the smell of the night queen wafting in through the bedroom windows on summer evenings –"

We would wander in the vermilion gardens till the children broke the spell. Brushing off the gold dust from our eyes, we would get up and drive home – past the lighted silhouettes of the boat houses along the river side.

We still go there. Every Sunday. The river still blushes as the sun slips behind the trees. The demigods still row past us, their paddles strung with pearls that catch the evening light. The ducks still paddle over to us. But the mango groves are abandoned, the peacocks have fled, and the gold dust falls no more.

"We must hurry back," Manish says, glancing at his watch. "I have to do a lot of work –"

"The traffic is getting so noisy," I complain.

"The conference begins tomorrow," he informs me, as if I don't know, as if I haven't lived with it day and night for months now.

"It's getting cold," I whisper, averting my face.

"I have to call Grace."

"Of course," I say.

"You don't have to get angry. After all –"

"Let's go."

I get up, brushing the dirt from my clothes. Holding the half-empty bag of popcorn, the children look at us in wonder. The autumn leaves turn and quiver and glide to the ground. We drive back in silence. The boathouses stand rigid and dull along the muddied waters of the river.

"What's daddy so busy with?" Mini has often asked me.

"He doesn't even play Scrabble with me anymore," Samir complains.

"Daddy is busy with a conference these days. When his

work is over, he'll play with you and talk to you," I assure him, but ask myself, "Will he?"

"He doesn't answer my questions, doesn't even hear what I say," Mini's dark eyes are puzzled.

"Everything will be all right," I tell her, though I don't believe it myself.

On the last day of the conference, Manish leaves very early.

"Be ready at six thirty," he flings the words at me as if he were casting away a banana peel. I simmer. What if I don't go? What if I take the children and go to a movie, instead? What would he do then? But as the afternoon wanes, I find myself choosing a navy blue chiffon sari with a delicate silver border. I have never worn it before. For a moment, I wish I could wear something different, a western dress, maybe. I might not feel a stranger, then. But my hands keep pleating and draping the sari around me. I look at my reflection in the mirror and think of Grace. What does she look like? I have never met her, but I know I will see her today. Carefully, I apply a delicate blush to my pale cheeks and darken the mascara around my eyes and stare at the woman in the mirror. She looks bewildered. Sometimes, I can't help feeling as if I were staring at a stranger. While the rituals of daily living go on, something seems to wither inside.

Then a car door slams. Quickly, I dab a little perfume and turn around just as Manish breezes in paying little attention to what I am wearing. Past the round-eyed children, he whisks me out of the door and into the car. We drive through the neon-lit streets into the luminous evening. He lowers the volume of the car radio, so that only a thin ribbon of a symphony curls around us. He is keen to acquaint me with the people I am going to meet for the first time.

"You're going to meet quite a few people today," he says, his eyes fixed on the road. I don't say a word.

"You haven't met Nancy and Bill, have you? Ellen and Terry

have been wanting to meet you so. Terry was in India a few years ago. And yes, Helen has invited us over for dinner next Friday. And you'll meet Grace. A superb woman —" He goes on, without waiting for my response. And I imagine Grace. A tall, blonde, blue-eyed woman winding her way gracefully through groups of people. I say nothing.

"– A great help in this conference."

I catch only a fragment of what Manish is saying. Driving in the privacy of our car in the violet evening, there is nothing that we share. Words keep bouncing weightlessly, like ping-pong balls, smooth, round, and hollow. For months, it seems to me, we have let them bounce between us. They hang so heavy in the air now, like deflated balloons.

Manish has turned the car into the parking lot. "C'mon. We're there."

I step out of the car and walk beside him.

As we enter the huge ballroom, my eyes take time to get accustomed to the unfamiliar faces and figures. For a moment, I pause, careening on the edge of a pit, breathless and nervous. So many people! The room is thick with the smoke of words flung lightly, incessantly, shot over one's shoulders. Laughter bubbles up around me and spills forth like champagne, clear and sparkling. In this entire din, I feel lost. Manish holds me by the elbow and steers me through the crowd.

"Let me get you something to drink," he says. I stand there, looking at the pretty women, at elegant men. A bearer comes up with a tray of hors d'oeuvres and from the dazzling array, I pick up a stuffed mushroom. I stand there, trying to relish the strange taste, inhaling the alien smells, hearing words I know and know not. Manish hands me a glass of ginger ale. I feel grateful to him for having given me something to hold on to, even if it is a fragile stem glass.

"Hey! That's Peter over there. Let's go meet him," Manish leads me through the groups of people.

"Peter. My wife, Anu." A pair of green eyes look into mine.

My lips fixed in a smile, my hand extended, I greet him.

"How nice to meet you!"

Words rise to my lips effortlessly as smiling, shaking hands, exchanging greetings, we move around.

"How are the children?"

"Isn't it a lovely evening?"

"Try stuffed shrimp, you'll love it."

"I'm allergic to cream."

"Where did you buy that dress?"

"As I was saying –"

Sounds rise and fall. Like marbles spilled from a box on the top stair, they bounce down each step, effortlessly. Shuffling through the crowd, I get separated from Manish and thread my way through people, past women with mascara-deepened eyes and glistening lips. On the wall hangs a reproduction of Van Gogh's Sunflowers. I have seen it so often that I have memorized every brush stroke, every shade, and yet I stand before it pretending to study it. Words keep whirling around me.

"O wasn't that cute!"

"I told Kathy she couldn't have it both ways, after all I couldn't take all the burden while she was having a lark of a time and –"

"We're going to the shore next weekend –"

"– And he ate all the rum chocolates and was so sick – had to be taken to the vet's. We were so worried. You know dogs can't –"

The conversation is punctuated by tinkling laughter or by clinking ice cubes. Half amused, half tearful, I stand with my back to the crowd, my neck arched, my eyes devouring the sunflowers.

"Excuse me," a voice says and I wheel around to look into a pair of gray eyes in a finely chiseled face.

"Where's Manish?" The question is direct, the gaze unflinching.

"He's here, somewhere."

"You're his wife, aren't you?"

I nod. "How did you – know?"

"Easy. There's no other woman in a sari here," she laughs, displaying a set of beautiful teeth. "I'm Grace Williams. I work with your husband," she extends a rather large hand. Somewhere in the depths of my mind the name clangs, reverberates...

"We've often spoken on the phone," she says. Her eyes grow a trifle puzzled.

And then I remember. I look at her. The generous mouth, the lovely eyes. But she's not slender as I had imagined her to be. She's tall and a bit stocky, with a slight stoop in her shoulders. We regard each other like two children whose parents have forced them to become friends with each other.

"So you've met!" I hear Manish's voice.

"Yes, we have and I think your wife's lovely," Grace says. I quickly look at her, to see if she is making fun of me. But there's no trace of mockery or jealousy in that honest face. "We must get together – and soon too," she says, holding out her hand.

"Yes, oh yes," I gasp, feeling my face burn. I watch her join a group of people at the far end of the hall.

"I'm hungry," Manish says looking around. "They're bringing in the food now." Then, suddenly, he turns to me and asks, "How about going somewhere else for dinner?"

"But you are supposed to be here, it's your –"

He takes me by the hand and leads me away from the crowd. The autumn evening has a slight chill. For a moment, I look back at the glass doors behind which people are laughing, eating, talking. Then I match my steps with Manish's easy stride. He doesn't let go of my hand till we have reached the car and he has unlocked the door for me.

In silence, we drive. It is as if all the words that had bubbled up to the brim have now settled down. I search my mind for something to say. But what shall I say? Talk about the children? About the weather? The party? Household chores? What? What, I wonder, is he thinking? We drive past the lit-up silhouettes of the boathouses along the Schuylkill River.

"Beautiful, isn't it?" Manish says. "I had almost forgotten the river."

I can say nothing.

"Anu!" There's tenderness in his voice. "You've been very patient these past few months."

Have I? I ask myself remembering all the bafflement and misery I have lived with.

"You know what?" He muses, "I'm glad the conference is over."

Then he turns to me. "Remember the houses lit up on Diwali?"

I nod my head in silence.

"And the fragrance of the night queen?" He is luring me back into the abandoned garden.

"Yes," I say at last. "I wish it were blooming here."

"It does bloom somewhere," he says, "and all the time too, whether you notice it or not."

I feel the sting of tears. The boathouses swing before my blurred vision and then grow steady and shine brighter.

"Marmalade?" I ask him at breakfast, next morning.

"Listen to this. Another leak in the nuclear plant. I tell you —"

About The Author

Born and educated in India and the States, Vijay Lakshmi, a critic and social commentator, writes of the psychological conflicts and moral dilemmas of the Indian women settling in western societies. Her fiction, lyrical and intense, portrays the alienation and the pathos of the life lived in a contemporary metropolis, whether American, European, or Indian.

Her awards include a Senior Fulbright Fellowship at Yale University, and Editor's Prize from *Orbis* (UK) for her story "Touchline." Two of her other stories – "Mannequin" and "Distances" – have been translated into French and Chinese.

Widely traveled in Europe, the States, and the Far East, a mother of two grown-up children, she lives with her husband in Glenside, and teaches college in Philadelphia.